# Midnight Muse

### Rii Finley

Book Cover by Rii Finley
Illustrations by Rii Finley
Proofreading by Stephanie Morales
1st edition 2025

*To all the girls who want a rich man...*
*on his knees, begging to please you.*

# Content Warnings

While the love in this book is not dark, the story contains several dark topics. Please check your triggers prior to reading. In this novel you will find:


Strong language
On-page explicit consensual sex
Kidnapping/captivity (in flashbacks)
Mentions of sexual assault (in flashbacks)
Degradation (in flashbacks)
Death of a family member (mentioned)
Self-harm/suicide (mentioned)
PTSD
Amnesia
Stalking/tracking
Gun/knife violence
On page murder
**BDSM and kinks including:**
    Praise
    Restraint
    Orgasm denial
    Cock warming
    Service submission

# Playlist

*Scan me on Spotify*

Dog Days Are Over - Florence and the Machine
Labour - Paris Paloma
Bad Blood - Taylor Swift
The Man - Taylor Swift
Praying - Kesha
Damaged - Plumb
Out of My League -  Fitz and the Tantrums
Monster - Meg and Dia
Perfect - Ed Sheeran
All of Me - John Legend
Sweater Weather - The Neighbourhood
Set Fire to the Rain - Adele
Zombie - YUNGBLUD
Alkaline - Sleep Token

Sugar - Sleep Token
The Middle - Jimmy Eat World
Face Down - Red Jumpsuit Apparatus
Yellow - Coldplay
Sunflower - Post Malone, Swae Lee
Die With a Smile - Lady Gaga, Bruno Mars
You'll be Okay - A Great Big World
Helena - My Chemical Romance
Marry You - Bruno Mars

# RUSSIAN TERMS

Ivan doesn't speak a ton of Russian in this book, but here's a couple nicknames.

Milaya – (Me-lie-ah): Sweetheart/Honey.
Solnyshko – (Sol-nish-ka) - Sun/Sunshine

# CHAPTER 1

## *Charli*

B ranches claw at my skin. My heart hammers wildly in my chest as I sprint through the dense undergrowth. Stones and thorns tear into the delicate soles of my bare feet.

It's cold, wet, and dark. Everything hurts, but I'm filled with hope for the first time in... well, I'm not even sure to be honest.

I couldn't tell you what year it is, or how old I am now. Hell, I don't even know where I am. Right now, my only option is to keep pushing myself forward through the pain.

I slow my pace to a brisk walk, traversing this unknown land through a dark, endless night. My body is weak, on the brink of collapsing. *You can do this, Li.* I repeat to myself, in hopes of bolstering any bit of remaining resolve I can.

Finally, morning approaches, bringing the comforting glow of dappled light as it breaks through the foliage overhead. Thoroughly exhausted from my night on the run, I stop to rest on a broken tree stump, allowing myself a brief moment to catch my breath. Inhaling deeply, I scan my surroundings and admire the waking world.

Afraid of the repercussions if I'm caught, I keep my senses alert, rise up on my tender feet and continue forward.

As the morning sun makes its presence fully known, the forest warms up and I slow my pace with the hope that I'm not being followed.

The world is quiet and still as I stumble upon a crystal-clear lake sitting undisturbed in a valley full of vibrant flowers. Snow-capped mountains serve as a picturesque backdrop.

Halting my steps, I drink in the beauty that surrounds me here. I haven't seen the light of day in so long, I'd forgotten what a fresh breeze felt like—how crisp and clean the natural air smells. A warm feeling I haven't experienced in a long while washes over me.

*Peace.*

For a fleeting moment I bask in this feeling of pure, blissful serenity. My body feels lighter than ever.

*I'm going to be okay.*

Dusting myself off, I wince as I get back on the move, following a river that runs off from the lake.

Several hours have passed me by, punctuated by the darkness of night beginning to creep in. I still have no idea where I am.

Technically speaking, I know that I'm lost in the

woods.

Lost isn't exactly the correct word, though, I was lost long ago.

What I really mean is that I have no idea, geographically speaking, where I am in the world. What I do know is now, being lost out here, I might finally be found. No matter how bad it hurts, or how tired I am, I can't allow myself to give up.

Not after what I've been through.

Along the river's edge a small cave tucked away into the cliff side catches my eye. A sob fights to break free. I pant. My legs tremble as I weigh my options. I'm torn between giving in and taking the risk of sleeping in this cave, or continuing and ignoring how desperately my body wants a break.

Time seems to simultaneously stop, and rush past me in a frenzy as the decision is ultimately made for me. In the distance, through the trees, I notice the faintest tendrils of smoke rising into the darkening sky.

*Smoke has to be a good sign, right?*

I just need to channel my remaining strength into reaching its source.

I nearly collapse, overwhelming emotions rack my body as I edge closer to the first sign of humanity I've encountered since my escape.

*This is it!*

The thought of putting myself at the mercy of unknown people sends waves of fear, coupled with anxiety, shooting through me.

*What if they aren't going to help me?*
*What if they take me back?*
It doesn't matter.
This is my chance to be saved, and I need to take it.
After another grueling trek through the dense vines and muddy forest floor, a small log cabin enters my view. Glorious smoke spirals from the stone chimney like a beacon of hope.
This place is clearly not lived in regularly, being in a slight state of disrepair. Tangled vines growing up the side, crumbled cobblestone foundation, and overgrown shrubbery give it an air of fantasy. It looks well loved, just certainly old.
Tears prickle the back of my eyes as I slowly bring myself up the weathered wooden steps to the front door.
*Am I finally safe?*
My feet are raw and bloodied. Weak legs struggle to keep me upright. Shaky and fatigued, I'm barely able to lift my arm and tap against the door. Trembling, I wait...
Nothing.
*Is anyone here?*
The fire's lit so someone must be, right?
Weakly tapping again, I faintly call out, "Hello?"
My voice is weak, unaccustomed to the use. I barely recognize the sound. My throat is dry and raw from several days without water. Still, nobody answers, not even a stir from inside.
*Maybe they're asleep?*
Whimpering, with the last ounce of strength I possess,

I knock as loudly as possible on the solid wooden door that has become my support. Shivers run through me. I feel myself succumb to the exhaustion and mental drain of being this close to safety after fighting to survive for so long. Everything goes dark as I slip down to the floor of the porch.

Warmth surrounds me. I feel a serene sense of relaxation as I float between consciousness and sleep. This must be what dying feels like. Slow and comforting after a life of cold and agony.

I startle, snapped from my spiraling thoughts by the sound of hushed voices.

"I don't know where she could have come from, there's nothing around for miles," a soothing, older sounding male voice says.

His slight accent catches my attention.

*Is he Russian? Am I in Russia?!*

"I know, but she looks like she's been out there a while, Dad. We need to try and wake her up," a rich, smooth female voice replies. Her lack of accent only serves to further confuse me.

"Caroline, she clearly needs some rest. The poor girl passed out on our front porch. Let her sleep a bit longer while the stew finishes, then we can wake her to eat. When we head back home, we'll get her checked out and take her to the police station."

"Dad, I'm just worried about her. What if she's sick, or worse. What if she's crazy or something?"

"I'm sure if she had any ill intent, she wouldn't have been nearly naked, torn up from a clearly unplanned trek through the woods, and passed out on our doorstep. Have a little compassion, Dear. I raised you better than this." He sighs in frustration.

I hear faint rustling around in the next room before sleep takes me again.

A scream tries to break free from my tattered, dry throat. Violently, I flail my arms, as I jolt awake at the feeling of a hand on my shoulder.

"Easy now, Milaya. I didn't mean to startle you, but you've been out cold for a while. I figured you would be hungry. You could also do with something clean to wear. You look to be about the same size as my Caroline, so she's offered to let you wear some of her clothes. I've put a few things over there on the dresser for you. I'll leave you to it. Come on out to the kitchen for some food when you're ready." He steps quietly out of the room.

I rub my eyes and examine my surroundings. Securely cocooned in an old wood-framed bed, the quilt I'm wrapped in seems to be handmade and well worn. Tears threaten to escape as I inhale the fresh scent.

The room itself is simple and cozy. Nothing more than a sitting chair by a large, lone window. A wooden chest sits at the foot of the bed, and an old dresser lines the far wall. Pink sweatpants and a bright splattered t-shirt sit on top of it next to a framed photo.

The man who woke me is in the picture, though definitely a decade or two younger. His now-gray hair is dark. While his face still holds the same kindness as he smiles, the lines that now occupy the sides of his honey-colored eyes are not present. His arm is wrapped lovingly around a beautiful woman. She has silky, long blonde hair and large striking blue eyes.

Smiling enthusiastically between them stands a young girl. Her long blonde hair is pulled back into pigtails, shimmering like that of the woman she's leaning into. Golden-brown eyes—that she clearly inherited from the man—shine brightly.

My stomach rumbles in protest to the time my investigations are taking as the smell of something earthy and savory wafts into the room. Holding myself up on unstable legs, I hurry to get dressed, then follow the scent.

Tentative steps lead me toward the rustic open kitchen. A small round table sits in the middle of the room, occupied by the man who woke me and the woman I immediately recognize as the now-grown girl from the photo on the dresser.

"Ah, so nice of you to join us. I've made stew and some toasted bread. Do help yourself. I'm Ivan and this is my daughter, Caroline." He gestures to the woman standing at the stove.

She smiles brightly and hands me a steaming bowl. "I hope my clothes are comfortable enough for you. They seem to fit alright. You've got a bit of room to grow into them though." She chuckles playfully, covering her mouth with her hand.

I'm noticeably shorter than her by a few inches and her curves are far more voluptuous than my current emaciated form.

With a wince, I sink slowly into the empty chair, my feet and legs sting with every move. My body aches from being neglected for so long and put through a cross-country endurance run with no training.

Ivan clears his throat. "Are you in need of some pain medication? I'm sure Caroline has some bath salts you can use after dinner to get yourself cleaned up. We also have more than enough first aid supplies to get you situated until you have to go." He inquisitively lifts a single brow.

"I don't have anywhere to go," I mutter into my bowl to avoid his gaze, realizing how absurd I must sound.

"Well, where the hell did you come from then?" Caroline quips.

I flinch at the sharpness of her tone. Ivan shoots her a stern look from his seat across the table.

Guilt flashes across her face. "Sorry, I'm not great at thinking before words come out of my mouth."

I attempt a weak, forced smile and begin engorging myself on the delicious beef and vegetable stew. The pain and uncertainty that plague my mind vanish with my first bite. I've missed real food.

*How long has it been?*

We finish our dinner in silence, serenaded by the low

hum of the old refrigerator. As I rise from the creaky wooden chair Ivan is quick to follow.

The cabin has one small, shared bathroom with a rustic wood and ceramic sink, a toilet tucked into the corner, and an old claw foot tub nestled in the middle.

Ivan sets out bath items and turns the squeaky brass knobs, starting the water.

*Is he drawing me a bath? Is this what being cared for feels like?*

"I know Caroline can be a bit much to take in at first, but she has a great heart. We're just worried about you, as much as we can be for a nameless stranger anyway."

Dipping his hand into the rising water, he nods, satisfied with the temperature. His presence is calming, warm, and comforting. The kindness I see in his eyes is convincing enough that he's trustworthy.

"I'm not nameless. My name is Charli, but I prefer to go by 'Li', and I don't know much about myself other than that, to be honest."

Ivan furrows his brows. The deep-set lines between them do more to showcase his age than the crinkles around his eyes when he smiles. "Well, Li, I guess we have some work to do when we head back home. For now, you go ahead and relax in a nice bath, and we'll worry about the details later."

Without another word he turns and leaves.

*Home.*

My head spins, the word feels foreign.

They don't live here regularly. That explains a lot.

My eyes skim over the selection of various bath salts and strange looking balls wrapped in plastic. I struggle to unwrap one, toss it into the tub—now filled with steaming water—and it begins to fizz.

Mesmerized, I stare at it and wonder how detached I must be to have never seen something like this before. What other normal, everyday things have I missed out on? Before long, the small bathroom is filled with steam and the sweet, floral scent of the bath.

The welcome burn of hot water bites at my wounds as I lower myself into the tub. Quickly, it begins to soothe my aching muscles. I submerge myself as far as I can manage and close my eyes. Long restrained tears begin to form. This time I don't fight them.

Barely above the surface of my bath, I lay back and silently weep. Tears flow steadily as I free myself of as many pent-up emotions as I can—grief, sorrow, anger, fiery rage—a torrent of feelings I've suppressed in order to stay alive.

Part of me hopes I'll be able to find answers. Part of me wishes I could remember anything to help find them, but the majority of my being is just glad to be here. I feel safe, cared for, and comfortable for what might be the first time in my life.

Do I really need to worry about the details?

What if nobody is still looking for me?

What if nobody ever was?

Tears continue to cascade down my face as I struggle to lather shampoo into my long, unkempt, black hair.

Gradually, I scrub and wash away the muck and grime from a lifetime of living in squalor.

I sigh, feeling nearly weightless as I rise from the now-murky water and wrap myself in a bathrobe.

An endless sea of knots and matting make it nearly impossible to comb my hair. Frustrated, I groan loudly enough that Caroline knocks on the door mere seconds later.

"Are you alright in there, girlie?" Her voice is soft, laced with concern.

"I don't even know what alright is!" I howl.

Without warning, the door opens. Her eyes soften as she takes in the state of me. My pale skin is bright red from the heat of the bath. A wooden comb is trapped in my tangled hair. Tears flood down my face as I hunch over the sink.

"Oh, Li. Let me help. Okay?" Gentle and soothing, her words extinguish my burning frustration.

My nod is so minor I'm not sure she even notices. Nobody has ever offered me help before Ivan and Caroline. I'm not fully sure how to accept it, or what to do. So, I inhale deeply, close my eyes and sit still.

Caroline massages thick cream into my hair, slowly working the comb through my knots. Methodically, she starts at the ends and ensures she doesn't pull any more than necessary. Kind eyes, identical to her fathers, meet mine in the mirror. So many questions can be seen swimming within them.

Minutes feel like hours, but she eventually manages to

get my hair completely combed out. Running my fingers through it, I'm awestruck at how long and silky it is.

Citrus.

The cream she used smells like citrus. *I* smell like citrus.

Biting my lower lip to stop it from trembling, I inhale the crisp scent, delighting in how soft and clean my hair is. At this moment I've decided that citrus is my favorite scent. It smells like crisp, vibrant relief.

"Oh my gosh, you have the most beautiful hair ever!" Caroline squeals and shimmies in some sort of cheerful dance. This new joyful expression makes her appear so much younger than the version of her I've been met with.

She looks like she is in her mid-twenties, but so far she's been reserved. She carries herself in a way that makes her seem more mature. Underneath it all she almost seems... sad.

This new side of her is lively and exciting, albeit a bit too loud for my liking. Sharing in her joy—even if I don't fully understand the reason for it—I offer a soft smile back at her.

"Let's get these scrapes and cuts all dressed up now that they're clean." Shuffling around the bathroom, she gathers various tubes of ointment and rolls of bandages.

Her thin blonde eyebrows raise slightly. A soft, sympathetic smile crosses her face as she begins applying them to my ragged legs and feet.

"Don't worry, I went to veterinary school... close

enough." She shrugs, which is not exactly reassuring.

The scrapes on my arms aren't nearly as bad as my feet, thankfully. Caroline wraps them loosely with bandages.

"Alright, don't scratch them if they itch. Those should heal in a week or so. Now, it's time for a movie. It's tradition." In a blink she takes me by the hand and drags me out of the bathroom.

Like the rest of the cabin, the living room shows obvious signs of age. Simple furniture, old photos nailed to the log walls. Warmth fills the room from the fireplace crackling away in the corner. My heart flutters as I realize this must be the source of the smoke that originally drew me here. On the thick stone mantle is a small TV with an old DVD player connected to it.

"We always watch mom's favorite movie the last night we're at the cabin," Caroline tells me as she drifts her way into the kitchen.

She and Ivan return shortly with bowls filled to the brim with fresh buttery popcorn.

"Where is your mom? I haven't seen her yet. Is she here?" My question immediately dampens the mood in the room.

Ivan and Caroline's faces shift slightly. I recoil at the thought of what their expressions must mean.

"Theresa passed away five years ago; it was sudden. We come to this cabin every year for her birthday, just like she used to love." Ivan's eyes glisten, wanting so badly to release the tears they're holding back.

"Oh, I'm so sorry for asking," I offer, not entirely sure

what else to say. This explains the innate sadness I sensed in Caroline. My heart aches for them.

"It's alright, you didn't know. We were so happy, and then our worlds got flipped upside down in an instant." Ivan's voice is thick with emotion.

"We always watch *The Notebook* the last night we're here. Mom loved this movie so much. She was such a sappy romantic and dad adored how much she'd ugly cry into his chest every single time," Caroline explains, her tone bittersweet.

Clearly, they were a loving family. My chest burns with envy.

Caroline and I take seats on opposite ends of the well-worn sofa. Ivan settles in a recliner off to the side, closer to the fireplace as the movie plays.

Despite the gloomy reason for the movie night, the fondness and love filling the room is palpable.

*I could get used to this.*

There's not a dry eye in the room as the ending credits roll. How beautifully tragic love can be. What I wouldn't do for the chance at a love like that.

Can I ever let anyone in though? After the things that have been done to me, I doubt it. Love like that doesn't exist in the real world.

Not for people like me.

"Well, girls. We had better get ready to turn in for the night. We'll hit the road early tomorrow. Li, you can have my bed again if you'd like, I can sleep out here in my recliner." Ivan yawns and stretches out in his chair, bringing my thoughts back from the depths they were drowning in.

"Oh, I didn't know that was your room, thank you for letting me sleep in there. I don't think I've ever slept in a bed so comfortable." I try to give him an honest smile, purposefully excluding the fact that I don't know the last time I slept in an actual bed to begin with.

"Don't mention it, you're our guest and you look like you need some good restful sleep. Goodnight, ladies." His eyes begin to droop as he relaxes into the old chair.

"Good night, Girlie, we've got a bit of a drive ahead of us so make sure you get rested," Caroline says in passing before slipping through the doorway to her room.

As I stare impassively at the ceiling, my mind races. I can't help but wonder where I'll go from here. I didn't think I'd make it this far. I wipe a stray tear as I process the thought of finally being free, my tired mind shuts off easily for once.

# CHAPTER 2

## *Charli*

I van wasn't kidding, we're awake before sunrise. Songbirds are whistling their springtime tunes. The rustle of leaves can be heard on the breeze outside, and the rich aroma of freshly brewed coffee wafts through the cabin.

I make my way to the bathroom to brush my hair, delighted by how effortlessly the comb goes through it. I pull my hair into a messy bun and change into some more of Caroline's excessively vibrant clothes.

Dragging my sensitive feet, I amble to the kitchen, where Ivan is standing in front of the small stove. Bacon sizzles on a cast iron griddle as he whisks eggs.

"Go ahead and eat up, we don't like to stop once we get on the road." He gestures to the spread in front of me.

*You don't need to tell me twice.*

I begin loading heaps of food onto my plate as Caroline emerges from her room, hair a mess from sleep. She wastes no time heading straight for the coffee.

"Good morning, my Solnyshko." Ivan reaches out, ruffling her bed head.

"Ugh, this is the worst part of this whole trip every year." She casts a bleary-eyed look my way, gasping at the sight of me eating pancakes and bacon with the speed and voracity of a competitive eater. "Holy shit, do you always eat like it's your last meal?" Her voice is still raspy from sleep.

"Oh, uh, sorry. I guess I just haven't had good food in a while. This is so delicious, Ivan. Thank you." Scrambled eggs almost fall from my mouth as I talk.

*Damn it, manners Li.*

Ivan casts a gentle smile my way and piles up his own plate before sitting down and directing his attention back to Caroline. "Now, let the girl enjoy her breakfast, you'd be wise to do the same. We leave in an hour. I know all too well how you get when you're 'hangry' as you say."

Caroline shrugs and yawns then proceeds to fill a plate of her own.

Forks gently clanking against ceramic and sips of coffee are the only sounds to be heard as we enjoy our breakfast.

"I'll clean up, you two make sure you're ready to go once I'm finished." Ivan stands and begins clearing the table.

Once he's satisfied with the cleanliness of the kitchen, we load their belongings into the back of his red SUV.

This whole situation feels so familial. Waves of sadness wash over me at the thought that I've likely never had an experience like this.

"Shotgun!" Caroline shouts, snapping me out of my self-pitying daze.

I jerk my head back in temporary panic, not quite understanding what she means as she hops up into the passenger seat. "Shotgun?"

"You don't know what calling shotgun is?" A dramatic gasp escapes her, as if I've announced that I don't know the color of the sky.

"Uh, no... I've never heard of that before. So, are you going to explain or just look at me like there's something on my face?" Still not used to talking this much, my voice cracks.

She maintains her shocked expression that makes me feel like some sort of alien.

*I think I might commit a murder today.*

"You call shotgun to claim the passenger seat, Silly. Whoever calls it first gets rights to the spot. It's like a fun competition because nobody wants to ride in the back. Shotgun also gets to pick the music!" With the press of a few buttons, she connects her phone to the car.

My head hurts as I try to understand the unknown technology.

Ivan huffs and offers that easy smile of his to me with a shake of his head.

I soon understand his reaction when Caroline's music begins to blast out of the speakers. It's some sort of bright, cheerful, bubbly sounding music. Belted out by women who are entirely too happy to be alive.

Exactly the type of music I'd expect someone as outrageous as Caroline to love.

I hate it.

We've been driving for about an hour. The roads so far have been dirt trails and gravel, barely even worthy of being called roads.

My eyes have been glued to the scenery out the window. I've never seen so many animals in one place, just carrying on with their day. So untroubled, wild and carefree.

*This is nature, huh. Who would have thought it was so... alive?*

The absurdity of that thought makes me chuckle softly, but I've never been in a natural setting before, that I can recall.

Not that I remember much of anything from before. My escape adventure excluded—I was a bit preoccupied with trying to survive.

Ivan breaks the deafening silence. "So, Li, where exactly did you come from? I know the area relatively well, and as you can see there aren't any other cabins or camps around for quite some time. You also looked like you had crawled out of one of those naked survival shows on TV." His probing eyes meet mine in the rearview mirror.

"Uh, well... I uh," I stammer, trying to find the best words to explain my situation, without divulging too many gruesome details. "I don't really know. I was, um, being kept... then I just got free and ran." A searing blush heats my face from my confession.

Ivan's eyes widen in question.

Caroline snaps around to face me, jaw slack from shock. "Got free?!" she shouts, "Free from where? From whom? KEPT! What?!" She sputters, shaking her head, blinking rapidly.

Ivan places a hand on her shoulder. "Relax, Caroline. You're yelling." His tone is soft and soothing, I'm not entirely sure which one of them he's trying to calm down.

"I don't know, and it's hard to think about. I don't remember a lot. I just know I got free and ran. There isn't much else. It was late and... and they forgot to shut the door. I can't remember anything else. Okay? I swear." Hot tears stream down my face as I ramble.

There's a considerable amount that I do, in fact, remember. I just don't want to haunt these kind strangers with the knowledge of those horrors.

The trauma I lived through is my own to bear.

Caroline pulls an incredulous face and turns back to face forward. Resting her head on the window, she sighs. "I'm sorry I was not expecting that *at all*. I don't know what happened to you, but you've got us now, so you're not alone." She glances over her shoulder at me.

Nodding, I offer her the faintest smile. We each return

our focus to the forest surrounding us as the drive becomes silent once again. Exhaustion overwhelms me and I doze off in the back seat.

"Dad, I have to pee so bad, can we please stop at the next rest area?" Caroline's whine wakes me.

We've evidently been on the go for a few hours now, finally on paved roads. The highway is packed with several lanes of hectic traffic. Signs pass rapidly as we drive, informing me we're in Washington State. I don't know exactly where, but it's all open roads and very rural.

*Not Russia, got it.*

"Caroline, you know I don't like to stop once we're on the road. I suppose we can make a pit stop once we get to the outskirts of Seattle. Maybe we'll grab some lunch while we're in the area. We have a bit to go until we get there. If we're going to stop, I'd rather do it where we can make the best of it." Ivan grumbles.

*So, he isn't always soft and cheery.*

An impish smirk crosses my face knowing I'm not the only one Caroline annoys.

"Okay, I can hold it 'til then, but only if we stop for coffee while we're there."

What is she, twelve?

Ivan nods in silent agreement and smiles back at her, apparently done with his brief irritation.

"Can, um, can I get a coffee while we're there too?" The heat of humiliation tingles my neck. I shouldn't ask, afraid to be a burden on these people who have already shown me more kindness than I deserve.

Ivan accepted me with open arms. Caroline is loud and abrasive, but she truly does mean well. Still, I'm only human, and so tired. A good cup of coffee sounds divine.

"Girl, of course. I'll order one for you. I promise you'll love it!" Caroline flashes a wide, pearly white grin at me.

I shrug and nod back at her.

I haven't known her for long, but I already get the sense that there's no room for argument.

About twenty minutes later we stop for gas, a bathroom break, and some overly sweet concoction Caroline promises me contains coffee.

Now we're set to embark on the final stretch of our journey to... wherever it is we're headed.

As if he can hear my snowballing thoughts, Ivan speaks up. "So, Caroline and I live in a small home. We only have two bedrooms and genuinely don't have space for a third person to live there comfortably. I promise we're not just going to drop you somewhere randomly though. Especially considering that you don't have the faintest idea where you live, or who you even are. We want to help you figure that out. So, once we get into town, we'll stop off at the police station. Then, we'll sort out living arrangements."

Caroline pops her head around her seat. "I've been texting my cousin, Nicky. That's who you're going to stay with." She immediately flinches from the shock and apprehension plastered on my face. "I promise Nicky is the absolute best. Okay? We were raised together. Do you like art? Nicky is an artist and works from home. The house is huge and so nice. You'll love it there."

Great. I can only hope Nicky is more tolerable than Caroline for long periods of time. "Sounds amazing," I manage to grit out through my clenched jaw.

"Theresa and I raised Nicky from infancy." I can clearly hear the adoration in Ivan's voice, mixed with a trace of sadness.

"You guys are close then?"

Ivan nods, his mouth corners rise slightly.

Caroline claps her hands together with far more enthusiasm than necessary. "Oh yeah, we are! Dad and I go over at least once a week, so you and I will have plenty of time to hang out and get to know each other."

I grin, as genuinely as possible.

We approach a large brick building. Marked police cars fill the parking lot.

*Here goes nothing.*

It's time to start figuring out who I am, and where I came from. Hopefully, whoever has been out there looking for me will be excited to learn that I'm alive.

Walking through the glass doors to the gray, lifeless lobby there are a few metal chairs, and pots with plants that look like they are about two days away from dying of dehydration. Directly ahead is a thick glass window. A young, disinterested looking woman sits on the other side. Her blank expression is unmoving as I approach.

My voice disappears when I try to speak into the little box on my side of the glass.

Clearing my throat, I try again. "H-hello."

"Name and the nature of your business?" She pops the neon green gum she's chewing.

"Oh. My Name is Charli. I... uh. I guess maybe I'm missing?"

*No, that's not right.*

"I mean, I'm not missing anymore but maybe I was? I don't really know."

"You got a last name?" Her tone is as dry as ever.

"N-not that I can remember." I wrap my arms around myself. I desperately want to curl into a ball and retreat into the secure depths of my mind.

Ivan rests a hand on my shoulder, interrupting my developing emotional overload. "Ma'am, my name is Ivan Koval. Miss Charli mysteriously landed herself on our cabin doorstep in the woods near Kootenai National Forest. All she seems to recall is running from captivity. We're not sure of much more than that currently. We're hoping for some help."

"Very well, take a seat and I'll have a detective come out to take an official statement." She presses a button on her desk and calls for assistance over the intercom.

A tall blond man in a deep blue fitted suit enters the lobby not long after.

*Don't panic. He's just here to help.*

He's fairly young—probably mid twenties—and

muscular. His clean-shaven face showcases a defined square jaw.

With an intense, shuddering breath, I look up at him and encounter genuine concern in his deep blue eyes.

"Miss Charli?" His voice is soft and unexpectedly comforting.

"Y-yes, sir."

"I'm Detective Theo Hastings. I hear you're not quite sure what happened to you. Would you mind following me to the back and we can talk about what you do remember? I'd also like to take your fingerprints and get a DNA sample so we can run it against the missing persons database." He holds his hand out, motioning toward the door he emerged from.

"Okay. That sounds like a good start." I look back at Ivan and Caroline, silently begging them to follow.

They recognize the pleading in my eyes and stand to follow.

Detective Hastings leads us back through a bland grey hallway, barely distinguishable from the lobby. He opens a glossy wooden door ushering the three of us inside. A large rectangular table fills the center of the room. The office is clean, neat and smells earthy. After motioning for us to sit he offers each of us a chilled bottle of water from the mini fridge in the corner.

Sitting across from us in a high-back leather chair, he opens a laptop, presses a few buttons, and asks his first question. "So, Charli. Would you please start from the beginning and tell me whatever you can remember?"

Swallowing a gulp of water, I dig deeply into my subconscious, willing myself to recall anything that may help. "I was in a room. It was always dark. There wasn't really anything in there for me other than a bucket to, well, use in place of a bathroom. I had a raggedy old pile of blankets to sleep on and there was a single door, no windows. A couple books to read and a TV on the wall playing the same cable channel forever."

I inhale deeply, suppressing the emotions that are trying desperately to burst free. "I uh, I remember there were men, three of them, but always  one at a time. I can't remember what they looked like. But I remember they... they..." A sob lodges itself in my throat as a mass of unpleasant memories flood into my mind.

"Hey, it's alright. I understand. You don't have to tell me about that right now, okay? We can move past that part." Detective Hastings' voice has taken on an even more comforting tone.

My shoulders relax, realizing that I'm being heard and taken seriously. Caroline and Ivan each take hold of my hands in support.

"I-I don't know how long I was there. I can't seem to remember much from before. One of them came to visit me. That's what they called it. He had been drinking and miraculously forgot to lock the door behind him when he stumbled out. I realized the door was left open and made a run for it."

"Was there anything around that was noteworthy? Any symbols or signs you can remember?"

"No, but I discovered that I was in an underground room. The door was connected to a small hallway that led up a flight of stairs. I didn't exactly think about exploring. I bolted and just ran. I ran and ran. Then when I was too tired to run more, I walked until I couldn't walk anymore either. I almost gave up. I was so close to curling up in a cave and just dying, but I saw smoke from the chimney of Ivan's cabin." Shaking, I finish the bottle of water. "I escaped two or three days ago now. I think I was on the run for a day and a half. I'm not sure."

"You did so well, Charli. We'll get your fingerprints and a DNA sample, then you can be on your way. I would love to give you the contact information of a great psychiatrist that works closely with individuals who have endured trauma. Hopefully she can help you regain some memories faster. I'm also going to give you my phone number so you can reach out to me directly, should you remember any details that may aid in our investigation." His business card is black and gold, sleek and professional.

*He's just doing his job.*

I give him a small smile and nod as I leave the room, heading straight to the car.

"That was... a lot to take in." Caroline is pale in the passenger seat. "We're here for you, okay?"

"Okay." My chin wobbles.

We drive to Nicky's house in silent commiseration.

# Chapter 3

## *Charli*

We travel down a long, paved driveway. Tucked away from the main road is a generously sized home. Stark white and modern. We're in a wealthy neighborhood from what I can tell, with my extremely limited knowledge anyway. Most of the homes we passed to get here were larger than any house I've seen. Even those weren't *this* stunning.

Tall, immaculately trimmed hedges and pristine, intricate landscaping cover the perimeter of the house. Flower beds fill every nook of the exterior. The backyard must look like a resort. You can nearly pinpoint that an artist lives here.

I don't know why I imagined Nicky living in some tall high-rise in the city. I pictured her looking out large windows of a penthouse over a bustling cityscape for inspiration, but this fits too.

The small suburb nearby is quaint and there are no immediate neighbors here. Hope flares in my chest as images of a bright, colorful future break through the darkness in my mind.

Stepping out of the SUV, my gaze sweeps over the sleek blue sports car parked in front of twin garage doors. The gorgeous sapphire color shines under the afternoon sun. She must take great care of it.

"You like the Corvette, huh? That thing is Nicky's pride and joy, I swear." Caroline rolls her eyes.

"Nicky likes cars?"

Caroline huffs out a laugh. "Nicky likes *that* car and tolerates the other two in the garage."

How many cars does one woman possibly need?

Rounding the corner to the front door, the blood in my veins turns to ice. The sight before me has been pulled directly from my nightmares. There's a man on the front step. At first glance I wilt.

*Does Nicky have a boyfriend?*

My hair stands on end.

Unease bubbles in my stomach.

My palms itch as they begin to sweat.

The stranger grins widely at us. He must be six feet tall, possibly a bit more. I thrust my gaze to the walkway, doing my best to disregard him.

Hopefully he's not here often. He makes me feel strange, tingly, on edge. His presence is terrifying. The urge to bolt rushes through me.

Caroline bounces up the steps and shoulder checks him. He laughs and pushes her back playfully. "Hey now, Parasite. Don't damage the goods. I need this arm."

"Oh, please. You're almost a whole foot taller than me. I'm not going to hurt your precious money maker, Nicky."

Time stops, my heart stills with it. I almost fall as my steps falter.

"Nicky?" His name is acid on my tongue.

*Oh no.*

"Last I checked." He looks himself over, adjusting his black framed glasses, then wiggles his fingers and waves at me.

Examining him closer I can see it, clear as day. He has the same dark-colored hair as young Ivan, only it's slightly wavy, down to his shoulders. He even shares the same easy smile, only I don't find it endearing like Ivan's. His eyes, while a sage green color, are just as gentle, outlined by dark full lashes.

I'm shaken, completely unnerved.

I cannot live alone with a man, not after what I just escaped. Especially not one that makes me feel like this.

The bagel I had at the rest stop threatens to eject itself from the vortex churning in my stomach.

"Nikolai, Charli. Charli, this is my nephew, Nikolai, but we call him Nicky." Ivan's attempt at a proper introduction is overshadowed by the terror building inside me.

*No. Nope. No way.*

This isn't happening right now.

"You can call me Nicky too, Sugar. I won't mind." An easygoing grin crosses his face.

Unable to stop myself, I scoff at him, averting my eyes. If I just stare at the ground, he won't see the pure disdain written all over my face.

*Pet names already, typical.*

I've found myself at an impasse.

Freedom really was too good to be true.

Everywhere I go there will just be another man in the way, looking to control my every action and use me for whatever he wants. Ivan is old enough that I don't perceive him as a threat, but Nikolai, he's going to be a problem. I can already feel it.

The jokes, the pet names, those dimples that could be weaponized.

*Great. Just great.*

Nikolai takes notice of how pale and clammy I've become.

*Of course he notices, creep.*

"Shit, are you okay?" He looks at Caroline with wide eyes. "Has she looked like this the whole time she was with you guys?"

"She's probably tired from the ride. She barely drank any of the coffee I bought her, and dad demanded we keep a tight schedule so show her to her room already, dickhead."

*She's standing right here, idiots.*

Nikolai rolls his eyes at Caroline's playful insult. Extending an arm, he motions for us to follow him inside. Chills riddle my body at the feeling of his eyes on me as I pass him.

*How the hell am I supposed to live here?*

Taking an unsteady step into the entrance of the house, my eyes widen in wonder. My first glimpse of the inside is just as beautiful as the outside.

Colorful canvases are scattered along the walls. Vases and small wooden sculptures fill shelves. Dark, polished wood floors shine brightly. My gaze trails over all the color and life in just this one room. Maybe this won't be so bad if Nikolai keeps his distance.

*Yeah, right.*

We make our way to the living room. The pale yellow walls are equally plastered with canvases. The couch along the far side is laden with plush blankets and pillows. A wide hallway parts the wall between the couch and fireplace that a TV is mounted over.

We continue down the hall to the bedroom I'll be staying in, not stopping to tour any of the other closed rooms. Shivers dart down my spine when I realize that one of them leads to Nikolai's bedroom.

I'm going to have to sleep here. He's going to be sleeping nearby. Possibly right next door.

*Run away. Get out now.*

Oblivious to the storm raging in my mind, Nikolai opens the door to a plain, cream-colored room. A simple large bed sits in the middle of one wall, a plain gray comforter and more pillows than I could ever imagine needing. A large walk-in closet and attached bathroom are across from the bed.

*At least I'll have privacy.*

"Sorry, I know it's really bland, compared to the rest of the house anyway." Nikolai rubs at the back of his neck like *he* is the nervous one right now. "We'll go shopping later and get things you can decorate it with. You're going to need some clothes of your own, aren't you? I didn't see any bags."

"I don't have clothes, or money." I'm increasingly aware that I sound ungrateful, but I don't care.

"Well, I figured you didn't have shit to your name, Sugar. Don't even worry about it. I love shopping. It'll be a blast." He beams.

"I highly doubt it." I curl my upper lip and roll my eyes.

*Again, with the damned name.*

"You haven't been shopping with me and the parasite here." He nudges Caroline with his elbow teasingly. "You'd better prepare for the best time of your life. We'll take you to the hospital tomorrow after you've had time to breathe."

"Shopping!" Caroline squeals, darting out of the room as if it's on fire. "Come on. Let's go already!" she calls out.

Lumbering down the hallway, I stand in the middle of the living room. It's so vibrant and warm I struggle to maintain my scowl.

"You aren't going to let me get out of this are you?"

"Hell no, Li! I can't wait to see you all dressed up. You're seriously stunning. I'm jealous."

"Are you blind, Caroline? Look at me. I'm covered in

scrapes and bruises and look like a starved rat. Nothing about me is stunning." My gaze falls to the floor.

The silence that swallows the room has me peering up at them. Caroline, Ivan, and Nikolai all stare vacantly at me as if I'm speaking a foreign language.

*Okay then.*

I scowl intensely back at them. Nikolai coughs to cover a laugh, shuddering as I glare daggers straight at him, making direct eye contact for the first time.

He looks away in an instant. A sneer pulls my face as I'm almost positive I see him blush.

*He's so strange.*

"Well, you kids have fun then. I'm going home to rest my old bones. Riding in the car that long does a number on my back." Ignorant to the silent conflict happening right in front of him, Ivan stretches and heads for the door.

"Okay, goodbye Uncle. Thanks for bringing me your vagrant," Nikolai teases.

*Forget Caroline, he's officially at the top of my mental hit list.*

Moving through the living room, to the opposite side of the house, we enter an outrageously nice kitchen. A double door stainless steel refrigerator is built into sleek black cabinets. Gorgeous wooden countertops contrast against gleaming white tiled floors. Why would one man ever need such a nice kitchen?

We step into the garage through a sturdy sliding door connected to the kitchen. Parked inside is a black SUV, and a deep blue truck with tires that must match the size of Nikolai's ego. Evidently, he just has a vehicle for every damned occasion.

*Ridiculous.*

I get into the back seat of the SUV, behind Nikolai so I don't have to look at him. Caroline can have her precious shotgun seat.

That does nothing to stop this man from trying to make conversation.

# CHAPTER 4

## Nikolai

*Holy shit. Holy. Fucking. Shit.*

I should have pushed Caroline harder when they showed up. What the *fuck* am I supposed to do with this fiercely captivating woman living under the same roof as me?

With the scar over her right eye, bisecting her dark brow, and her tiny frame swimming in Caroline's baggy hoodie—glaring as hard as possible at me—she's a vision.

*Fucking hell Nikolai play it cool.*

"So... What do you like to wear? Or do you want to go to the furniture store first?" I'm annoyed that I have to look at her in the rearview since she's behind me. Caroline just *had* to steal the passenger seat, that brat.

An ice-cold gaze meets mine momentarily, before she swiftly flicks it back to look out the window.

*Great, she hates me.*

I have no idea why I'm seeking her approval so

damned badly. All I know is she's ferociously timid, like the mean old raccoon that got trapped in my garage last spring. Razor sharp claws, menacing growls, and raised hairs. Ready to tear me apart if I get too close.

*God, do I want to get too close.*

"Whatever you want." She interrupts my internal spiral and crosses her arms over herself, still staring out the window.

*Maybe I just make her uncomfortable?*

"I always feel best when I'm dressed to kill."

She stiffens at my words and I instantly want to cut my own tongue out for saying dumb shit.

Typically, I can talk forever, rambling on about nonsense. To be honest, I don't know how to handle someone who would presumably rather drive spikes into her ears than have me utter another word in her direction. "Sorry, bad wording. Anyway, let's get you some nice things to wear. You'll feel better when you're in something that's more your style. Whatever that is anyway."

"Oooh good point Nicky! Li, what is your style like? I just realized you've been wearing my clothes pretty much the whole time I've known you. The scraps you showed up in don't really count." Caroline vibrates with excitement next to me.

My hand twitches with the urge to smack her for being a social bulldozer. Doesn't she see how shut down Charli is? Does she even know what she likes? I'm dying to learn all her favorite things.

No, I can't think like that right now. Charli is lost and

confused and doesn't need me creeping on her.

"Ahem—" I narrow my eyes at Caroline. "—what she's trying to say is that she's excited for you to spoil yourself."

"Oh, well, I don't really know what I like. You'll have to show me some stuff if that's okay, Caroline?"

"Girl, I got you! Nicky can go do whatever nerds like him even do at the mall, and we'll blow all his money on cute shit!"

"You mean *Charli* will blow my money on whatever *Charli* wants. You have a job, and your own money. You don't need mine."

"But you always buy me stuff." She folds her arms over her chest.

"You're twenty-four. Please act like it, brat." My smirk gives me away. I can't be too hard on her, and she knows it.

Uncle Ivan and I have given her everything she wants since Auntie T died. It's done absolutely nothing for her mental maturity. She has a serious case of resting bitch face that makes her seem far more reserved, until she opens her mouth.

I love her to death, though. Even if she's my little parasite. I can't help that gifts and acts of service are my love languages. I bought her a brand-new car last year for her birthday for God's sake.

Even now, after being scolded she just looks at me with pleading puppy dog eyes knowing damn well I can't deny her.

"Fine, if you help Charli get some nice things to wear that *she* likes, I'll take you to the bookstore and buy you some new romance novels so you can ease some of the yearning in that sappy ass heart of yours."

"SOLD!" She yells.

As soon as we get to the mall, Caroline grabs Charli by the arm and damn near drags her through the doors, toward the escalators.

Now, I have a special stop to make while they're busy.

I don't even realize how much time has passed since we split off, until my phone vibrates in my pocket.

**Parasite:** *OH MY GOD Nicky. She's so pretty!!!*

**Me:** *Calm down... and please tell me you let her pick things out. Do NOT force the poor woman to wear more of your pink girly shit.*

**Parasite:** *Hey! She picked her own things once I warmed her up to the idea and showed her how much fun it is. Apparently, our girl likes dresses and comfy oversized sweaters. Cute, right? Anywayyyy she's almost done getting her hair cut!*

A haircut?

Excited flutters fill my stomach.

**Parasite:** *Why the heck don't you have a girlfriend,*

*Nicky? Women would do a lot of dirty things to spend your money so freely ;)*

**Me:** *I'm blocking your number.*

**Parasite:** *Oh, come on! You know you love me too much to do that. Your life would be boring without me you hermit!*

**Me:** *Just meet me at the food court when you're done at the salon. Ask Charli what she wants to eat, and I'll have it ready.*

**Parasite:** *Hubby material I swear! I'd swoon if you weren't my annoying ass cousin. Also, she said she doesn't care.*

I snort as I put my phone away.

A creeping feeling tells me Charli just doesn't know what she likes, and she's too shut down to work toward finding out.

Twenty minutes later I'm sitting at the food court looking like a complete idiot. I've bought food from four places so Charli can take her pick or have a little of everything if she wants.

Caroline's chattering catches my attention before I see them. My throat tightens, heat flushes over my cheeks. I don't give a shit that I look like a complete and utter loser blushing like a teenager when I see her. Caroline isn't wrong. Charli is pretty.

No, not pretty.

She's striking, radiant, mesmerizing.

A midnight blue dress with little white stars is

wrapped around her frame in a loose but well-fitting way. It's so intentional and comfortably cute I can't breathe.

*Fuck me, I'm in trouble.*

I've only known her for a few hours, and I'm so gone it's got to break at least a couple world records.

My thoughts jumble as they approach. "I, uhm..." Caroline sits down next to me and pats my shoulder. I shake my head, willing my brain and mouth to get back on the same page. "Sorry, I like your dress... and your hair looks lovely."

*Lovely? What is wrong with me?*

Charli stares blankly at the mountains of food on the table, ignoring the fact that I even exist.

"I know you said you didn't care so I did what Caroline and I always do and got us what I like to call 'build your own buffet'."

Caroline raises an eyebrow at my absolute bullshit lie. We don't do this. We always just split a pizza and get boba.

*Fuck. I forgot the boba.*

"Thank you." A barely-there whisper. One that I would have missed if I wasn't so zeroed in on her presence. It takes all my willpower to reign in my delight and not act like a total fool over two words.

This feels like some sort of colossal win, even if it's only a microscopic one. A couple of hours ago I thought she was going to run away from my house at the first chance she got. Now she's at least acknowledging my efforts.

"Oh, Charli, I know I told you Nicky was an artist, but he also really likes to cook and dance. You should see the way this man can move!" Caroline wiggles her brows and I elbow her in the ribs.

I know she's on to me and how absolutely enamored I am. She squeaks and pokes me back. We're both giggling like kids while Charli sits across from us at the food court table. If I thought she looked displeased before, I was wrong. The glacial scowl on her face would make a weaker man cry.

Clearly, she has some extremely deep-seated issues. It doesn't deter me the slightest. I want to help her find whatever happiness she can. It's going to start with getting her an appointment with that psychiatrist my uncle mentioned.

I'm personally familiar with how much of a relief it can be to have your own space. So, first, we'll get her some furniture in an effort to make her feel at home.

Charli is currently standing in front of me, frozen, staring at herself in a floor length mirror. She's had her hair cut and styled and is completely lost in her own reflection. Perhaps furniture shopping wasn't a great idea after all.

"She probably hasn't seen her reflection in a while, at least not all at once. You know she told dad and I that she has no clue who she is?"

"Yes, Caroline. I remember everything you've told me about her. Showing up randomly in the middle of nowhere, scratched and bruised, torn up feet. I also re-member you telling me how quiet she is. So, it is very possible she hasn't seen herself in a while. I hope the police investigation sheds some light on her situation."

Charli finally snaps out of the trance she's been in and slowly turns our way. She looks at Caroline, still refusing to acknowledge that I'm standing *right* here.

"Can we go, please?" Tears fill her eyes.

Caroline rushes over and wraps her in a hug and jolts of envy surge through me seeing how freely she accepts her comfort. There's no time for me to get caught up in my own emotions though. I've got to get my girl out of here.

*She's not yours, you idiot, she can't even look at you.*

On the way out the door, I stop by the checkout counter to pay for the things Charli managed to pick out—before the mirror ruined everything. I also make a mental note to cover all the mirrors in the house so she can take time to work herself up to seeing her reflection.

Charli is asleep in the back seat of my Tahoe by the time we get back to the house. She's had a long day, and I know she's probably bone tired. She's so thin and frail, it looks like she hasn't had a good rest in years.

Caroline hops out and opens the back door, softly nudging her. The frantic flailing and heart shattering screams that accompany her waking moment are not for the faint of heart.

My body shakes, holding back how desperately I want to hold her and tell her she's safe now. If only I could reassure her that whatever shit she endured before is over and I'll never let anything happen to her again. Instead, I give her space and let Caroline take her to her room while I head to the kitchen.

This is going to kill me.

I can't handle watching others suffer, and Charli's anguish is like none I've ever seen. I thought Caroline breaking after her mother died was awful. Charli is here to prove that it can always be worse.

Whistling echoes through the room as the electric kettle finishes heating. I don't know if Charli likes tea, but some chamomile and honey with a splash of milk always helps me feel better.

Standing outside Charli's door feels like I'm not even in my own house anymore. As far as my mind is concerned this is her space and I'm an intruder here.

The last thing I want is to encroach on any comfort she may have found, but Caroline left once she got Charli settled in. Now it's just the two of us in the house and for the first time I feel like I'm drowning.

"Knock, knock." I creak the door open and await a response. Silence. Hesitantly, I step into the dimly lit room. Charli is in her bed curled up, still crying softly.

"I brought you some tea. I'm not sure if you even like it but the L-theanine in the leaves is scientifically proven to aid in the production of dopamine and serotonin. So, it should help you feel better. The apigenin in chamomile is also helpful for relaxation of the mind and body." I scrunch up my face as she vacantly stares past me.

"Sorry I ramble when I'm nervous." I chuckle humorlessly and rub the back of my neck. "Please try to get some good rest. I know it was a tiring day, and tomorrow is going to be another. Uncle Ivan and Caroline will meet here. Then we're going to get you checked out at the hospital to make sure you're not sick or injured. Sweet dreams."

She doesn't respond. Not even a nod to let me know she heard me. Alright then. I take the hint and leave her alone.

I slept like shit. I'm up at an unreasonably early hour. All I can think about is the devastating look of overwhelming sadness on Charli's face as she stared at herself in that damned mirror.

I made sure to cover up the one in her bathroom, and the one in the main bathroom as well.

My emotions are all over the place, so I head to my studio for some therapy. Lo-fi music fills the room as I load my palette with a variety of colors.

Navy blue will be the star of this piece. Inspired by images of yesterday. How delicate Charli's pale, rosy complexion looked wrapped in such a rich, deep hue.

The way her expressive golden flecked hazel eyes stood out in stark contrast against it. Onyx black hair, freshly cut and layered to delicately frame her soft, round, face.

She's the embodiment of pure, ethereal beauty. Intense as a vibrantly burning nebula, illuminating the darkness that has engulfed my universe.

The stars on her dress matched the ones in my eyes. I have absolutely no business feeling like this about her after one day, but it would seem that I'm trapped in her gravitational pull.

Before I even realize, a wild and wondrous scene has materialized before me. Cyan and sea foam waves swirl through an unruly starry night sky. Flecks of gold fly about in the abyss.

This is Charli.

All the abstract chaos immersed in waves of beauty I could lose myself in.

I clean up my paint and head down the hall to my bedroom. After a quick shower I make my way to the kitchen and begin cooking breakfast.

It's nice having someone else to cook for now. Uncle Ivan and Caroline visit for dinner, but breakfast food reigns supreme. You just can't beat a good waffle.

Sausage sears on the griddle beside me as I finish whipping up some eggs. Movement in the doorway catches my attention.

She just stands there, hair rumpled, eyes half open, empty teacup in hand.

*She drank the tea.*

My heart damn near throws itself out the window.

"Good morning. I hope you slept well. Did the tea help?" I smile softly at her. She doesn't respond, so I slide a plate her way. "Eat up. We've got a big day ahead of us. The cavalry should be here any minute."

On cue, the door opens and an all-too-cheery Caroline bursts into the kitchen. My poor old uncle is trailing behind her. "Yesss! I love your waffles, Nicky! Dad, why don't we come over for breakfast more often?"

"Are my waffles not good enough, Caroline? I'm sure Nicky wouldn't want you in here screaming at him every morning."

Wide-eyed, I shake my head frantically.

Caroline loads her plate, completely ignoring our teasing. "So, Girlie, are you ready for the doctor today or what? Whose car do we want to take, Dad's or Nicky's?"

"Does *he* have to come?" Charli's voice is stony and flat. It doesn't take a genius to know she's referring to me. My shoulders drop, taking my stomach with them.

"Well, no I can stay here. If you don't want me to go, I won't impose." Looking down at my own breakfast, I wish my tone didn't sound so pitiful.

At this point, I shouldn't be surprised she doesn't want me there. Hearing it out loud still stings, though. Foolishly, I had believed her drinking the tea was a small victory, progress even.

"Well, Milaya, Nikolai is paying for your medical care. But I suppose if he's fine with it, I'll borrow his card while he stays home." my Uncle places a hand on her shoulder.

"That'll do perfectly. Thank you for taking the day off to help Charli." I nod, forcing down my envy.

"The day off?" Charli looks curiously between my uncle and cousin.

"Yeah, Dad is a kindergarten teacher, but he used some of his vacation time so he can accompany us today. I work part time at a vet clinic and I'm off today, so it all works out!"

"Oh, you didn't have to do all of that for me," Charli mumbles, staring down at her untouched plate.

"Milaya, I want to. Part of me feels responsible for your well-being. While I don't have room at home to take you in, or the finances to take care of you like my nephew, here. I have enough room in my heart to be here for you," my uncle tells her with a warm tone.

Charli tears up at his words, her expression lighter, full of gratitude.

Here are my uncle and cousin, making her feel welcome, comforted and cared for. Then you have me, banished to the shadow realm.

Having such deep feelings is difficult and not being allowed to express them for fear of rejection hurts. In this case that fear is clearly warranted. Every time I look at Charli, she makes it well known that I'm unwanted.

This isn't about me, or my feelings, though. I'll give her the world, unconditionally. I don't know what she's been through, but I don't need to.

I see her.

I steady my thoughts and clean up our breakfast mess. Charli nibbled on a waffle and drank a cup of coffee. My need to nurture her has been satisfied for now.

Waving them off, all I can focus on is the tug in my chest urging me to beg to go with them.

# CHAPTER 5

## *Charli*

Pulling away from the house, I stare at Nikolai standing awkwardly on the front step. The look on his face is unreadable. He's peculiar.

Men are strange in general, but I can't seem to get a read on Nikolai. Deep down I don't feel like he's all that bad, unlike the ones I broke free from. Still, I don't trust him. He's just so...odd? Unsettling? I don't know.

When I look at him, I just feel *different*.

I don't like it.

Fortunately, he's been keeping his distance.. The cup of tea he brought me last night, and breakfast this morning were nice gestures and all, but I can't overlook the way my stomach flips when I catch him staring. At this point I don't know what to make of it.

We check in at the hospital and take our seats to wait.

My clammy complexion alerts Ivan to the storm in my mind. As if the dread I feel over Nikolai isn't bad enough, the lobby to the hospital has me quivering as I try to reign in my panic. My fingers ache from my death grip on the plastic chair I'm sitting in.

*Don't pass out.*

"We need to make sure you don't have internal damage, or any sort of illnesses. We also don't know if you've been, well, exposed to anything. They need to make sure you're healthy, Li. Just breathe, okay?" Ivan pats my leg.

"Yes, Dad." I poke, trying to distract myself.

His face lifts into a tender smile.

"Oooooh just imagine if we were sisters. I've always wanted a sister! Nicky is the closest thing I have to a sibling. He's super supportive and fun, but he doesn't like girly stuff." Caroline lets out a snort. "Imagine Nicky getting mani-pedis with me."

"Is he genuinely a good person?" I don't know why I care. But there's something different about Nikolai. For some strange reason, part of me wants to care.

"Oh, totally. He loves with everything he has and wears his emotions all over his face. The poor guy has had the worst luck with women though. I give him hell for it all the time. He gets flustered easily." She giggles.

"It's got to be challenging though. He has the whole hot nerd vibe going. He's a successful introvert with enough feelings to make a statue cry. You'd expect him to be the broody, silent, rich guy. But he's so passionate, full of snuggles, deep conversations, and quirky facts."

"So, he *wants* to pay for my stuff then? Or are you pushing him to do it?" I scrunch my face.

"Girl, he practically forced us to let him pay for your

things. Trust me, nobody is twisting his arm about it."

*Interesting.*

The hospital visit is as routine as it gets. I'll have to wait for blood test results, but all my physical exams go well, miraculously.

I had an IUD during, which explains how I never got pregnant. I had it removed though, since I have no idea when it was implanted. A new prescription for birth control pills takes its place. Thankfully I have no lasting physical damage.

Hours have passed by the time we finally return to the house.

Nikolai is seated at the kitchen table with a small box in his hand. "I bought this for you at the mall yesterday while you were shopping. It took a bit to get it all set up and everything, but I figured you'd need your own phone for important calls and things like that."

My hands shake as I cautiously open the box. Inside is a brand new, sleek phone. It comes to life as I press the button on the side, just like I've seen Caroline do with hers more times than I can count.

"I've already programmed my number, as well as Uncle Ivan's and Caroline's. I can show you how to use it if you'd like?"

I stare at him longer than I should.

For the first time I allow myself to look at him, truly *look* at him.

His jaw is strong and defined, peppered by a hint of stubble. His face is angular, with high cheekbones, yet there's a hint of boyish softness, I think it's the dimples. Long lashes encompass his dusty green eyes, framed by black square glasses that really work for him. Thick and shiny, dark hair falls in waves across his brows.

I fully understand how women would find him attractive. It's almost a shame I can't stand to be in the same room as him.

I offer a tired smile to no one in particular and take this new contraption to my room.

I rested and settled in for the last few days. Nikolai has left me alone for most of it, except to bring me food, which I don't really eat.

The thoughtfulness is nice, I suppose. He's trying to show me some sort of hospitality. My appetite is just completely absent with everything going on.

My blood work results came back yesterday. I'm deficient in a lot of vitamins, which isn't shocking. Aside from that I'm healthy. Thankfully I'm free from any diseases.

I've been bored out of my mind all week with nothing more than a single book to read. The phone Nikolai gave me has sat unused on the stand next to my bed. I don't know how to operate most of the features on it, and I'm not about to ask him for help. The twisting deep in my gut that happens when I'm around him overpowers my need for entertainment.

It's Friday now. Waves of unchecked emotions consume me. I've been free for a week.

I have an appointment to see the psychiatrist Detective Hastings recommended. I'm fidgeting in my seat at the thought of trying to relive the things I've endured. The fact that Nikolai is the only one available to take me only exacerbates my panic.

We're taking the Corvette, which means I have no choice but to sit in the passenger seat. Nikolai is wearing a deep blue T-shirt and some nicely fitted jeans. The clean, casual way that he dresses is different from the men who locked me away. The cologne he wears also smells a lot better than their stench, so that's a bonus. Especially in such close quarters.

He avoids eye contact while handing me his phone.

"Uh?" I stare down at it.

*Does he expect me to read his mind?*

"It's connected to the car. I figured you could play some music you like. You know, since my pest of a cousin isn't here hogging DJ rights."

"Oh, uh I don't know—"

"Shit, I'm sorry. Of course you don't know what app it is. God I'm a complete idiot." He delicately swipes a long finger across the screen, careful not to make contact with my hand.

*Is he shaking?*

When he taps on a green circle the image changes. There are endless lists filled with tons of music options. Open-mouthed, I try to make sense of what I'm seeing.

"Tap that magnifying glass in the top and type out the name of a song you like, then play it." He shifts in his seat.

"I don't know any songs." Burning embarrassment creeps up my neck.

"Oh." Nikolai stares at his lap for a second, then sends me an intense look that makes my entire body tingle. "We'll have to figure out what you like then."

He immediately chokes on the words. "I'm sorry, that sounded so fucking desperate. I swear I mean music. Not, uh, anything else." His face is ablaze with red blotches. I don't know what his problem is, but I want out of this damned car.

I blindly tap the screen of his phone, and a random song fills the car, something about sunflowers.

Nikolai clears his throat. "Right then, let's get you to this appointment."

I silently observe the world as it passes by. So many people go about their daily lives, never having to worry about a thing. Such a state of ignorant bliss I wish I could accompany them in.

The white brick building we park in front of is far nicer than I had expected for a psychiatrist's office. The front lobby is nothing like the police station, or even the hospital.

Pillars, waterfalls on the walls, trays with swirled white sand and gray stones adorn the tables. If this is just the waiting area what the hell is in store for me on the other side of the door?

Shortly after checking myself in, a tall slender woman appears through the dark wooden door of the office. Sleek blonde hair pulled into a high ponytail, her slate-gray pencil skirt and blush-pink blouse are easily the most expensive clothes I've ever seen. I can't even imagine how much this is going to cost Nikolai.

I'm going to be in debt to him for the rest of my life.

Maybe that's his whole plan.

"Charli? I'm Doctor Hastings. Would you like to accompany me to my office?" She tilts her head toward the door.

"Hastings?" My eyes grow wide.

"Yes, Detective Hastings is my husband. Though I can assure you his recommendation has nothing to do with our marital status, and everything to do with my accolades and capabilities. You're in the very best practice this side of Seattle."

"Oh, I wasn't thinking about that, I just didn't expect it at all." She watches me, analytically, as I wrap my arms around myself.

"It's no bother. Now, right this way. We mustn't dawdle. We've got mysteries to unveil." She grins and turns back toward her office. I rise to my feet and scurry to follow her, leaving Nikolai behind.

Once we're inside, she has me sit on a chaise lounge.

"Okay Charli, this won't be a typical session. I'm not going to load you up with medications to mask your issues. I'm also not going to have you lie there and tell me how it makes you feel to have no recollection of your past. We're here to help you discover your past, and that requires acting accordingly. So, without further ado, please lay back and close your eyes."

She strides around the room, turning on soft, subtle music. The rhythmic clacking of her heels on the tiled floor soothes me like a metronome. Almost immediately the scents of lavender and something herbal fill the air around me.

"This is an essential oil blend designed to calm your emotions and allow you to open your mind. Based on your file, and our brief introduction, you've show-cased classic signs of PTSD, as well as dissociative am-nesia. Some practices would promote hypnotherapy or EMDR therapy to aid in the recovery of repressed mem-ories. I prefer a more natural meditative approach, one you can manage while at home, should you desire. Now, relax yourself. Allow your mind and body to fall into a state of bliss."

I'm filled with tingles as I immerse myself in the seren-ity of the room around me. A sigh escapes me involun-tarily.

"Focus on breathing slowly and calmly. Allow your mind to accept your newfound safety and security."

I'm weightless as my mind relaxes and the room be-gins to feel cold and damp. Dread begins to overtake my senses. The familiar electric zing of panic shoots through me as distressing memories crash into my subconscious.

*My head pulses. The blood pumping through my veins*

*sounds like thunder in my ears. I'm young, unsure of where to go or what I'm going to do. A faceless man is here with me.*

*I'm devastated, my world feels fractured as I'm brought to a concrete room and left there, alone in the dark, without another word. "Uncle V-Vinny please don't leave me down here!" I stutter through violent, pleading sobs.*

Tears fight to evacuate my tightly sealed eyes. "I-I can't." Frantically, I sit up and bolt out of the room. Doctor Hastings makes no effort to follow, as if she anticipated this reaction.

My hands shake at my side as I rush out the front door. Nikolai follows silently behind me. His face is tight, filled with questions and worry as we load into the car. I know he wants to ask, he doesn't.

We drive to the house in silence. His stray glances burn like fire, scorching my already stinging skin.

I barely give him time to put the car in park before I dash to my room, curl up in my bed and sob through the blazing panic until I fall asleep.

# CHAPTER 6

## *Charli*

I don't know how I'm supposed to feel. I spent so long dreaming of freedom. Now that I have it, I'm immensely overwhelmed by everything. Therapy was utterly terrifying.

I don't know if I can re-experience all that suffering. The small flashbacks I've had since my attempted appointment last week are unsettling enough.

Trauma is a funny thing. I don't mourn the life I lost, probably because I don't remember it. What I do mourn is who I could have been had my life not taken such a dark turn.

I have no idea why I went to live there, or who Vincent really is. I vaguely remember calling him my uncle but can't begin to place the connection to me.

I haven't left my bedroom all week. Every time Nikolai comes to my room pure terror guts me. His presence is something I may never get used to. My mental capacity to try is non-existent at this point. Despite his continued kindness, he still makes me irrationally nervous.

Fortunately, after my appointment he began texting me and announcing his approach before entering my room. Such an effort would likely be endearing to anyone else. I just don't know how to not be furious at him for simply existing.

I'm not sure where he gets all the food that he brings me. The tiny bites I've managed to stomach over these past two weeks have all been delicious though.

I love food, I only wish I could enjoy it more. My appetite, like my emotions, just won't let me appreciate his acts of kindness.

Vibration rattles the stand next to my bed.

*Great, what does he want now?*

I sigh and feel my muscles relax as Caroline's name lights up on the screen. Up to this point she has mainly checked in to see how I was getting along with Nikolai. The rational part of me feels a bit guilty that I don't think as highly of him as she thinks I should.

**Caroline:** *Good morning! I hope your last couple of days have been better. I want to take you to the bookstore today. Are you feeling up to it?*

That's right, Ivan isn't feeling well so they aren't going to come for dinner tonight. Sappy romance novels are my one weakness, thanks to Caroline for introducing me to them. A small smile pulls at my lips.

*__Me:__ I'll always feel up to book shopping. You don't have to buy me anything though. We can just go and look around.*

*__Caroline:__ Girlie, there's not a chance in hell Nicky would ever let me take you anywhere and have you come back empty handed. He's already told me we can use his card.*

My eyes hurt from how hard I roll them. Of course, Nikolai is paying.

*__Me:__ Is he going to be there?*

*__Caroline:__ No... but I'm sure he would love to go with us.*

*__Me:__ I'm just not in the right headspace for that.*

*__Caroline:__ I know. I'm sorry. I just want you to like him. :(*

*__Me:__ Maybe someday. For now, I'll stick to fictional men.*

Fictional men never hurt me. Sure, they might do dumb things and don't always communicate the best, but they always make it right.

*__Caroline:__ I love a good book boyfriend. Real men tend to pale in comparison huh?*

*__Me:__ Yeah, that's an understatement.*

*__Caroline:__ Okay, I'll be there in 20. Get readyyy!*

Nikolai beams at us as we make our exit from the house. I doubt I'll get used to how cheerful he always is. Nobody has ever smiled at me nearly as much as him. Unless malicious sneers count.

A trio of evil grins flash through my mind.

With a shudder I shake off my building anguish.

Caroline's little red car is the physical manifestation of her personality. Loud, flashy, and not a hint of practicality to be found. Further proving my point, she presses a button on the dash and the roof retracts.

Music that can only be described as listening to lollipops and bubblegum blares from the speakers as she weaves wildly through the bustling traffic. She's so carefree, it borders on recklessness.

I envy her ability to push aside the hurt and anger she's lived through. She may be off-putting at times, but deep down I want to be more like Caroline.

An SUV with a few men around our age stops beside us at a red light. Whistles and whooping ring out from them. Caroline blows a kiss their way, followed by a middle finger. Darting off as the light turns green, her long golden hair blows wildly behind her.

"Why did you blow them a kiss then give them the finger? It doesn't make any sense." My voice strains against the wind.

"Gotta keep 'em on their toes, Girlie."

I shake my head and laugh.

We wander around the large bookstore for hours. Caroline shows me her method of reading the first and last chapter of a book before deciding whether she'd like to buy it. It's genius and takes the guess work out of making the final decision.

The café inside has fresh baked, flaky croissants. My stomach rejoices as I manage to eat most of one. Finally having the chance to order my own coffee guarantees I actually enjoy the cinnamon sugar latté I order. We leave with full stomachs, and a few new romance novels.

A more subdued version of Caroline accompanies me on the drive back home. The look on her face is distant as if she's lost in thought. The roof of the car is back in place, and the music is at a much more reasonable volume.

"Charli," she starts, her tone tentative, "you're such a wonderful person. I already care so much about you. Please just give Nikolai a chance to care about you, too." Her gaze flashes over to me.

"I'm trying. If I wasn't, I wouldn't be here." Not that I have other options.

"I'm sorry, it's just..." She sighs. "We've all had such terrible luck in life. My grandparents moved here from Russia when Dad and Nicky's mom were just teenagers. They had to overcome so much." A stray tear breaks free as she sniffles. "Dad met my mother in college, they fell head over heels for each other instantly. They were the picture of deep, endless love."

"I was wondering why Ivan has a hint of an accent, but

you and Nikolai don't."

"We were both born here. Nikolai's mom was my dad's twin sister."

"Oh, I didn't realize. That explains how Nikolai could pass for Ivan's son."

"He basically is. Which is why I know dad has some...reservations about your current living situation." She fidgets with her fuzzy steering wheel cover.

"Reservations?"

"Yeah, he loves Nikolai, he also feels a fatherly sense of protection toward you. If he had it his way you'd live with us. It's not that Nicky isn't amazing. I think dad is just afraid that you two are not a good fit. Given your very apparent aversion."

Now it's my turn to squirm.

I've made no attempt to conceal my unpleasant reaction to Nikolai. I never stopped to consider the effect it would have on Ivan and Caroline, though.

"It's not that I don't want to get along with him." My brows pinch.

"I know. Nicky also has some, well, Dad calls them quirks. That's probably the best way to put it."

"As long as he's not going to force me to have sex with him or anything."

"It'd pretty much be the exact opposite." Caroline shrugs dismissively, not bothering to offer any sort of explanation.

I screw my face up as I try to figure out what she means. Part of me wants to ask her to elaborate, but the sensible part of me decides that it's better if I don't.

"I can sense your curiosity. Nicky's business is his own so I'm not going to put it out there. Get to know him and you'll figure it out. He's an open book. Just know that he's been through some difficult things, too."

"I can't make any promises, but I will try," I mumble.

*Damn it.*

"Fair enough. I don't want you to push yourself too hard either. You've been through a lot. Focus on you. Just don't take him for granted." She squeezes my hand before pulling into the driveway.

Once I'm inside, I make a swift retreat to my room, avoiding any potential interaction with Nikolai. Despite Caroline's efforts to convince me he's sweet and harmless, being in the same room as him still makes my skin crawl.

After taking a warm, relaxing shower I promptly slip into a large cozy sweater paired with some leggings and fuzzy socks.

My bed has become my sanctuary and I waste no time falling into it. The plush duvet and feather pillows are paradise after spending so long sleeping on a concrete floor. I had thought they were overkill but I completely understand the appeal now.

My phone vibrates on my bedside table.

*What now?*

The contact scrolling across my screen this time makes me pause. I haven't talked to Detective Hastings since Ivan and Caroline took me to meet with him.

*Hastings: Good evening, Charli. I hope you're doing well. Have you remembered anything new? Don't hesitate to stop by any time. Or call me. I can also come to you if it's easier.*

God, no. I can't think of anything worse than having him here, too.

*Me: I have had a few flashbacks, but nothing I feel is going to help your investigation. Mainly memories of my childhood resurfacing. It doesn't appear that I had much of a childhood to be fair.*
*Hastings: There's no rush. I have forensics cross checking your DNA and fingerprints in the meantime.*
*Me: Thank you, Detective.*
*Hastings: Please, call me Theo. I'm here to help however I can.*

*Theo.*
It feels so informal to call him by his first name. I'm not sure if his intention is to make him feel more approachable, but it doesn't.

*Me: I'll let you know the moment I have anything worth sharing.*
*Hastings: That sounds perfect. Be safe.*

Safe. Such an unusual concept. I never felt safe before.

Every new day was just another battle in an endless war. One I had to fight alone. My mind did what it could to protect me, while my body struggled with the constant onslaught of abuse and neglect.

Now, a measly couple of weeks after escaping, the concept of true safety still feels foreign. Fear of being taken advantage of prevents me from feeling truly safe and secure. Someday maybe I'll be able to accept it.

Yet *another* text lights up my phone.

My face automatically pulls into a grimace as I read Nikolai's name. He's on his way to my room.

*Great.*

A heartbeat later, he gently taps on my door before slowly opening it. "I brought you some pizza. I'll be in the living room eating while I watch TV if you'd like to join me," he speaks softly, timidly. Even still, his voice is deep and velvety.

I spare him a quick glance, which doesn't go unnoticed. This man is so annoyingly attentive and observant, it's agonizing.

He passes me a plate with two slices of pepperoni pizza, and a dipping cup of ranch dressing. Our fingertips graze as I reach for the golden, gooey peace offering, and a zing of energy passes between us. When his eyes land on mine he promptly looks away. A bright pink blush stains his cheeks.

*What the hell was that?*

I want to cut my fingers off.

With my pizza in hand, I turn myself away and flip

open one of my new books. Nikolai gets the message that I'm done entertaining his attempt at friendliness and leaves, clicking my door closed behind him.

My chest feels oddly tight, almost with...sympathy? No. I can't feel bad for him. Tomorrow he'll do the same thing.

Every day he brings me food, tells me where he's eating, and tries to lure me from the comfort of my bed.

*Hell no. Not happening.*

A good book, cozy blankets, some hot tea, and my own company are all I need. Oh, and pizza. Pizza is the closest thing I've experienced to pure ecstasy.

# CHAPTER 7

## Nikolai

What. The. Fuck?

Those have become my three favorite words since Charli barreled into my life. I just want to hold her, damn it. Why doesn't she like me? How can I fix this?

If Caroline were here, she'd let her comfort her.

I just want to be good enough.

Fuck. My. Life.

The agony and suffering in her eyes as she bolted from that psychiatrist's office broke me. She was so scared. I don't know if she remembered something or if the psychiatrist said something to upset her. I know she wouldn't tell me if I asked though.

So, I didn't.

It's been a week. Every day she's more of a shell than the last. I need to break through to her somehow, I just can't. I'm not good with people in the first place, let alone guarded little warriors who loathe the air I breathe.

She's been holed up in her room since that day, except for her outing with Caroline. She has barely spoken to me, only out of pure necessity. I am ecstatic to see she's been eating more though.

I turn the music up in my studio, letting it flow through me. Warm, golden yellow, burnt orange and scarlet are today's colors of choice. Recklessly moving my paint-soaked brush across today's victim—a large black canvas—I release all of my pent-up turmoil.

Colorful starbursts splatter across the surface. It's pure emotional chaos, perfectly represented. Beauty found in the madness. Flaming desire partnered with shock and a touch of precaution.

*God what is she doing to me?*

It's been a weird day. Charli is in a peculiar mood and has decided to sit on the couch and read a book while I'm in the same room. Suddenly, this documentary about ancient Egypt is significantly less interesting.

Somehow my stupid ass heart sees her presence as a small triumph. Just enough that my mouth decides to ruin it.

"Did you know that mummies weren't always so rare? Medieval Europeans ate them all. Well, not exactly. They believed in this practice called medicinal cannibalism. They thought that consuming embalmed bodies would cure diseases. There was also a paint color called mummy brown that used ground up mummies to make the pigment. It was discontinued though."

*Fuck. I'm rambling.*

By the apathetic look on her face, she probably wishes she was a mummy right now.

*Say something normal, idiot.*

"Did you know the Mona Lisa has her own mailbox at The Louvre? People literally send so many love letters to a painting that it has its own mailing address. Crazy right?"

*No, dumbass, you're crazy.*

I stand, far too quickly, wiping my sweaty hands on my shorts before darting off to the kitchen for some air.

At least she didn't leave, that's a good start. Right?

She's still reading the same worn-out book as I walk back into the room, a cup of hot tea and some cookies I made late last night in hand. "You haven't finished that book yet?" I ask, tilting my head.

"I've finished it four times. I only bought three the other day." She mumbles into the pages, as if she doesn't want me to hear.

"Why didn't you say something? Put some shoes on, we're going to the bookstore."

Panic flashes across her face. She resists for a moment before unpacking herself from the blanket nest she's surrounded herself with.

A giant grin splits my face as we walk to the car. I'm going to take any little victory I can get. Right now, I'm on cloud nine.

"When we get there, you pick out as many books as you want, I mean it. You don't really watch TV so if reading is your source of entertainment, I want you to have enough to be happy with. Then, when you read all the ones we buy today, we'll just come back and buy more."

"Okay."

Another word barely whispered in my direction. It may as well have been a love declaration judging by how mushy my heart feels right now.

*She's letting me take care of her.*

Even though it's only books and food. It's a start.

We drive to the bookstore in silence, I'm too excited to put music on.

"When we're done here, do you want to find a drive through and get some food? I didn't sleep well last night." I intentionally exclude the fact that I barely slept at all. "I just don't feel up to making a whole meal tonight. Especially when tomorrow is family dinner night. I'm going to be making lasagna until my hands fall off." I laugh to myself.

"C-can we get burgers?" She flicks her eyes my way for a second.

Is she afraid to ask for things?

*Damn it, please just ask me for everything.*

"Sugar, we can get whatever you want. Burgers from one place, fries from another and dessert at a completely different spot, it doesn't matter. All you've got to do is tell me. Don't ever be afraid to tell me what you want."

Feeling daring I give her a long look, hoping my sincerity is apparent. "Now, go crazy in there."

"Wait, you said you don't feel like cooking tonight. Have you been cooking the things you bring me every day?" Her eyes bulge.

I take a breath, struggling to control my reaction. This is by far the most she's ever said to me at one time. "Yes... Why? Is it bad? I'll do better if you don't like it. Just tell me what you want, and you've got it."

"N-no. It's uh. It's all been delicious. Thank you."

"It's my pleasure, really. Now, books." I tip my head toward the door.

We roam around the bookstore for over an hour and Charli doesn't disappoint. She manages to find a nice selection of books, some mystery/thrillers, but mostly romance novels.

She's glowing with excitement. Even though she's trying to hide it I see a slight rise in her mood. This lighter version of her is precious and I want to do everything in my power to keep it.

We bring our food into the living room, deciding a casual night on the couch is fitting for our casual dinner. We only ended up going to one place, despite my insistence on Charli's freedom to spoil herself.

I watch her, entranced as she holds a new book in one hand, bringing fries to her mouth one by one with the other. She glowers my way when she notices.

A lump catches in my throat.

Rattled, I stand up and dash to the kitchen.

When I return to the living room after grabbing extra napkins, she watches me like a hawk with the deepest scowl I've seen yet darkening her face.

It's as if my brief absence reminded her that she was getting too comfortable, and now she needs to do damage control.

*Not on my watch.*

"Listen, I'm not going anywhere no matter how hard you try to scare me off. I'm invested." Foolishly, I lean toward her as I place a few napkins on the end table.

"But I *want* you to go somewhere. Literally anywhere else will do," she grumbles into her book.

"But if I leave, I'd miss out on the cute little faces you make while you read." I pout, trying to bring the lighter mood back.

Her eyes burn into me with blazing fury. Before I can lean away, she reaches out and slaps me. She actually *slaps* me, hard, right across the face.

*I think I'm in love.*

I knew she was fierce but holy hell do I want more of that energy. When I stand up, with my hand pressed against the angry mark on my cheek, I see penetrating fear and panic in those big round eyes. The sight makes me hurt.

In hopes of easing her worries, I offer her a chuckle and a—hopefully—playful smile as I straighten my glasses.

Returning to my seat, I redirect my attention to the TV, hoping she doesn't look at my lap and see how fucking hard she just made me.

# CHAPTER 8

## *Charli*

I can't believe I slapped him. I don't know what came over me. It was something about the way that stupid face he made had me reeling in a way I can't explain. I panicked and acted reflexively. There's nothing to do now, except prepare for the fallout.

Internally, I'm berating myself. I expected him to immediately tell me to pack my bags, or worse. God knows I'm used to so much worse.

I still don't have a good read on Nikolai, but I can tell you that the last thing I expected from anyone who just got bitch-slapped was a chuckle.

*Oh god he's got to be a psychopath.*

Shrinking in my seat, I brace myself for whatever comes next. My teeth grind watching as he sits down, places a pillow in his lap, picks up the remote and begins watching TV—like it's just a normal Friday evening, and he didn't just get assaulted in his own home.

"What is wrong with you?" I squeal.

*Why am I even asking?*

"Huh? Oh. Are you talking to me? I thought you were asking yourself why you hauled off and slapped the shit out of your gracious host." He smirks, showing off an infuriating dimple. There's not an ounce of seriousness in his tone.

Resisting the urge to slap him again. I put my nose back in my book, deciding a second time may just be his breaking point.

He resumes the Egypt documentary that was on before we left.

I struggle to sleep. Some part of me is still panicked over slapping Nikolai. He took it in stride, and I want to feel secure in the thought that, if he was going to retaliate, he would have done it already.

My dreams are filled with vivid, horrendous recollections of a childhood that I've decided isn't worth remembering.

Scenes filled with images of my parents lying passed out on ragged couches with needles in their arms haunt me all night. The memories where they were conscious are so much more upsetting. The beatings, the name calling... all I've ever known was abuse and neglect.

Meditation does me no good, either. Every time I close my eyes I see *him.* Vincent haunts my subconscious. I don't know who I was before he got his hands on me, but I know he's a very big part of the reason I'm like this.

I wish I knew what the warm, comforting embrace of a loved one feels like.

As I sit here, mulling over my past, the smell of garlic and herbs wafts into my room, drawing me out of hiding. I wander to the kitchen and my breath catches in my throat.

Knowing now that Nikolai is the source of all the delicious food I've been eating, I should have expected him to be here cooking.

What I wasn't expecting was *this*.

Upbeat music is playing, Nikolai is swaying along to the tune, shirtless, as he kneads pasta dough.

My mouth goes bone dry. Looking at him like this I can't ignore how lean and muscular his body is.

The contracting waves of his biceps and chest while he presses forward and works the dough is captivating. Low hanging shorts show off a defined Adonis belt. Dark hair scatters across his chest and lower stomach.

The tingly, uncomfortable feeling I get when I'm in his presence returns.

*No.*

I can't be this detached.

This whole time, I've thought that Nikolai makes me feel a sense of unease, disgust even. Only now am I recognizing that it hasn't *all* been a disturbing feeling, like I had thought.

I'm officially convinced that I find Nikolai attractive.

As in, I'm breathless while I watch him.

My body superheats as the veins in his forearms bulge.

Holy shit, is this what arousal feels like? Has this ridiculous, awkward man actually been turning me on this whole damned time? Sure, he's nice to look at by most standards, but why the hell would I want anything to do with any man?

My body is a traitor.

I need to leave.

"Are you enjoying the show?" He snickers, peering at me through his thick lashes.

Oh god.

He definitely knows I was having some very heated and confusing thoughts. "Wh-what? Uh. Why are you shirtless?" I try to sound disgusted, only for my cheeks to betray me, flushing red-hot.

"I think my apron is in the washer, and I didn't want to get my shirt covered in flour making the pasta. By the look on your face, I should cook this way more often." His full lips tilt into a crooked smile.

My knees wobble in response.

*Whores.*

What the hell is wrong with me? Every man I can remember has betrayed me. Why am I lusting after my new pseudo-captor?

Nikolai hasn't hurt me, but I still can't fight the feeling that he's only helping me for his own gain. Then again, he did cover all the mirrors in the house when I had a crisis over my reflection. I've uncovered them now, though.

No. There's no way I can let him in and risk it.

Not happening.

Curling my lips, I clear my throat with a grunt and rush back to my room.

Caroline and Ivan will be here for dinner soon and I still haven't changed out of my pajamas.

My hair is tossed in a still-damp messy bun atop my head. I'm wearing a flowy dark blue dress that Caroline lost her mind over. I feel...cute.

When was the last time I felt anything positive about myself? It may only be Ivan and Caroline, but this is our first family dinner, and I feel like dressing nicely.

"Buckle up bitches I brought wine!" Caroline throws the door open with excessive force.

"Easy now, don't break my shit you heathen! Uncle, please leash your feral beast." Nikolai grabs the wine from her and places it in a bucket of ice at the center of the table.

"Li, Girlie! I've missed youuuu. You look freakin' stunning!" She wraps me in a hug so tight I can hardly breathe.

"Caroline please sit down. I knew I shouldn't have let you drink before we left." The humorous pitch of Ivan's voice gives away how entertaining he actually finds her antics. "Charli, milaya, are you well?" His palm squeezes my shoulder.

"I am, thank you. I think I've gained about ten pounds

from Nikolai's cooking though, so I'm glad you're here to help eat it tonight." I let out a small, sincere, chuckle.

Fortunately, my appetite returned earlier this week and I've taken full advantage of Nikolai's cooking skills.

We gather around the table and before I know it we're devouring gooey, meaty lasagna, homemade garlic knots, and sipping glasses of red wine. They all talk about everything and nothing at once until my phone buzzes with a new message.

Curious expressions address me from across the table. "Oh, it looks like Detective Hastings sent me some information. I'd better check this. Excuse me."

I read the message four times, scanning the files Detective Hastings sent me. Reading it over and over doesn't make the words less shocking.

My expression must broadcast my distress because three sets of probing eyes are glued to my face. I lean back in my chair, inhaling deeply to hold back my building tears.

Ivan approaches me. "Are you okay Milaya?"

"They figured out who I am." Having completely lost my appetite, I slide my lasagna around aimlessly.

"Charli Hilda Thornton. I'm twenty-two years old. Apparently, I'm from Seattle. What are the chances?" I try to force a smile. "My parents, Dot and Jeremy... Well, they were not good people, they both had records, mainly drugs, petty theft, and DUI's from what I can see. They drove drunk and died in a head on collision five years ago. That's when my dad's stepbrother got custody of me since I was still seventeen... He's the one who took me. I don't know what led to it, or how I ended up in that room. But I know he was one of my captors."

Ivan rubs my back in small calming circles.

"I have no other family. I'm not even an official missing person because, for the last five years, nobody has missed me. Five years... I-I was in that room for five whole years. Locked away, nobody was looking for me."

"Wait... A car accident?" Shrill words cut through the room in a bitter tone I've never heard from Caroline. "Your parents were Dot and Jeremy Thornton?!" She's crying and shaking as she storms out of the house.

Ivan and Nikolai's faces both fade to a matching shade of ghostly white. I can only assume they've reached the same conclusion Caroline has.

"What was that all about? Is she okay?" I bounce my gaze between them.

Ivan pats my shoulder one last time, before turning away slowly. The wounded expression dimming his typically bright features is the most heartbreaking sight I've ever witnessed. "She'll be okay, Charli. Your parents... Oh sweet girl. Your parents caused the accident that took our Theresa away from us. It's not your fault, please know that, but Caroline is still in a bad spot over losing her mother and I'm sure she's just shocked, like the rest of us. I need to go be with her. Nicky, my boy, please don't let Charli cry alone." A solitary tear travels down his face as he steps out the door.

Nikolai blows out an uneven breath, his face now

planted in his palms, fingers tangled in his hair.

Once again, I can't look at him. Only this time it's from my own shame. His aunt was like a mother to him, and I know, like Caroline, he must be hurting tremendously.

"I'm just going to bed." Trembling, I slide my chair out to escape the tension.

"No, Charli, please. Just know that none of us blame you, okay? It's not your fault. Hell, you got it way worse from their fuck up than we did. Please don't feel bad. It's just a lot to process, okay?" His eyes are glossy, I've never seen the look of sorrow written so clearly on someone's face before.

Caroline is absolutely right; Nikolai wears his emotions openly for the world to see.

"Good night, Nikolai." My breath stutters as I fight to hold back a sob.

Not only do I have no family—excluding the monster who did the unthinkable to me—now, I feel like my only chance at having a familial bond has been shattered.

I spiral for hours, sobbing into my pillows until I heave uncontrollably. All the progress I have made has been reversed with one simple text message.

Nikolai brings me a cup of tea and checks in intermittently, which I find myself strangely thankful for.

Numb and lonelier than ever, a small part of me wants to reach out to him for comfort, but I force it back into the recesses of my mind. Yet another evening ends with me lying in bed, curled up under the blankets sobbing

alone.
Always alone.

# CHAPTER 9

## *Charli*

*"Uncle Vinny, why are you doing this?" Sobs bubble out of me through heaving breaths as he forces me into the basement. My body shakes furiously.*

*"Women'r only useful for fuckin' and we aint had one 'round here in a while. The boys'll be excited when they get back from their run. That good for nothin' stepbrother of mine finally came through for somethin'."*

I'm jolted awake, swinging blindly at the figure above me. "Hey, easy there, it's just me. You're safe."

*Nikolai.*

Disoriented, I stare up at him as I gather my thoughts and realize we're in my room.

I was asleep.

It was only a dream, a memory.

After a breath I become fully aware that I'm only wearing a tank top and a pair of barely-there shorts. Panicking, I try to tear my arms from his grasp to get away, but he calmly holds me in place.

"Easy now. Whatever you were dreaming about seemed violent, terrifying actually... Listen, I know you've got some shit to work through. I also know talking and meditating haven't helped. You can take it all out on me if you need to." His gaze is sharp and glued to mine.

"Wh-what?" I breathe out.

*Oh god here it comes.*

"You've been wronged in the worst way possible by a man, or several men, that much is obvious. I could sit here and coddle you, try to tell you how to get over it. Tell you to keep talking it out. Blah, blah, blah. But I don't think that would do much good since you'd rather chew your arm off right now than talk to me about your pent-up feelings." He licks his lips, exhaling a heavy breath through his nose.

"So, let's work through it then. Take it out on me. I know slapping me across the face made you feel something, I saw the fire in your eyes when you did it. So, claw at me, tie me up and slap me, spit on me if you need to. Whatever you can do to feel something again. Allowing yourself to feel is a source of strength, not weakness. After what you learned last night, you need an outlet. Let me be that for you. Please. I...I don't know how else to help."

Molten heat works its way through my entire body. Sensations and emotions that have long lain dormant stir to life.

Softly, I brush my fingertips across his cheek.

*What the hell is wrong with me?*

Fighting with myself, I try again to free my arms from his grasp.

"Ah-ah, not yet. Here's how this works. Based on how you gawked at me in the kitchen, I'm going to trust that you don't want to seriously hurt me and will just use me to release some of that stored rage. Just in case though, my safe word is baboon." He kisses my hand softly before letting go.

I stare up at him in a stupor.

*Safe word? Baboon? Is he serious?*

Nikolai steps away from me slowly, tentatively, awaiting my next move. "We do as much, and go as far as you want here, Charli. You have full control over this situation. If you want me to leave I will, and we'll never speak of this again. But if you want to *feel*... use me."

His words cut sharply through the tension in my room. With shaky legs, I rise from the bed and walk toward him. Only now do I notice he's only wearing pajama pants, which are doing absolutely nothing to hide his arousal.

Looking from his obvious erection up to his languid grin, I scoff. "Strip and get on your knees."

Shocked by my own demands, I stare at him, unsure of what my actual goal is. Subconsciously, I just want him to feel weak, ashamed, powerless. Exactly how I felt locked in that basement.

He drops his pants and boxers in a swift, smooth motion before kneeling eagerly at my feet. His eyes drift up to meet mine through heavy, hooded lids. "Just getting straight to the fun part huh?" The crooked smirk on his face makes a single dimple show up.

Rage builds inside me at his insinuation. I grab him firmly by the hair and tug his head back swiftly so that he's looking up at me. His eyes widen as I lean in closely.

Intensity I'm sure he's never seen before fills my narrowed eyes as I glare directly into his. "You'll only speak if I give you permission, do you understand? If you don't like it, get out." He nods as much as my grip allows. "That's a good boy"

*What the hell?*

As the words cross my lips he inhales sharply and whimpers, trying to suppress a moan. I don't know why, but I'm desperate to hear it. "Don't strain yourself. You're allowed to make noises. Just don't talk. All you ever do is talk."

His cock twitches, dripping with precum. His unmistakable enjoyment makes my head spin with a confusing flurry of need and anger. My self-control sways on a dangerous ledge.

"You're all the same. I know what you want. I see how you look at me Nikolai," I spit his name out, like it's caustic on my tongue. "Men are only good for causing pain and suffering. You all just want to fuck me and treat me like an object, using me to fill a need and nothing more." The last few words jumble as my emotions begin to boil over.

Nikolai shakes his head, brows furrowed, with a pleading look on his face. "No? You don't want to fuck me?" He shakes his head again. "What is it that you want then? Tell me."

From where he's knelt, he stares intently at me with sincerity and passion swirling in his eyes. "I want to lift you up, put you on a pedestal and worship the ground you walk on. You're a fucking warrior, a goddess, a *survivor*. You deserve to be bowed down to, without question or complaint. I want to please you *so thoroughly* you forget any hurt or pain you've ever felt. I want to make you feel sensations you've never dreamt of and devour you until all the hatred and rage you carry is dripping. Down. My. Face." His chest heaves from the intensity of his declaration.

With a shiver, I let out a trembling breath. The air in the bedroom grows increasingly heavy, filled with desire. For the first time in my life, I want a man to satisfy me. I have never experienced this feeling of pure arousal before.

Something about Nikolai kneeling at my feet, begging for the right to please me is empowering and thrilling. Releasing my hold on his hair, I stand to my full height.

As he leers up at me, the smart-mouthed man I've known is nowhere to be found. This is different, new, and... hot.

*Holy shit, I like this.*

Glancing down I take in the sight of his *very* erect cock. Clearly, he's turned on by this in some way I don't understand.

"You want to satisfy me Nikolai?" I raise my hand to the waistband of my shorts. He tracks my movement, the heat in his eyes intensifies as I begin to slip my them off. "Careful, I might think you're going to enjoy this, and we can't have it that easily, you've got to earn it. You'd better beg me to let you put your mouth on me."

Biting his lip, he looks for permission to speak.

I nod once.

"Please, Sugar. Please let me worship you and show you how good I can be, just for you. Let me make you feel so amazing that you forget where you are. Please let me taste how delicious you are. I want to make you soak my face so badly. You deserve to be savored." Raw hunger fills his voice, sending sparks through my body, straight to my throbbing clit.

*Holy shit I'm actually about to do this.*

Slowly, I slide my shorts and panties down and circle him. Grabbing both of his arms, I bring them behind his back.

His breath catches as I slip his hands through one of the legs of my thong and loop the other through to tie his arms in place.

I lean into him, ghosting my lips over his ear as I whisper my demands. "I don't want you touching me with anything but your mouth, understood?" He swallows loudly and gives a short nod of agreement.

I strut back to my bed, filled with self-confidence I've never previously possessed, lean back and close my eyes.

"Worship me."

# CHAPTER 10

## *Nikolai*

I'm breathless. My sanity hangs by a delicate thread. If I die right now, I wouldn't even be upset. Well, maybe give me this, then I can die happy.

The scene before me is pure magic. Charli, spread out on her bed, glistening and ready for me to luxuriate in her excellence.

In what may have been the boldest, dumbest move ever, I told her I wanted to worship her, and she told me to do it.

*Holy. Shit.*

I walk on my knees to the edge of her bed. She isn't looking at me. Her arm is draped loosely over her face. I can only guess it's a defense mechanism.

I want to talk to her so badly and tell her how spectacular she is, and how lucky I am to even breathe her air, but I need to behave and listen to my muse.

This is the sweetest form of torture and I'm salivating at the thought that I get a taste of her.

Fuck, I hope I don't come just from being this close.

Once I'm nestled securely between her soft, smooth legs, I gently skim my lips along the innermost part of her thigh. My reward is a shy moan. Her hips jerk slightly out of instinct.

Slowly, I move in closer, so I don't overwhelm her from the start. If I do this right, she may just let me do it again sometime.

I'll do it every day if she'd give me the honor.

Breathing in her mouth-watering scent, I trail my lips higher, taking my time to memorize all her little noises. She's so far removed from the situation, I'm not sure she's even aware that she's making them. For the first time since she arrived, she's completely at ease. All those walls she built have crumbled, if just for the moment.

Kissing right above her clit, I let out a guttural groan at the first hint of her on my lips.

God damn. I have to bite my tongue, resisting the urge to tell her how exquisite she tastes.

I'm so hard I could beat someone to death with my dick right now.

When I finally slide my tongue over her swollen clit, she gasps. "Oh god, that feels so good."

With that bit of encouragement, I swirl my tongue even deeper into her, moaning against her as I work.

Her need takes over and she grinds herself against my face. The sound that escapes me is full of pure heated passion. Letting go of my lingering reservations, I bury my tongue deep inside her.

Her hands snap to my hair and grip with vigor. The raw desire I've unleashed from her drives me to seek out even more. Her empowerment is erotic as she finds her pleasure, driving me closer to the edge of madness.

Dragging my tongue slowly up to her clit I swirl around it and flick with deliberate movements, paying attention to what makes her squirm and moan even louder. Together we create a slippery, delicious mess.

Once she's twisting, squirming, and on the verge of pulling my hair out, I suck her clit into my mouth and run my tongue around it.

I damn near explode when she screams my name and falls apart on my face with a trembling orgasm.

"Oh my—" she pants, "—fucking god... I-I didn't know anything could feel that good."

Overwhelmed by her release, she relaxes her hold on my hair. Her arms lie limp on the bed over her head.

I groan at the sight of her, taking in her flushed cheeks and wild hair. I'm overcome with the need to break her down even more.

She's about to learn what I meant when I said that I wanted to worship her.

With a rumble I lean back in and keenly slide my tongue through her wetness.

Our eyes meet as she cries out, "N-Nikolai, oh god. Yes. Make me come again."

Her order is music to my ears. There's no holding me back this time. I'll never get enough of her.

I bury my face between her luxurious thighs until I

fear I may suffocate.

Her legs wrap around my shoulders, and she rocks her hips to guide me exactly where she wants.

*That's my girl.*

I consume her like a man starved, as if she's the only thing keeping me alive. We're nothing but a symphony of groans, moans and the sounds of me devouring her, working toward a roaring crescendo.

I drag my tongue from her entrance up to her clit and suck her into my mouth again and she screams. I scrape my teeth against her sensitive, swollen clit before driving my tongue deeply back inside her.

She tightens like a vice and grinds herself into my face even harder.

Feeling daring, I pull back, tilt my head and nip at her inner thigh, careful not to bite down too hard, getting a read on her response.

She responds with a squeak of pleasure and desperate mewls. I nibble at her sensitive skin, kissing the marks I've made as she thrashes.

Eventually, I slide my tongue back through her wetness, slowing down my movements to a more relaxed, sensual pace.

At this point I'm thoroughly coated in her juices, slowly and passionately making love to her pussy with my entire face.

How badly I wish I could thrust a couple fingers inside her and feel her tightening around them when she topples over the edge.

Fuck. If only I could record her scream as she comes undone the second time. I want to remember the sound, just in case this is the only time I ever get to hear it.

Charli lays boneless before me, panting and whimpering. "Wow… I don't even know what to say." She looks down at me through barely open eyes. "You, uh, can leave now. I don't want you getting the wrong idea."

Okay, understood.

She needs to process what just happened and I'm not going to fight her on it. This was a lot, and very unexpected for both of us. I can't say that I anticipated this result at all when I came to investigate what had her shrieking in her sleep.

I work my way out of the restraints she fashioned from her panties. They didn't actually hold me back to begin with, but I would never touch her after she made it clear she didn't want me to. This was for her after all. The experience of being restrained was also hot as fuck, so I'm not going to complain.

I pull my pants back on and move to leave. As I'm about to slide her door closed, she clears her throat. "Oh, and Nikolai. If you jerk off tonight, don't you dare think of me."

Ouch. Okay then.

My plans for the rest of the night just changed. There's absolutely no way I could think of anything but her if I get myself off, so I'll have to do the next best thing.

My studio is still cloaked in darkness from the night. I don't often paint when I'm so turned on. We'll see what kind of emotion I can capture in this piece.

Pinks ranging from fuchsia to bubblegum, vivid orange, and a vibrantly pigmented candy-apple red are what speak to me. The blistering passion coursing through my veins is the tour guide for my brush as it traverses the canvas. Waves and blooms of vibrant colors appear before me, as if I'm not even the one painting.

This is what I live for. Or, what I used to live for, anyway. I've been lost for so long. Charli has helped reignite my passion. I owe her a lot of thanks if she ever lets me give it. Maybe someday I'll have the balls to show her these. I just hope it doesn't freak her out.

It's entirely too early when my phone vibrates. I peel my eyes open to read Caroline's message.

*Parasite: I'm sorry for my outburst last night. I hate to ruin dinner like that. But I know you of all people can understand, right?*

*Me: I do understand. Charli looked completely devastated though. I know this is hard for you but look at what she's been through. Please, I'm not trying to pick sides here.*

*Parasite: I know. Dad sat me down and gave me a very 'wise-old-man' talk. Meaning he pretty much told me I was a giant asshole.*

*Me: I wouldn't say GIANT, but you definitely reacted pretty harshly. I still love you though. But the look on*

*Charli's face was heartbreaking.*

***Parasite:*** *I'll be over in a bit to try and apologize. The last thing I want is for her to think I hate her :(*

***Me:*** *I guess I'd better get my ass out of bed then.*

***Parasite:*** *It's a bit late for you to be lazing around still. Get up you bum!*

I'm in the kitchen making breakfast when Caroline arrives. Charli is still hiding away in her bedroom. Internally, I wonder if last night's events were helpful, or if she's just going to shut me out even more now.

A carrier in Caroline's hand pulls me from my thoughts. "What do you have there?" I raise a curious eyebrow.

"There were a few dozen dogs that got rescued from a puppy mill and a bunch of us at the clinic are fostering them. This one's a cuddly little guy. I wish I could keep him, but I'll take what I can get from fostering him for now." She opens the door, and a fluffy ball of orange and white fur stumbles out. "Isn't he the most adorable thing ever? Corgis are the cutest, I swear."

I squat down to pet him. When I hear Charli shuffle into the room, my nerves immediately run amuck.

Naturally, she's overlooking me and is fixated on the cuteness overload at my feet. A small breath escapes her as the pup makes his way toward her. In an instant she's sitting on the floor and he's in her lap. Charli smiles brightly as the puppy licks her face and paws at her.

Caroline giggles at them while pouring herself a cup

of coffee. "So, Li. Dad is still asleep, it's Saturday, and the world is our oyster now that we're just waiting for more information on your case. What do you say we steal Nicky's card and go get the royal treatment at my favorite spa?"

"Oh. Sure, that sounds nice." The uncertainty in her voice is loud, she clearly has questions.

I would too if someone stormed off on me the night before and just showed up offering a damned spa day like nothing happened. But I know Caroline, she'll make it right.

I grab the card from my wallet and hand it to Caroline, at the same time the puppy decides to pee all over the floor. Charli scoops the little fur ball up into her arms. Holding him protectively against her chest, she gives me a pleading look.

"Please don't hurt him." Her eyes are watery, worry consumes her face.

"Charli, he's a puppy. It's a quick and easy cleanup. I'd never be mad at him for having an accident. He's just a baby and doesn't know any better." I'm mystified that she thought I'd be upset. What kind of hell has she lived through?

"I'm not the type to get mad about anything, really. It'd have to be a lot more than a little puddle for me to even bat an eye." I wipe up the mess and disinfect the spot on the floor.

"Now let me see the little rascal and you two go get ready for the spa." I hold my arms out so Charli can pass me the puppy.

As they leave, I notice Charli watching me carefully as I snuggle up with the little fur ball on the couch. I don't know exactly where we stand after last night, but at least she talked to me.

I can only hope she'll continue to let me in.

# CHAPTER 11

## *Charli*

Caroline and I load into her little red sports car. She's decided to keep the top up and the music down today. This time, I have the mental power to appreciate the sleek interior.

Clean, black leather. Pastel pink inlays. The sweet smell of cherries and vanilla lingers in the air. How did I not notice how nice it is before?

I have no idea what to expect from this spa day. My face falls as I think of her storming out last night, only to immediately heat from visions of the gigantic mess I let myself get into with Nikolai.

*God, I'm an idiot with no self-control.*

"You look lost in your thoughts over there, Li. Is everything okay?"

"Uh, yeah I'm fine." My voice is rough from sleep, and all the exertion last night. I wasn't aware that moaning like that would be such a strain. My cheeks flush again. "Sorry I didn't sleep well... flashbacks kept me up."

"So, you're having luck remembering more?" Her tone is cautious.

"Well, I'm not sure if I'd call it luck, exactly. Some stuff is coming back to me though. I just wish I had pleasant memories to look forward to. It doesn't seem like that's going to be the case." I pick at my nails again.

*Stop that.*

"Are you going back to see Doctor Hastings? Do you feel like it helped?"

"I barely went the first time. I have been practicing meditation like she showed me, though. That's what's bringing back the memories that haunt me at night." I know the half-hearted smile I offer her is not convincing in the slightest.

Caroline takes my hand in hers. "We don't have to talk about it. Just know that I am sorry for all that you're going through, and I'm so, *so* sorry for how I reacted last night. It wasn't fair. I know you need all the love and support you can get right now."

I nod slightly, gaze fixed on our linked hands. "I agree that I need support. I think I will go back to see my psychiatrist. As long as Nikolai will keep paying for it anyway." With a shudder, I shake off the tingles brought on by memories of last night.

"Girl, he'll pay. Don't worry. He's got a heart of gold. He's just got his own past issues, so he's not very good at expressing his feelings anymore. I promise he doesn't bite though."

*If she only knew.*

"Well, I guess I'll have to talk to him about it when we get back then."

"Just tell him you want to go back, it's easy. Trust me, he likes to be bossed around."

I choke on my spit.

"Oh my God! Are you okay? Do you need a drink? Should I pull over?" She pats me on the back, hard.

"No, I...just swallowed wrong," I manage to wheeze out between coughing fits.

"Okay then. We're almost at the spa. Get ready to experience pure bliss." Her bright white grin is blinding, spanning her entire face.

When she said "spa day" she wasn't kidding.

A woman with mousy brown hair, and a soothingly soft voice greets us as we enter. My eyes double in size as I scope out the reception area. This place is extravagant.

I thought Doctor Hastings' office was classy. This lobby looks ten times as expensive. The air smells like mint and fresh linen. Everything is stark white with oak wood accents. We're provided with luxuriously soft white robes to wear during our visit.

The receptionist leads us back to a candlelit room. There are two massage tables in the center, and privacy curtains on the back wall.

"Please get changed, your masseuses will join you shortly. Help yourselves to some cucumber water and get comfortable." She bows her head and steps out of the room.

Caroline and I change into our robes, lay on our

respective tables and wait. Colorful, abstract paintings adorn the walls that I can't help but admire. They're... familiar?

"We kind of have a connection here," Caroline whisper-yells over to me, "Nicky painted all the art for this place." Her grin is filled with admiration.

"Oh, wow. So, he's an actual professional artist?" The shock in my voice makes her chuckle.

"Yeah, haven't you seen his studio? How did you think a twenty-eight year old affords all the stuff he's got?" Her face morphs with confusion.

"I don't know, I guess I don't really know how much things cost. I also don't snoop around his house."

"Oh, yeah that's pretty fair, sorry."

As she wriggles, her visible discomfort makes me laugh softly. "It's okay, I just didn't know. It's really cool seeing his work here though."

"Yeah, he's so talented. When he was nineteen, he painted one piece for some fancy guy who put it in his dental office lobby. Then it's like the whole city found out and he was frantically painting for years trying to keep up with the demand. Businesses all over wanted large canvases. He did murals for the city, hotels, even some celebrities. It was insane! I don't know much about art, but he was smart about it and made a lot of money in those few years" Pride radiates off her.

"Oh, and don't worry, Li. I made sure to book us masseuses, so it'll be just women in here. I may not know everything you've been through, but it's evident that you're not a fan of men."

I blink at her, stunned that she's taken my feelings into consideration.

*Say something already.*

"Oh... Thank you. I appreciate that, Caroline. You're right, I don't like men touching me at all, so it means a lot that you were looking out for me."

"You let my dad touch you though, so that's something at least." She raises a single shoulder.

"He's different. I've felt nothing but comforted by him since I met you guys." My voice cracks with the emotions welling up inside me. "He's really the only father figure I've ever known, even if it's only been a couple of weeks. From what I've remembered about my parents I can't imagine that I had much of a father figure in my biological dad."

"Don't worry, Charli. My dad's got enough heart for you too. He took Nicky in with no question when his mom died. He'll do the same for you." She smiles at me.

"Nicky's mom died, too?" I turn my head to the ceiling in hopes that she can't see the slew of added questions written on my face.

"Yeah, it's not really my story to tell, but she died when he was a baby. That's why my mom and dad raised him. He never even knew her really. His dad wasn't ever in the picture. My parents were only newlyweds. I hadn't even been thought of yet when it all happened."

"So, you really are like siblings then?" I turn my head back to face her.

"Yeah, we argue like siblings too, but we'd both die for each other. I know that sounds dramatic, but when your family has suffered as many losses as ours, you hold the ones you love a little bit closer."

*Interesting.*

Our masseuses enter the room with a plethora of items. We each elect for the hot stone treatment with a deep tissue massage and aromatherapy.

My stomach burns and twists with concern at first, unsure what to expect. Closing my eyes and inhaling deeply, I push myself to relax and live in the moment.

Caroline most definitely knew what she was doing by bringing me here. Weightlessness washes over me from the released tension. A blissful smile stretches across my face.

*This is the best day of my life.*

After our massages, we splurge on manicures. I decide against getting a pedicure since my feet are still relatively scuffed up from my barefoot run through the woods. They are healing well though. All thanks to Caroline's initial treatment, and the medicated cream from the hospital.

Caroline stretches and buckles her seatbelt as we return to the car. She drifts her attention to me with a slight frown. "Girl, listen we're going to go get boba and then you can unload any additional resentment you may have onto me."

"I don't have any resentment to let go of. Well, not toward you anyway. I'm actually pretty at peace right now. The spa was as magical as you made it out to be. I also feel like a 'baddie' as you put it, with my nails done."

"I told you! It's so nice having someone to do this type of thing with. I used to have a couple friends when I was still in veterinary school, but we don't talk anymore."

"Why did you stop going?"

"Well, I took a break after Mom... yeah." She shifts in her seat. "Anyway, I took a year off, then went back for a couple of years but my heart just wasn't ready. There's a lot of emotion in caring for sick and injured animals, and I couldn't cope."

"Do you still want to go back some day? I know you said you work at a clinic right now, so you must still have the passion."

"I do, I think I'm almost ready. I only have a couple more years before I can complete my DVM and can get certified. If I opt for year-round school, I can expedite the process."

"I wish I could work with animals in the future. I'm too messed up right now though. But playing with that puppy earlier was the best medicine." I huff, wrapping my arms around myself, warding off the creeping sadness.

So much more than just my memory has been taken from me.

"Well, for now focus on getting better. Then you can always volunteer at the shelter. They'd love to have you, I'm sure. As long as Nicky is around, you'll never have to worry about money or anything. Take time to find yourself." Her smile is soft, warming my insides.

An unfamiliar feeling of kinship fills the moment. We've had a great day so far. I could see myself getting comfortable with a life like this.

The afternoon sun is high in the sky. We're sitting outside a food truck in a nice plaza sipping on strawberry boba. The peace I had felt has now vanished. An uneasy feeling drifts over me in its place.

My eyes dart back and forth, my breathing is choppy. I swear I see movement out of the corner of my eye, but there's nobody to be seen when I turn my head toward the tree line. A questioning look crosses Caroline's face.

Sensing my rising tension, she looks in the direction of the trees as well. "Are you okay Charli? Do we need to go?"

*When did she get so observant?*

"That would be great. I just started feeling uneasy out of nowhere. Sorry."

"Well, let's get you back home then. I'm sure Nicky is ready to be free of the little pee monster anyway. We've been gone for quite a while." She giggles as she stands from the bench.

I toss one last look over my shoulder as we head toward the car. Still nothing to be seen but I can't shake this eerie feeling.

Thankfully, our drive home is fast and uneventful.

Caroline doesn't press me for any more of an explanation, and I'm relieved. My internal panic subsides by the time we park in the driveway.

The first thing I hear when we enter the house is the sound of Nikolai playing with the puppy. Lighthearted laughs filter through from the living room. As we approach the threshold, my stomach does a strange little swoop.

Sitting on the floor, cross-legged, he makes a claw shape with his hand and bounces it around the floor. He's talking to the puppy with a high pitched, gentle voice and playfully attacking him with the claw.

I'm engrossed in the moment, until Caroline bumps me. "Don't drool over my cousin, it's weird."

I lurch, snatched from my daydream. My shoulders tense up and guilt covers my face.

"I'm just kidding, Girlie. I mean it is strange, but you can drool if you want. I think it's adorable that you're crushing on him." She sticks her tongue out and I want to cut it off.

So much for her mature side I met this morning.

Nikolai pauses and looks over at us. A warm smile filled with adoration lights up his face.

Damn it, he's strangely attractive right now.

I need to leave the living room immediately or I'm going to literally drool. "Uhm, I need to pee... be right back!" I bolt, basically running down the hallway.

There's absolutely no way I'm going to allow myself to fall deeper down the rabbit hole of my growing attraction to Nikolai.

What happened between us last night was, and will only ever be, a one-time lapse of judgement. I simply cannot let myself indulge in the carnal desires I've started to feel toward him. He's my only source of housing right now, and if I let my recently awakened hormones do the thinking it'll only complicate things.

I splash my face with cold water, pull my hair up and take in my appearance. My collarbones protrude, the sharp points of my bony shoulders stick out. I'm still so thin I look like I'd break if the wind blew too hard.

*How could anyone want me in this state?*

Burning envy fills my stomach at the thought of Caroline's full figure. My skin does appear to be more vibrant than it was days ago, though. I can see some minor improvements.

When I return to the living room Caroline has the puppy all loaded up in the carrier and is saying her farewells. My spine stiffens as she walks out the door. I'm abundantly aware that it's just me, Nikolai, and an excess of unspoken questions.

"So... did you guys have a good time today?" He asks as he drops down onto the couch.

I take my seat on the chaise that I've claimed at the other end, grab my book off the end table, and curl up under several plush blankets. "Mhmm."

*Wow, Charli. Such a well thought out response.*

"That's good, I'm glad you guys made the most of your Saturday. I was beginning to think you weren't coming back." He chews his lower lip and offers me a timid smile. "Did, uh, did Caroline apologize? She told me she was going to."

"Yeah, she didn't really need to though. I totally understand her reaction." Casting a glance over the top of my page, my face pulls into a remorseful expression.

The way Nikolai sits, shriveled into the arm of the couch causes a pang of hurt in my chest.

*I really haven't been fair to him at all, have I?*

Caroline has told me several times that he's just a big softie and has horrible luck with people because he's awkward. Having allowed myself to truly see him, the legitimacy of her claims is obvious.

I shift in my seat, turning my attention completely to him. "Hey, Nikolai, I have a question for you. You don't have to answer, but please don't get upset with me for asking." The acid bubbling in my stomach threatens to burn straight through me.

This is the longest conversation I've had with him, aside from my vengeful outburst last night. I square my shoulders before speaking, this is about to get very personal.

"Charli, I won't ever get upset with you. Not for any reason." The tenderness and honesty in his eyes almost shatter me.

"Well...Caroline told me a bit about your mother today. In a roundabout way it was part of her apology process. But she wouldn't really tell me much about what happened." I pull on a stray thread that's broken free from a blanket. "What exactly *did* happen?"

Nikolai blows out a powerful breath and adjusts his glasses.

My shoulders tense up. I instantly want to take back my question.

"Damn, I didn't picture this being the first real conversation we had." He lets out an uneasy laugh. "It's not as sad as you may think, though. My mom suffered from depression. My dad was never there. I don't even know who he is. She left custody of me to Uncle Ivan and Auntie T before she..." He swallows the lump in his throat, averting his eyes. "She took her own life."

The blood drains from my face. His revelation hits me like a runaway train. "I understand now. Caroline told me you're loyal and would do anything for people you love. It's because you couldn't do anything to help her."

Nikolai casually shrugs. "I mean, I was a baby. I didn't really know her. I can see how you could draw that conclusion, I guess. Way to psychoanalyze me."

"Oh, that reminds me. I made a call today. Going forward every Monday I have an appointment with Doctor Hastings. I'll need you to take me." My freshly polished thumb falls victim to my anxiety as I pick at my tattered cuticle.

It's terrifying being so direct, offering my wants as an order instead of a request, but I like it . I feel in charge of something for a change.

A satisfied twinkle shines in Nikolai's eyes. He sits up straighter, nodding enthusiastically.

Apparently, Caroline was telling the truth once again. He really does like being told what to do. Even outside of the bedroom...I'm not familiar with calling the shots, but I want to be.

A ridiculous idea flashes into my mind. My new-found bravery makes me feel adventurous. "I also want spaghetti for dinner tonight... and I want you to cook shirtless again."

*I guess adventurous is an understatement.*

Instantly, an inferno burns in Nikolai's eyes as he stands and discards his shirt. He may be awkward in conversation, but he's certainly not shy about showing off his—very enticing—body.

He wastes no time sauntering to the kitchen to start gathering ingredients. Silently, I watch him from the doorway. Rock music plays from the speaker on the counter preventing any awkward silence.

Occasionally Nikolai will aim a tentative look my way. A playful grin crosses his face when he notices my ogling. I move to sit at the counter and study him as he finely chops fresh herbs, adding them to a simmering red sauce, and rolls out fresh pasta.

The man can cook and my body reacts as expected. I know this turns me on, but part of me wanted proof.

The thrumming pulse between my thighs is infuriating. I'm getting hot just thinking about all the random things he does that make me tingly. I don't know what the hell he awakened in me last night, but it needs to go back to sleep.

Afraid of what will transpire if I spend too much more time around a shirtless Nikolai, I opt to eat dinner in my room. I desperately need to get my urges and desires under control. I'm not a damned teenager.

My jaw ticks and I grind my teeth, painfully aware that my angst-filled, hormonal teenage years were stolen from me.

Storm clouds brew in my mind while I finish my food.

I manage to avoid Nikolai when I take my plate to the kitchen. After returning to my room I flop onto my bed, worn out from the day.

Tears drench my pillow while I lay here and reel, alone in the dark.

# CHAPTER 12

## *Charli*

"*Sit down and shut up, Pet. You should be seen and not heard.*" *A swift slap across my face stuns me.*

"*B-but Vincent, I just want to leave. Please let me go and I promise I won't tell anyone that any of you even t-touched me.*" *Tears pour from me. My left cheek stings. I have no idea how long I've been here, I just want out of this nightmare. I don't even call the monster looming over me my uncle anymore. Family would never do the things he's done.*

"*Yer not goin' anywhere, whore. Yer earnin' yer keep just fine. Ain't nothin' for ya outside of this room. Ricky's lookin' forward to his visit so ya better eat up 'fore he gets here.*"

*My stomach lurches as I stare into the bowl of mushy gray slop he's trying to convince me is edible. They bring me one bowl a day, at least I think it's once a day. Everything has blurred together. I beg to be let go every time one of them comes through the door. They just ignore my plead-*

*ing, use me, then leave.*

*Defeated and broken, I want to die, but I can't. They give me nothing to even think about using anymore. Not after the last time I tried with a fork. Inhaling a deep, ragged breath I mentally try to prepare, knowing I'm in for a rough time with Ricky.*

*He's always the most ruthless. I think he broke one of my ribs once. The others just use me for their sexual release and go, as if I'm not even a person. Ricky likes to torture me as he does it. Not enough to "damage the goods" as Frank called it. Meaning, if I don't bleed, they don't care.*

*I have a scar now from one time when I almost lost an eye. He got too rough for their liking then and they let him know it. Bruises are just fine though, so are welts. Anything that won't leave a lasting mark is fair game.*

*I finish choking down the last few globs of my mystery meal as the door opens and the short, round silhouette in the doorway turns the blood in my veins to pure ice.*

*"Ah, perfect you done finished eatin' just in time, Princess." I wince at his pet name for me, they each have their own. "Time to see if you can keep it down today." His venomous tone coupled with the stench of his body odor is almost enough to make me lose it before he even gets his hands on me.*

*He stalks closer, handcuffs in one hand and a riding crop in the other. "We're lookin' to have a bit of fun, Princess. Ole Ricky's gonna have a real good ride tonight."*

Sweat coats my body.

I wake up choking on a scream, trembling uncontrollably.

My door slowly opens. Nikolai stands on the threshold, wearing plaid pajamas with ruffled up hair. Electric bolts of panic flood my system when I realize I must have woken him.

Surely, he's upset by the disturbance I've caused. I don't know what time it is, but the sun hasn't risen yet.

"I-I'm..." I stutter through uneven breaths. "P-p-please." Wide eyed and feverish, I can't get the words out.

"Charli, I—"

"Nikolai, I'm s-sorry!" Scrambling, I clutch my blanket to my chest and wither against the headboard, shrinking into myself as much as possible.

"Charli, oh god, how can I help? What can I do?" His panicked eyes dance across my face looking for answers I can't give him.

"I'm just s-so cold." My words break as I clamp my eyes closed as tightly as I can, afraid to look at him. "I didn't mean to w-wake you." Tremors shake my body.

"Sugar, it's more than alright. Please just hold on, okay? I'll be right back." In a flash he disappears through the doorway back into the darkness of the hall.

I lean back, panting in an effort to calm my breathing. I shiver through the sobs, bracing myself for his impending retaliation.

Nikolai returns a few minutes later, with a hot cup of tea in hand.

*Oh.*

"Here, please drink it. I'm going to go start a nice warm bath with some of those lavender bath salts you bought. The linalool in it is great for easing anxiety and promoting relaxation." He slips into my bathroom leaving me on my bed, utterly speechless.

I woke him up in the wee hours of the morning—freaking out like a crazy person—and he just makes me tea and a bath.

*What?*

My chest feels fuzzy and strange.

Tiptoeing back into the room, the tightness pulling at his features can only be described as a mixture of pity and uncertainty. He grabs my teacup from the stand and turns back toward the bathroom.

"I'll put this on the tub tray you have so you can sip it while you warm in the bath. It's ready whenever you are. I'll give you some privacy, but please yell if you need me." He places my tea in the bathroom and leaves me to finish calming down.

Tonight's events have been eye opening. For the first time, I believe he's really just trying to care for me.

There's no way I'll ever be able to properly apologize for treating him so coldly the past couple of weeks.

I drag myself to the bathroom, shed my shorts and tank top and slink into the steamy water. Sparks ignite inside me when I notice he also moved the book from my nightstand when I wasn't paying attention.

Somehow, I need to thank him for this. Even if he

doesn't want me to. Maybe it's just my heightened emotions, but a small part of me wishes he was still here. Just to fill the emptiness.

I'm getting tired of being so alone.

I spend the entire day wallowing in self-pity from the comfort of my bed. Nikolai, as usual, only comes to bring me food. I manage to eat the loaded turkey and cheese sandwich around dinner time.

I'm thankful for the space he's giving me, but also desperately want to be comforted. The brief moments of compassion Ivan and Caroline have shown me made me realize how much I love being held and consoled.

I wish either one of them were here.

I perk my head up and grab my phone. I'm so unfamiliar with the ability to freely communicate with anyone I want, I forget about it. Caroline told me to text her if I ever needed to. So, I pull up her contact and try to not sound like the needy, emotional disaster that I am.

**Me:** *I had a horrible dream last night, woke up in a panic and haven't been able to brave going back to sleep all day. I've been sitting here staring at the wall and wanting to be held. Are you busy?*

**Caroline:** *OMG Girlie! I'm sorry to hear you're having a rough day. Nicky did mention you woke up all freaked out earlier and haven't left your room. I'm work-*

*ing a late shift at the clinic taking care of the overnight patients. Sorry :(.*

***Me:*** *It's okay. I thought I'd ask. I just really liked how it felt when you hugged me at the furniture store the day we got here. I guess maybe I'm just desperate for basic contact. I don't know. Sorry to bother you.*

***Caroline:*** *Don't apologize. You're going through shit. If I wasn't working, I'd come over and we could curl up and watch videos on my phone together.*

***Me:*** *That would have been great. Maybe some other time.*

***Caroline:*** *Nicky has a laptop. Text him and I'm sure he'll come to hang out with you. He's got long arms and throws off more heat than a furnace. I promise his hugs are magic.*

***Me:*** *Oh. I think I'll leave him alone. I already did enough damage by waking him up early this morning. I'm sure he doesn't want anything to do with me.*

***Caroline:*** *He'd be in there ASAP if you just ask. Don't be afraid of him. I know we kind of forced you to put up with him but he's not THAT bad ha!*

***Me:*** *I guess I'll think about it. Thank you for responding anyway.*

There is no chance in hell I'm asking Nikolai to come comfort me. I can't imagine he'd want to anyway. I'm also not entirely sure how comfortable I would be snuggling up against him. Chills run up my spine just thinking about it.

A soft knock on my door pulls me from the train wreck happening in my mind. "Charli, Caroline sent me a text. If you don't want me to come in, that's fine. But…I have ice cream, and a movie loaded up on my laptop."

*Well shit.*

His voice sounds so earnest and tender. I can't send him away, but I need to mentally prepare myself to be so close to him. This is going to be awkward as hell, I can already feel it. The deep ache in my chest grows, and my need for support takes precedence over my reservations.

"Okay." The two syllables sound like bullshit as they leave my mouth. Still, Nikolai gradually edges my door open.

His hands are ridiculously full. He wasn't kidding when he said he had ice cream—two heaping bowls of it to be exact. His laptop is securely tucked under his arm. He's wearing a different pair of pajama pants and a plain black T-shirt.

"I didn't know if you liked chocolate or vanilla, so I brought a bowl of each. We can always share if you like both. I like both." His face flushes as he rambles.

I snatch the bowl of chocolate ice cream with super-human speed and drop back against the headboard.

"Okay, chocolate for Charli then, noted." He laughs and tentatively slides up next to me on the bed, close but not touching me. "Is this alright?" Tension fills his entire body.

This is the closest we've ever been…if you don't count the other night.

I look over at him, offer my most convincing smile, and awkwardly nod. He presses play on his laptop and we dig into our ice cream. In all honesty, I didn't know which ice cream I would prefer, but chocolate was in the hand closest to me.

I sneak glances at his bowl every so often. Naturally, he takes notice, and a spoon full of frozen vanilla goodness is lifted to my mouth before I realize it.

With a quirked brow, he hesitantly nudges the spoon in my direction. "Go on, try it. I don't mind."

*He's so close.*

Timidly, I open my mouth.

With anxiously held breath, he feeds me the spoonful. The whole interaction feels so domestic, almost intimate in an innocent way.

"Oh wow, that's delicious, too." staring at my empty bow, I frown as regret fills me. I should have offered to share my ice cream, so I could have more of his.

Nikolai continues offering me spoonful after spoonful of his ice cream, until we've finished it together, anyway.

Over time the distance between us closes on its own. Eventually, I find myself leaning into him, making the faintest bit of contact.

Inhaling deeply, he slowly wraps an arm around me and softly rubs my shoulder. "This isn't too much is it?" His breath is warm against my cheek. The sweet smell of vanilla fills my senses.

My body vibrates, unable to offer a response.

Recklessly, I give into the urge to be closer and curl myself into his side, seeking out his warmth. Pressed against him, I can feel the stress he carries. He's holding back, and I appreciate him for trying not to overwhelm me.

Would I prefer curling up with Caroline? Yes. But this has proven to be a surprisingly decent alternative.

An optimistic warmth fills me. I have a long way to go but tonight's progress feels monumental.

Warm, golden light filters through my room as the morning sun peeks through my window. My head hurts from all the crying I did yesterday. I don't remember falling asleep, but I don't want to get up.

Half-conscious, I scrunch up my face, struggling to make sense of why my bed is unnaturally warm. It feels like the heat of the morning wrapped me in its embrace. With a drawn-out sigh, I relax my body.

Then I feel it.

Something is poking me in the back. Something hard. I peel my eyes open and freeze when I realize that Nikolai is wrapped around me, snoring softly in my ear.

Holy shit. I fell asleep in his arms watching some movie about talking cars. Now his dick is prodding me in the ass.

*Don't panic. It's a natural thing. He's not trying to take advantage of you.*

I inhale deeply, determined to calm the explosion of thoughts shredding my mind apart. I nudge Nikolai gently with my elbow.

He stirs slightly, nuzzling his face into my hair and scooting closer... just enough to grind his morning wood into my ass.

A grumbly sigh rolls from his throat as he squeezes me, placing a soft kiss into the crook of my neck. His body goes rigid in an instant.

I hold my breath, assuming he's awake and finally aware of the situation we're in.

I'm simultaneously reeling with panic and the need to protect myself, but the throbbing between my legs craves for him to continue.

*What the hell?*

I need to have a serious talk with my hormones.

"Nikolai, uh." I clear my throat. "Are you awake?"

"Fuck! Shit! Damn it." He throws himself from the bed, raking his fingers through his hair. "Charli I'm sorry Oh god, I swear I didn't mean to—"

"Nikolai, it's okay. I mean, I freaked out a little bit when I realized what was going on, but you were literally sleeping and couldn't help it." I get out of bed and walk toward the bathroom and he visibly relaxes.

I swiftly close the bathroom door behind me. With a death grip on the marble countertop, I brace myself—hoping my shaky legs keep me upright. I need to get ready for the day. It's my first real appointment with Doctor Hastings, and I'm determined to not look like a

complete mess.
    No more running from my fears.
    Today I start taking my life back.

# CHAPTER 13

## *Charli*

Squaring my shoulders, I hold my head high and try my best to stroll into the living room as casually as possible. Awkwardness buzzes in the air like a swarm of angry wasps. Nikolai stands abruptly from the couch and grabs his keys without a word.

I'm not exactly upset that he isn't chatting my ear off. I'm anxious enough about this appointment, I don't need him to add fuel to the fire.

We're in the front seat of the Corvette. Again, Caroline was on the nose about Nikolai loving this car. It's always in such pristine condition. He doesn't even eat or drink in it.

My whirling mind takes in details I've never noticed before. The air freshener clipped to the visor above my head. His interior lighting must be custom, it matches the exterior too well to be manufactured this way.

When he hands me his phone this time, I know which icon to tap for music. Looking through his recent searches, I snort when I notice he's been listening to some interesting sounding songs.

I side eye him, taking note of how red-faced and clearly embarrassed he is by the history. "There's a song called 'Sugar'?" I press play before he can protest.

The lyrics are undeniably intimate, about effectively being addicted to the subject.

Nikolai snatches his phone from my hand and fumbles to turn the music off. "Actually, I have a headache, it'd be nice to ride without music."

"Nikolai, It's—"

"No, I'm sorry, okay? God, I'm pathetic."

"That's not what I was going to say." I jerk my head back, confused by his self-deprecation every time we talk. Then again, I've been nothing but hostile toward him. Maybe others have interpreted his awkwardness for creepiness in the past as well.

I plan on bringing my reservations up in my session today.

"I don't think you're pathetic, Nikolai." My voice is barely audible as I force out difficult words. "I just, clearly have issues and I-I don't really know how to be comfortable with you. It's not your fault though."

He blinks at me rapidly, mouth slightly open. "I thought you just hated me. I mean, if you do that's okay. I don't want to pressure you to reciprocate my feelings or anything like that... Not that I have *feelings*. Jesus, I'm bad at this." He swallows roughly and runs his fingers through his hair.

"About this morning...I should have never fallen asleep in your bed. I know I was in the wrong, but I just couldn't handle how perfect it felt to have you curled up in my arms."

My heart beats harder in my chest. "Don't worry about it. I slept remarkably well for the first time ever. It wasn't as terrifying as I would have thought."

"Either way, I promise I won't touch you again." A shy, crooked smile crosses his face. "Unless you give me permission, or an order."

*Is he flirting with me?*

He recoils as the words cross his lips. "Sorry I just can't help it, I'm so dumb."

"Don't do that. You're always 'joking' at your own expense. I'm mean enough. You don't need to berate yourself, too." I smile over at him as warmly as I can.

"It's just a force of habit, I guess. When you live your life being made fun of and excluded from things, you eventually just follow suit." He shrugs dismissively, but the sadness clouding his eyes is evident.

For the first time I consider that maybe we aren't as vastly different as I had originally assumed. Sure, he wasn't taken and abused physically like I was, but clearly his emotional scars are abundant.

A feeling I'm not accustomed to takes over—empathy. Before I have the chance to consider my actions, I lay my hand on his jean-clad thigh. He peers down, slack jawed.

I immediately start to pull back, flustered by an unexpected tingling sensation. "Sorry. Uh. I—"

"Don't apologize, please. Let me just have this moment... Please?" Deep pools of sage consume me.

The remainder of the drive is filled with amicable silence. At his request I leave my hand lying gently on his thigh. My mind races with thoughts of Nikolai—how badly the deepest parts of me yearn to let him in.

After we park he slides his gaze back down to our point of contact. "Blue is proven to help you stay calmer, regulate your breathing and emotions."

"What?" I tilt my head, completely puzzled.

"The psychiatrist's office uses a lot of blue. Probably because of the tranquilizing properties. I imagine it helps." His eyes are still fixated on my hand.

"Oh, Dark blue is my favorite color. I never really understood why, but maybe that's got something to do with it." I lightly trace circles on his thigh with the tip of my index finger.

"It also brings out the vibrancy of your eyes and accentuates the pink undertones of your skin." A fierce blush stains his cheeks and ears. "Sorry, there I go, putting my foot in my mouth again. We should go get you checked in."

"You're something else, Nikolai." Other words elude me as flutters bloom inside my stomach.

Doctor Hastings starts the aromatherapy machine, and motions for me to take a seat. "Charli, I'm so glad to see that you've decided to give this another attempt. I sincerely apologize for the fact that I may have been overzealous in our first session."

She sits opposite me. "I was not well informed on the complexity of your situation when I had originally formulated a treatment plan, for that I am immensely sorry. For today's session we're merely covering the basics of meditative therapy."

"Oh, I have done a little bit of meditation since I was here last. That's uh, kind of why I'm back. I've been having flashbacks, mainly in my sleep. They're pretty disruptive to be honest. I was hoping for some help with managing them."

"Ah, yes, nightmares can be an unfortunate side effect. Luckily there are some medications that can help, many of which are also sleep aids. I will gladly prescribe you one to try if you'd like to go that route. It can be a bit more immediate than behavioral therapies. Ultimately, it's your decision as to which route we take."

A wave of relief washes over me. "I think the medication would be fantastic. I also was wondering if there's some way that I can work on my uh, intimacy issues? I don't know if that's the best term." I wrench my hands together. "I mean, I want to be more comfortable with people."

In reality, I just want to be more comfortable with Nikolai, but she doesn't need to know that.

"In what sense are you meaning?" Her perfectly shaped brow rises in question.

"Well, I just get all itchy and panicked whenever someone comes too close."

"Charli, that's a completely valid reaction, especially in survivors of sexual assault and abuse. Perhaps talking about what you endured, that you can remember, would be a good starting point. Coming to terms with what you went through won't come easily, but it could prove to be therapeutic. You also need to allow yourself time to process everything and embrace the newfound control you have over your life."

"Control? I feel like I'm not in control of anything." My nose burns as emotions threaten to overflow.

"Look back at where you were two weeks ago, as difficult as that may be to remember. Compare it to the situation you're in now. Do you have autonomy? Or is there something going on at home that needs to be brought to the attention of authorities?"

"Oh God, no! Everything at home is actually great. I just wish I wasn't harboring so much resentment. I feel horrible for the way I'm treating my...roommate." The word feels wrong, but I have no clue how else to define my living arrangements.

"Is this *roommate* pressuring you into anything you're not comfortable with?"

"Not exactly. He's not who I originally thought he was. I judged him based on my experiences and now I'm starting to see how damaged he is as well, but I feel like he's so intimidated by me. I don't know how to relax around him though."

"It's not an easy process. There are also no right or wrong methods. Perhaps a direct approach would be a wonderful starting point. Tell him how you feel. Set clear boundaries. You also need to open yourself to offering him the same respect."

"We. Um. We don't really talk all that much," I mumble.

"We've all got to start somewhere, Charli. I'm not asking that you welcome him as an immediate confidante. Simply extend the invitation of basic communication his way, with no expectations."

"I think I can try." Staring at the floor, I pick at the skin of my thumb.

"As a parting gift I'll offer you words of wisdom from the late Walt Disney. 'The way to get started is to quit talking and begin doing.' I'll have your prescription sent to the pharmacy for you to pick up later. Do enjoy the rest of your day. I'll be looking forward to our session at the same time next week." She stands gracefully and ushers me out of the room.

Meeting Nikolai in the lobby, we silently head to the car.

"Can we get food, that was so draining." I slump into the passenger seat as he starts the engine.

"Charli, you can have whatever you want. I'm just proud of you for going back." The warmth in his smile breathes a bit of life back into me.

"She helped me clear my mind. I've had so much going on up here—" I tap my index finger to my temple. "—I thought I was going to drive myself crazy."

"Shit, maybe I should schedule myself a session too." A full, genuine grin lights up his face. "So, what does the lady want?"

"You were doing so well." I glare, folding my arms. "I'm not a lady."

"Okay, my bad." He raises his hands in surrender. "What does 'not a lady' want?"

"You're insufferable. Do you know that?" I roll my eyes, only half kidding.

"Hey now, cut me some slack, I'm not used to you acknowledging my existence. The last couple days have rocked the boat." His shoulders stiffen at the tension building between us again. Our easygoing conversation is rapidly devolving into familiar discomfort.

*Do better, Li.*

"I'm sorry. I really am trying to not take all my issues out on you." I soften my features, hoping my expression conveys authenticity. "We can go get a pizza and maybe watch one of those superhero movies you like? I want to see what the big deal is."

"Prepare to have your mind blown!" His face lights up with another smile, crinkling the corners of his eyes.

*Wow, he's adorable when he's actually happy.*

"But first, pizza. Feed me or I'll get... What does Caroline say? 'Hangry'?"

"Oh no. I can't imagine you being any meaner. I'll buy you a whole pizza place if it saves me from ever having to experience you being hangry."

"Are you being serious?" My mouth hangs open.

"About you being mean? I, uh well—"

"No, not that. I know I've been downright vile. Would you really buy me an entire pizzeria?" My eyes must be twice their normal size.

"Well, I don't know exactly how much that would cost. Do I have to pay staff too? Can I just buy a brick oven and be your own personal pizza chef? I mean, I have money but I'm not sure I'm personal pizzeria rich. So...maybe?"

"You'd be my private pizza boy?" I perk up.

"*Man.* Charli. I'm a man, not a boy." A hungry look pierces me as his voice drops an octave.

I can't peel my eyes from his. Tingles run rampant through my body. "I, uhm. Okay. Be my pizza man?"

*What is going on?*

"Is that a question, or an order?" The familiar heat in his eyes is unmistakable. His desire to be bossed around burns white hot.

"I'm uncomfortable right now." My words are meek whispers—barely breaking through the tension in the car.

Nikolai's expression softens immediately. He scrubs his hand over his face. "Damn it. I'm sorry, Charli. I don't know how to act around you and I just fuck it all up. I really am a giant loser. I'm pretty sure I'd still be a virgin if I didn't have a second of minor fame." His knuckles are bright white from the force of his grip on the steering wheel. Black, polished leather squeaks in protest.

The remorse in his voice is believable enough to calm my unraveling nerves. "I'm sure if I wasn't so messed up, I'd have ended up in your bed by now."

"If you weren't 'messed up' as you put it.—" He makes air quotes with his fingers. "—You'd never even know I exist. So, no, you wouldn't be in my bed. You wouldn't be in my life at all." He leans against his head-rest and exhales a shaky breath.

"Nikolai, I promised myself, and Doctor Hastings that I would do my best to communicate with you. She said I need to be open and honest and set clear bound-aries. She also mentioned that I need to allow you to do the same. I'm really trying but it's just...going to take some time."

"All of this is at your pace, okay? There's no pressure for anything to transpire that you don't want. I'll do better at controlling my...impulses. I swear. If I make you too uncomfortable, and you want your own place, I'll pay for it."

He puts the car in park outside of a plaid painted pizza place, giving me a curt nod before getting out to pay for our order.

I don't want my own place. I don't dislike living with Nikolai. I just dislike him, by no fault of his own. I really need to push myself to do better.

For now, I'm going to try and make it through this movie.

# CHAPTER 14

## Nikolai

Charli sits on the far side of the couch, changed into cozy pajamas. "Okay, tell me again. Why are we watching this particular movie? What exactly is an Avenger?"

"This is the first movie in correct chronological order, Captain America is also my favorite! This is his origin story. He's the skinny blonde guy, Steve Rogers. He was a nobody before he signed up to test a secret government serum that made him a super soldier, but that's coming. Just sit back and try to follow along. I'm more than happy to answer any questions." While I'm waving my hands at the screen, Charli listens intently trying her best to seem interested.

"Why do you like him so much?"

"I know it's silly, but canonically he was an artist. He went on to work for Marvel after his retirement. It doesn't take much more than that, sadly."

"Oh, well that other guy looks like a more rugged

version of you, he should be your favorite." She points to the screen.

"You think I look like Bucky? Winter Soldier?" The nerdiest possible snort escapes me.

*As if.*

"I mean, kind of. Your chin is more pointed. You also have slightly fuller lips, but I can kind of see it. He's quite attractive."

"You compare me to him, then call him attractive. Are you hitting on me right now, Charli?" My attempt at poking fun falls short. I immediately notice her mood shift, the distant expression I've grown accustomed to overtakes her features.

*Shit.*

"I'm sorry if that was too far. I know I need to tone it down. Please just enjoy the rest of the movie. I'll keep my mouth shut." I shift in my seat, adjusting my glasses.

"It's just...I think maybe I was?" Her eyes drop to the plate in her lap.

"You were what? Hitting on me?" My eyes must be bulging out of my face, they physically hurt from how wide they are.

"Don't think anything of it, okay? I didn't even mean to do it. I was just drawing a comparison. I wasn't trying to make your ego any bigger than it already is."

"You think I have an ego? What?!" Pausing the movie, I gasp, unironically.

Judging by the way her eyebrows have acquainted themselves with her hairline, it's apparent that my shock is equally shocking to her.

"You don't think you have an ego? You're so full of yourself it's crazy. How many other men would have come into my room after knowing me for two weeks and, you know—" She waves her hands, motioning to her lap with exaggerated movements. "—done what you did."

"I honestly wasn't planning on any of that. I promise. We also don't have to even acknowledge that night if it upsets you. I was trying to help, and it sort of just happened." My face falls before I can reign in the hurt. I hoped she enjoyed it, too.

"It doesn't upset me, okay. God this conversation sucks. I don't really want to talk about...us. Not that we're an *us*." Her arms cross over her chest.

The hard truth hits me.

I upset her. *Me.*

Everything about being here is uncomfortable for her and I'm the world's biggest asshole for trying to push her out of her comfort zone.

"Are you sure you don't want me to find you an apartment? I'm so sorry for always making you uneasy. I just want you to heal. I want you to grow and thrive. I want to see you find yourself. But it feels like I'm just making it all worse."

"You're kicking me out?" Her lower lip wobbles.

My heart hits the floor and crumbles at the sight.

"No, I just want whatever you think is best. It was just a suggestion. I lo—" I bite my tongue, stopping myself before I say the dumbest shit ever. "—I like having you here and I want to watch you succeed. The small victories you've made have been the highlights of my week. I just don't want you to feel trapped."

"But I don't want to be alone! I was left cold and alone for years." She blows out a ragged breath. "Fine, we're doing this now then. Can I be honest, without you getting mad at me?"

"Charli, again, nothing you say or do will ever make me mad. I'll keep reminding you of that forever," I explain, making sure to keep my voice level.

"When I first saw you, I couldn't figure out why I was filled with this eerie feeling. It was horrible and made it nearly impossible to even look at you. The day you made the lasagna I was watching you and it became evident to me that not everything I felt was dread or anger. I was actually feeling butterflies, and chills from my attraction toward you." Her hands are fisted at her side, apparently she's unhappy about this discovery.

"I'm confused. Should I be sorry that you find me attractive? Do I need to be less attractive somehow? I'm just trying to understand the issue. It's not exactly something I've had to deal with before."

"No, it's not that. There's something else. I also realized that some of it *is* a subconscious fear response. You remind me of Frank. After my last dream, I remember him having hair like yours. I think that was what originally made me uneasy around you. The other feelings were from attraction. It's all a confusing combination."

Tears stream down her face as she figuratively slaps me with this nauseating fact.

"I'll shave my head if it'll help. I don't want to remind you of any part of what you went through. Damn it, Charli I'm so sorry." My voice wavers.

"Don't apologize. I like your hair, really. It, uh, it's soft and shiny and I, um. I liked pulling on it." She's bright red, nibbling on her lip and won't look me in the eye.

My dick takes notice.

*Not now damn it.*

"You can pull my hair any time you want." I give her a playful wink, trying desperately to lighten the mood. "In all seriousness, though, I understand your reason for being upset. I know this must be so much to take in, especially when it's all coming back to you whenever, and however, it pleases. I'm not even the tiniest bit upset at you for sharing. I'm proud of you for opening up, and thankful that you're starting to feel safe enough here to talk to me."

A small smile crosses her lips as she wipes tears away. "Can we finish the movie now? I was starting to enjoy it." She turns back to the TV.

With a smile I press play and we snack on pizza in peaceful silence for the rest of the night.

The rest of our week is uneventful. Charli reads a couple books, I paint a few new canvases and do my best to keep her company while I watch TV and doom scroll on my phone.

We haven't talked a ton since the movie, but when we do, I'm learning it's best to just smile and nod instead of saying something she may find off-putting.

It's Friday afternoon now and Charli has just finished a cup of tea and made her way back to the couch to reclaim her reading nest.

*She's so adorable I can't stand it.*

"So, what should I make for our family dinner tomorrow? Uncle Ivan and Caroline will both be over early so they can spend a good bit of time with us," I ask during a commercial break.

"Oh, do you think we could do something fun but easy? I'd like to try cooking. If you'll show me how."

"Of course we can. I'd love to teach you something. You name the dish, and we'll make it happen." An overly excited grin engulfs my entire face.

"Well, we could make roast chicken and vegetables. That should be easy but also fun to prepare right?" She tilts her head as she asks.

"You got it, Sugar. I'll order all the ingredients tomorrow." She turns her attention to the show I'm watching. "Did you finish the book you were reading?"

"Yeah, I have more to read but this show looks fun. You seem to watch cooking competitions a lot."

"This is *Cake Wars*. It's one of my absolute favorites. I love cake, and the artistry of the competitors is amazing! Some of the things they pull off blows me away."

"So, they just try to one-up each other and make the bigger cake?" She puts her book down, leans forward, and watches intently.

"No! It's got nothing to do with the size of the cake," I reply with a bit too much enthusiasm.

"Is that a dick joke?" She's frowning, but it's laced with a hint of humor.

I'm slowly learning to pick up on her micro-expressions. Tiny lifts of her mouth corners, little quirks of her brows. She's subtle, but obvious if you pay enough attention.

"Uh…it wasn't meant to be but it's accurate." I shrug.

"Well, I haven't seen a lot of different cakes. But after seeing yours I can tell you that the other three were cake pops at best."

I choke on the soda I'm drinking.

*Did she just compliment my dick?*

The damn near neon pink color staining her cheeks tells me that, yes, she definitely did. Taking what I've learned into consideration, I decide to play it smart and not let my mouth ruin the moment for once.

Huffing a laugh, I offer her a smirk instead.

I'm fully aware of *who* she's comparing me to, and the fact she can make jokes at the expense of those sick bastards is an improvement.

"What's your favorite flavor of cake? We can make one for dessert tomorrow."

"I'm not exactly sure…I didn't get cake while I was sealed away down there. The memories of my childhood that have come back didn't make it seem like I was part of a very loving family. Cake was most definitely *not* present in any of them."

I shrink back in my seat. She hasn't shared a lot with me regarding the memories she's regained. The more I learn, the more I want to shield her from a life where she'd ever have to experience such horrors again.

Her drooped shoulders and the sullen look on her face have me dying to comfort her.

*Fuck it.*

I scoot closer to her and lift my arm up. When her gaze connects with mine, I hesitate at the mixture of longing, fear, and uncertainty I see.

Determining that it's worth the risk, I slide ever-so-slightly closer until she gradually begins to lean into me. She tucks her head under my chin and starts to sob and I hold her like the world around us doesn't exist.

It's just her.

I'm the shield protecting her from everything else. She's in a safe place where her emotions can run free, and boy, do they ever.

Gripping the front of my shirt, she wails. The heart wrenching cries piled up from years locked away in that hell escape all at once. As if possessed by someone else, her body seeks mine out. In a breath she's curled up in my lap.

Cradling her securely in my arms, I rub small circles on her lower back with the lightest touch of my fingers.

As her cries begin to subside, she nuzzles deeper into

my chest. My heart squeezes from our closeness. This is my first time holding her while she's awake and I never want to let go.

She looks up at me through damp lashes, with glossy eyes. Still poking out her bottom lip, her nose is cherry red from crying. She reaches up and presses her soft palm to my cheek.

I lean into it like an attention starved cat. Her eyes move to my mouth and immediately dart away before she curls back into me.

Shit, she thought about kissing me and my dick immediately got the memo. I shift underneath her to reposition my obvious erection. Fortunately, she either doesn't notice or doesn't care.

"Why are you so nice to me?" She mumbles into my chest.

"Because you deserve to be loved." My lips brush against her hair as I whisper to her. Within minutes she's asleep and peacefully resting in my arms.

I carry her to bed, kissing her temple as I tuck her in.

# CHAPTER 15

## Charli

*A* tall, scrawny man with greasy, dark, scraggly hair looms over me like an ominous cloud. Frank. He licks a trail from my chest up my neck and behind my ear while he gropes me with his grimy hands. Of the three, he's the strangest.

*While Vincent is fairly bland, and just spews hateful words, Frank makes me feel filthy. This whole shit show that has become my life makes me feel dirty, but Frank somehow manages to make it even more disgusting.*

*He's just finished, and I know what to expect next. His—literal—signature move. The man is repulsive and deranged. Every time he's done, he writes his name on me somewhere with his release.*

*He'll literally dip his finger in it as it leaks out of me and sign my body like he's autographing his work.*

*My body may belong to them, but my mind still holds itself hostage. I've begun forgetting things, things I think I should remember. I can't recall the color of my eyes, my birthday, or even my last name. Hell, I'd have forgotten my first name if they didn't use it when they were angry with me.*

*"Such a beautiful little doll. You're the best toy ever." Frank rasps while pinning me down to sign off on his work. "Someday we'll get a new doll. You're getting a bit worn out and aren't as fun as you used to be. But we've still got plenty of play time left." He takes a picture with the camera he always brings.*

*I don't even want to know what he does with them. He'll pose me just the way he wants and if I move before he gets the perfect shot, there's hell to pay.*

I wake in a cold sweat. I must not have screamed this time. Nikolai isn't here to check on me.

Shit...Nikolai.

How did I end up in his lap crying my eyes out?

Why did I feel the urge to kiss him when those tender green eyes melted into my soul?

Why did I slightly enjoy the feeling of his erection pressed against my ass?

*Get a grip.*

Do I want to work on building up my comfort with him? Yes. But I do *not* need to have fantasies about him in the process. How did I get to bed anyway? I hope I didn't fall asleep in this man's arms for the second time in a week. I really need to get my shit together already.

I step into my steamy shower and stand under the scorching hot spray. The crisp, sweet scent of my citrus body scrub invigorates me. I'm not prepared to face Nikolai today, but a good scrub and some pampering should at least imbue me with a little strength.

Ivan and Caroline will be here before I know it, and I'm supposed to help make dinner.

In short, today is going to be an emotional circus.

On heavy legs, I head to the kitchen after my shower to get a glass of water. I haven't cried that hard in a long time. I feel emotionally drained and relieved at the same time. Cuddling up on the couch with Nikolai wasn't a horrible experience. In fact, I may have to take him up on it again sometime. Hopefully with less tears involved.

There's a large white box on the kitchen counter.

When I open it, a sharp laugh rushes out of me. Inside is a variety of cake pops. Over a dozen of them, all different colors.

*This man.*

"I figured you'd find humor in that."

With a jolt, I whip around to face the doorway behind me.

"Sorry, I wasn't trying to spook you. But we never did figure out what flavor cake you wanted, so I ordered a few for you to try." He smiles softly.

"They just *had* to be cake pops, huh?" I prop a hand on my hip.

He looks like a dream leaning on the doorway with that teasing little grin on his face, dimples on full display. His shorts are hung low and the black V-neck shirt he's wearing is perfectly fitted.

Biting my tongue, I suppress a groan.

Damn it, I hate Frank even more for subconsciously making me dislike this man. I hate all three of them, but Frank is at the top of my list right now.

With the slow return of my memories my hormones are also going wild. I definitely need to talk to Doctor Hastings about this on Monday, before I do something I can't come back from. There's no reason I should have the urge to climb this man like a tree.

"You're drooling again," he comments.

"This is the ego I was talking about. It's not cute." Stomping my feet—like an absolute child—I storm past him.

He lets out a lighthearted chuckle.

I've noticed that he's been minimizing his verbal responses to me. I love and hate it at the same time.

Nikolai's silky voice is soothing to listen to, but he says the most out of pocket things I want to glue his mouth shut. It's a real conundrum.

"You're not going to help me get the snacks ready for Caroline and Uncle Ivan? They're bringing board games," he says from the kitchen

I stop my retreat. "Board games? Like what?"

"I don't know, Caroline loves *The Game of Life* so I'm sure that will make an appearance. Couldn't guess what else though."

"Nikolai, I've never played any board games. I don't think I'll be any good at them. It sounds like it's going to be a horrible time," I grumble, returning to the kitchen.

"They're fun, I promise. We'll show you how to play. You're smart and witty. I believe in you."

I dig my nails into my palms, resisting the urge to cry at the sight of his genuine, affectionate smile, combined with his compliment, as simple as it was.

"Well let's make these snacks then. I don't want a hangry Caroline when dinner comes around." I step next to him and busy myself laying out cheese slices, crackers, and miniature pickles on a wooden board. Apparently, this is some sort of dinner party staple. It's just cheese and crackers, but I suppose that's all it takes.

"We're heeere!" Caroline sing songs. "I brought the puppy too! He'll be leaving next week though. The rescue said they found him a home, but we need a little more time to make sure he's clear of his worms and that pesky ear infection first."

"Puppy!" He bounces up into my arms and licks my face all over as I drop to the floor. "I've missed you too, you little wiggly baby."

Everyone's eyes are trained on me, filled with adoration. My happiness really does seem to bring them all joy.

This is beginning to feel a lot like family, even if I still barely know any of them.

"We brought some games, Caroline insisted on *Pictionary*, *UNO*, and of course *The Game of Life*, but I also brought some playing cards for good ole poker if we feel like it."

"Charli doesn't know how to play poker and that's a bit more complex than UNO," Nikolai hisses, scolding

Ivan.

"No, it's okay, I want to learn. You said it would all be fun, right?"

"Yeah, you're right. I'm sorry. I wasn't trying to make it seem like you couldn't learn to play. I just don't want your first family game night to be frustrating." Nikolai's cheeks darken with red spots.

Caroline notices immediately and nudges him in the side. "You're lame, nerd. What are you, fifteen at your first house party?"

"Excuse me for trying to help Charli have a good time." He plops down at the table with a dramatic huff.

"Now Li, Milaya. As the guest of honor, what would you like to play first?" Ivan asks as he sits at the table

"I don't know, Ivan. They all sound like fun. Let's start with *UNO*."

We play games, snack on cheese and crackers, and chat for hours. It's easily the most fun I've ever had.

Nikolai unintentionally puts his hand on my leg and immediately removes it, giving me a remorseful look, surely expecting an adverse reaction. When I pat his leg in return, I swear he nearly sheds a tear of joy.

We're about to make dinner for everyone now, and I'm buzzing from nerves. I know this will require being close to each other and cooking together feels almost romantic. I take a few seconds, breathe deeply and remind myself that this is for all of us. It's not anything more than him teaching me a new skill. I literally asked for this.

"I'll prepare the chicken if you want to wash and chop the veggies." He hands me an apron and points to the pantry where the vegetable baskets are kept.

"You've got such an extravagant kitchen. I had no idea people actually lived like this." I look over the shelves in wonder.

"Well, I don't really care for most material things, but I do love to cook, and I love good food. So, I made sure the kitchen was state of the art when I had this place built."

"Wait, *built*?" My jaw falls open.

"Yeah." He scratches the back of his neck, shying away from my shocked stare.

He does this a lot and I've begun to find it adorable.

"I didn't like any of the houses in the area and decided my big reward for my success was going to be my dream home."

"And the Corvette." I scrunch up my nose.

"You don't like my car? You wound me." He places his hand over his heart with a playful gasp.

"I didn't say that. I just don't think it's practical. What about the winter?"

"I have a truck and SUV for that. They get the job done when I need them to." He lifts a single shoulder.

"Ah, so they're second best. Got it. A man's got to have options."

"Charli—" I swear I hear him growl. "—I don't need options. I'm a man who knows *exactly* what he wants.

I also don't change my mind once I've decided I like something."

"Uh, am I cutting these potatoes, right?" I squeak out, attempting to ease the growing awkwardness.

Nikolai blinks a few times, looks over at my mess of potato chunks, and huffs out a laugh. "They're very abstract. I love it."

His familiar smirk returns, allowing me to breathe easier and relax back into the moment.

Cooking dinner isn't a bad experience at all. Dare I say everything turns out delicious, even though Nikolai does most of the actual cooking.

We all clean our plates and sit around the table snacking on cake pops. "So, Charli, my nephew tells me you've decided to revisit your psychiatrist. How was your appointment Monday?" Ivan asks around a mouthful of red velvet cake.

"Oh, it was very enlightening and helpful. She gave me some medicine to help with my nightmares, and it has. I don't have them every night anymore, and when I do, they aren't as intense. So, I'm considering that a huge step in the right direction." My smile still feels strange, but it's becoming a more regular occurrence.

"That's great, Girlie! I know you texted me a couple of times about the bad dreams, so I'm glad they're helping. I'm sure Nikolai wouldn't mind comforting you again though." Caroline elbows me, wiggling her brows.

Ivan stiffens in his seat. "Now, Nicky. You're being a gentleman, right?"

"Yes, Uncle. I've come close to scaring her off, but luckily, she's stubborn enough to put up with my shit." Nikolai's expression doesn't quite sell the story he's telling.

Thankfully Ivan doesn't notice. I don't know how we'd begin to explain the mess we've found ourselves in.

"Nikolai has shown me some music and movies. He also took me book shopping. I'm working with Doctor Hastings about my, uh, underlying issues with men in general and Nikolai has been very patient with me and my emotions. It's been nice, really." I place my chocolate cake pop on a napkin and squeeze Nikolai's hand. He gives mine a small squeeze back with a warm smile.

He seems to genuinely enjoy the little bits of contact I've been giving him and it's slowly helping me overcome my fear of being touched.

"I told you he's a giant sweetheart, all six foot three of him. He's also the best man I've ever met. I don't know where I'd be without him. You're in the best hands." Caroline pats Nikolai on the head, messing with his hair. He swats her away playfully.

"I'm honestly so thankful that it was your doorstep I passed out on. I don't know where I would be if it was anyone else. I know it's only been a few weeks, but I feel so much better and really am hopeful for the future." A stray tear streaks down my face. I wipe it away quickly.

"It's too heavy in here. Let's play with the puppy for a little bit and lighten the mood. It'll probably be his last time coming, so we should enjoy it. He's going to his new home Friday." Caroline scoops him up and we all shift to the living room.

Nikolai sits opposite me on the floor. We take turns doing the claw move he showed me. The little puppy loves it, bouncing around on his tiny legs. He rolls like a tumbleweed when he reaches us.

When my eyes meet Nikolai's across the room, I can't read the emotion I find in them, but it makes my whole body feel warm.

# CHAPTER 16

## Nikolai

Yesterday was a dream. Sure, there's still tension, and I still manage to make Charli uncomfortable by merely existing, but now I know the reason.

I was only partially joking when I said I'd shave my head. While I didn't go to that extreme, I needed a good change anyway. So, I went this morning and got myself a trim. I hope it helps her feel more comfortable.

When I walk through the front door Charli appears to be just waking from a long night's sleep. "Hey there, you look well rested."

Her eyes scan my freshly cut hair. My wavy locks are off my shoulders now, but still long enough to curl around my ears. "Your hair." She reaches out to touch it.

Instantly realizing what she's doing, she pulls back.

I school my features, hopefully concealing my disappointment. "Yeah, I figured it was time for a trim. I got sick of it getting in the way to be honest."

"It looks so different, in a good way though. Much livelier." Her pink cheeks and soft smile are all the confirmation I need to know this was the right choice. It feels like the first time she's been able to look at me and not feel even slight disgust.

The small reassurance gives me a huge boost of confidence. "Would you like to go get some lunch? We can take a trip to the pet store first. I like to go and look at the little animals and daydream about owning a giant fish tank someday."

"I do love animals. That would be fun. Maybe there will be dogs there that I can pet!" She flashes me a blinding smile.

As much as I want to spend more time with Charli, I absolutely have ulterior motives. This shopping trip will be helpful in more ways than one.

Once we're in the car, I hand her my phone, silently telling myself not to be embarrassed over what she plays this time. As I study her, scrolling mindlessly through the music choices, I realize that I'm falling more and more in love with the woman I'm watching her become.

*I'm in so fucking deep.*

She decides to spare me on the embarrassment front and finds a top 40 playlist instead of investigating my recently played songs again. Her hand rests securely on my thigh the entire drive as she sings along to *Taylor Swift*—decidedly her favorite artist.

When we enter the pet store, I lead her directly to the back where they keep the small animals. I truly do like the thought of having a pet rat or maybe a ferret eventually, but just looking will have to do for now.

"Oh my gosh, these fluffy little guinea pigs are so cute! I want to get a pet someday." Charli has her face practically pressed to the glass as she fawns over the little fuzz balls.

"You'd want to get a guinea pig? I took you for more of a dog person. You sure are a huge fan of the puppy Caroline is fostering."

"Oh, I love him. Knowing I'll never see him again breaks my heart. But I know the shelter will make sure he gets a great home. He came from such a horrible situation, the poor little guy deserves all the affection in the world. He's such a sweet little thing." The hearts in her eyes are the most precious expression I've ever seen.

"Let's go look at puppy supplies then. Show me all the things you'd buy for him. We can put together a care package for Caroline to send him off with."

Charli makes quick work of finding the dog aisles. "Look at this Nikolai!" She holds up a dog sized denim jacket.

I snort loudly.

Of course, Charli is the type who would want to dress her dog up. "What about a little bowtie for him? So, he can make a proper impression on his new home. Bowties are cool, as The Doctor said."

"What doctor?" Her head does an adorable tilt. "But, yes. A bowtie is now a must, do you think the blue one will look cute with his orange fur?"

"Yes, the blue would be adorable. Also, we need to get you into *Doctor Who*, because it's one of the greatest shows on the planet. Next to *Cake Wars* and other cooking shows anyway." I wink at her, she sticks her tongue out playfully in response.

She's in such a fun, light mood today. I've never experienced this side of her before. Well, not directed toward me anyway. It's enough to make my face hurt from my permanent smile.

The rest of our shopping trip at the pet store goes smoothly. I'm fairly certain this is the first time we've been together for an extended time without anything getting awkward, or me making shit weird. We joke back and forth and manage to get genuine laughs out of one another. I'm on top of the world.

Charli admires the baskets overflowing with puppy gear, toys and a really cushy bed she picked out. "He's the luckiest little guy ever! You're so amazing for doing this Nikolai."

"You said it yourself. He deserves the best. Now, let's go get sushi for lunch. I bet you'll love it. If not, I'll eat it all for you." I chuckle loudly.

"Wow, how generous." She rolls her eyes and nudges me with her elbow. I feign injury and push her back. "You're the worst, Nikolai. But in all seriousness, thank you for everything."

"It's nothing, I promise. I'm more than happy to do it. It's a bonus that I get to see you happy, too." I beam at her, and she smiles brightly straight back at me.

*I'm officially done for.*

The sushi spot is busy today—Sunday specials will do that. The small red and gold pagoda is packed with people.

As we work our way through the line, Charli begins slowly falling into a mood of some sort. I can't read her expression, but I've made a promise to myself to leave her to her thoughts and not press for answers, because that's when I ruin shit.

"Does this place make orders to-go?" Her pleading gaze pierces mine. She looks terrified, darting her eyes around, never lingering on one spot.

"They do, if you don't want to eat here. Is it too soon to eat one on one in public with me? Or is it just too busy here? We can go somewhere else if you want." The whine in my voice makes me sound so insecure, but I truly don't understand her sudden shift.

"No, I just want to order and leave please." She tucks herself up against me.

"Okay, whatever you want, Sugar."

She resumes her frantic examination of our surroundings as we wait for our food. I scan the tree line outside where she seems to be focusing a lot of her attention. Nothing seems out of the ordinary that I can spot. I'm at a complete loss.

In an attempt to shield her from the invisible threat outside, I shift myself between her and the windows.

"Thank you." The tension in her face softens slightly. "I just have this uneasy feeling, like I'm being watched.

I felt it when I was out with Caroline too. Maybe I need to tell Doctor Hastings about it."

"I'm here for you. You don't have to hide your feelings from me. Tell me about things when they bother you. I'll do whatever I can to try and ease your mind. Alright?" I murmur.

"You're really just going to enable my paranoia?" Her brows knit together.

"I'm not looking at it as enabling anything, I'm just trying to make you feel safe, and protected. Nothing bad will happen to you as long as I'm here to get between you and trouble. Even if it's just some shadows in the trees."

"That really means a lot. Thank you, Nikolai." She grabs our bag of sushi, and we head straight home.

"Wow, shrimp tempura is amazing!" Charli stuffs another piece of the roll into her mouth.

"Slow down, it's not going to run away." I laugh, grabbing a dumpling. "Have you even tried any of the other rolls yet? Or are you just hooked on that one?"

"Uh, no comment." Her cheeks bulge from the amount of shrimp tempura roll she's hoarding in them.

"Charli, this isn't the only time you'll ever have sushi, it happens to be one of my favorite foods, after tacos. So please try some of the other rolls, too. That way we'll know what to order next time. There's going to be a lot of sushi in your future, gorgeous."

*Shit.*

Charli pauses mid-chew and stares at me slack jawed.

"Damn it, I have been doing so well all weekend, here I go fucking up again." I pinch the bridge of my nose and blow out a heavy breath.

"You... You think I'm gorgeous?" Her voice wavers.

"No, Charli. I don't *think* you are. It's not an opinion. It's a fact. I'm sorry for accidentally saying it, but I mean it just the same. Don't think I'm just trying to talk my way into your pants." My voice comes out more stern than I intended.

"Oh, I-I didn't take it that way." She inhales deeply. "Sorry, I just don't think I've ever been called gorgeous. I sure don't feel like it, or even pretty. I feel grimy, tainted, weak, unwanted...all sorts of negative things." She chews her bottom lip.

Her downturned mouth and dimmed eyes damn near wreck me.

"You're so much more than gorgeous. But I'm not going to scare you away with declarations of that magnitude right now. So, eat the sushi and I'm putting on *Doctor Who.*"

"Yes, Sir." She mumbles.

"Hey, what was that for? Please don't call me sir. I'm not your boss or your dad."

"Sorry, force of habit, I guess. I had to refer to them all as 'Sir' when they allowed me to talk, or they'd rough me up." She swallows hard.

I think back on her telling me not to talk while she had

me on my knees. It wasn't that long ago, but it feels like a lifetime. "That explains a lot, actually." With a nod, I turn to the TV and press play, not elaborating further.

We make it halfway through the second episode before Charli speaks up. "This is...different. I don't know if I like it to be honest. Sushi is phenomenal, though."

"You've got to give it more than two episodes. There's a lot of lore to learn about. Trust me," I beg.

"Nikolai, thank you for the shopping trip, and dinner. It was an extremely domestic sort of day. For a while there I almost felt like a normal person, minus the paranoia at the restaurant. I'm exhausted and I have therapy in the morning. So, I'm going to bed." She unwraps herself from the throw blankets she's bundled herself in and stands.

"Want me to come tuck you in?" I quip.

*Fuck why did I say that.*

Blank faced, she addresses me, "You know, you were doing so well. We had such a great day, I'll let that slide. Good night. Don't stalk me to my bedroom." The dryness of her tone makes it impossible to misread her disapproval.

"Good night, Charli. I won't." I stare at my clenched fists and contemplate kicking my own ass.

"I know." She drops her shoulders, letting out a sigh. "I'm sorry for reacting so coldly, I really need to give you more credit. Hell, you cut your hair on my account and everything."

"You don't owe me, or anyone, any sort of understanding. Just know that I am sorry for not being able to stop the bullshit before it comes out of my mouth. I've been trying though...so fucking hard. I'll do better." I fiddle with the hem of my shirt.

"I promise that I don't hold it against you. I just need to work on my reactions in the moment." She taps her fingers on the wall beside her, temporarily lost in thought. "You're fun to be around, Nikolai. I know you're harmless and really do have good intentions. Your efforts haven't gone unnoticed. So, be a good boy and take care of yourself tonight. You deserve it." She quickly flies down the hall to her room.

My jaw is on the floor.

I'll be damned if those aren't the most erotic words she's ever uttered in my presence. My legs move on their own, racing toward my bedroom.

I spend far too long in the shower. I'm not ashamed about the way that I ferociously fuck my hand because Charli told me to. I come so hard my vision blurs..

As I lay in my bed and stare at the ceiling, I let out a sigh of blissful contentment.

I'm going to sleep so goddamn good tonight.

# CHAPTER 17

## *Charli*

"*Listen here whore, you been slackin' on yer duties. We're gonna have to start punishing you if ya keep it up,*" *Vincent spits.*

*I know now not to say a word. He only gets angrier when I try to defend myself.*

*"What kind of useless bitch uses us like this and doesn't even have the decency to give us a smile or a 'thank you'? You been here leechin' all this time and yer still just a stuck-up bitch. Would it kill ya to appreciate our hard work?"*

*I cry silently as Vincent storms out of the room. He tore up one of my favorite books in his rage. I don't know how much longer I can survive here before I lose what's left of my fractured sanity.*

Nikolai stands sheepishly at my door as I wipe tears from my face. "I heard you crying and wanted to make sure you're okay. Have something to eat." He sets a plate with a delicious looking omelet on my nightstand.

"You brought me breakfast in bed?" I sit up, clutching my blanket to my chest. I'm wearing a very thin tank top and am not interested in giving him a free show, despite his efforts.

"I was already cooking when I heard you. I figured I'd just bring it to you so you could take your time getting ready. We have to leave in an hour though." As he closes the door behind him, my heart flutters.

I've been pushing myself to be more appreciative of his generosity and friendliness. My comfort levels regarding him have improved significantly, but the side effects are rather troublesome. The boldness of telling him to pleasure himself last night was unexpected. Even *I* was shocked by my sudden command.

Curiosity strikes me as I savor the fluffy egg, stuffed with pockets of gooey cheese and salty ham. There's no way I'll have the gall to ask him face to face, so I pull his contact up on my phone.

*Me: Did you have a good time last night?*
*Nikolai: Uh... I'm gonna need a bit more information to formulate a response.*
*Me: You know what I'm talking about. Did you do as you were told?*

*Who the hell am I?*

*Nikolai: ...Are you asking if I fucked my fist for you,*

*Sugar?*

**Me:** *That's exactly what I'm asking. Were you good for me?*

Okay, I absolutely need to stop reading all these filthy romance novels. But the things I've read recently have got me feeling risky.

My blood is on fire as images of Nikolai, naked and hard, flash through my mind. Eagerly, I watch my phone, staring at those three dots awaiting his response.

**Nikolai:** *Yes, ma'am. I wasn't sure if I was allowed to think of you, so I didn't.*

Searing waves of arousal pump through my veins. Some dormant section of my brain takes over as I type out my reply.

**Me:** *You're such a good boy even when you're giving in to your desires. It's...exciting.*

**Nikolai:** *I do as I'm told. My pleasure is yours to control.*

**Me:** *I like that. I didn't know I would. I don't know this side of myself, but getting to know her is empowering.*

**Nikolai:** *You're so much more powerful than you realize. Your presence alone is commanding. You're a badass, Charli. Don't ever second guess yourself.*

I can't reply. My need for release is too intense.

I'm reeling, imagining Nikolai stroking himself for me last night as I step into the shower.

My attempts at pleasing myself fall short. I don't know how to play my body the way he did.

*Damn it.*

How can I be so out of touch that I can't even make myself come?

*What a joke.*

I don't have time to keep trying, I dry myself off and get dressed quickly.

My heart rate increases and panic attempts to settle in as I approach the kitchen. Nikolai is bound to be there. It was only thirty minutes ago that I sent that first text, initiating the scandalous conversation about last night.

Much to my relief, the kitchen is empty. When I put my plate in the dishwasher, the front door opens. Nikolai walks in, wearing a gray plaid flannel shirt and jeans.

I've grown fond of his style. It's so well suited to him.

"Hey there, are you ready to go?" My body relaxes as he breaks the silence.

"Yeah, I was just washing my plate. Thank you for the omelet. It was delicious."

"Don't mention it, really. Taking care of you is what makes me happy. I promise you'll get sick of it eventually." The dimples on his cheeks pop as he grins at me.

"I don't know, I can't imagine not appreciating you. Well, we won't talk about me from weeks ago." I wince at the thought of all the uneaten food.

"Hey, I didn't take offense back then and never will.

You're perfect exactly the way you are."

His words lessen my panic.

"Charli, my favorite patient! How are you feeling?" Doctor Hastings greets me.

"Well, I feel pretty good. I have a lot I want to talk to you about and I need some advice as well." My voice is more confident than the last two times I sat in this chair.

"That's wonderful to hear. Where would you like to begin?" She clicks a pen and folds a paper over on her notebook.

"I guess the first thing I'd like to ask you is how normal it is for someone like me to have, uh, feelings."

*Really?*

All the shit I've been through, and I can't even talk about sexual topics without feeling like a child.

*Ridiculous.*

"What is the nature of the specific feelings you're questioning? It's also important to keep an open mind and realize that no two scenarios are alike. Factually speaking, there are no others just like you."

"Well, I mean. Is it normal for someone who went through what I did to feel arousal? Horniness? Turned on? I'm not sure how else to put it really." Red hot embarrassment burns my neck.

"The concept of normalcy is all a matter of perspective. With that being said, arousal is a natural human reaction. It's also important to note that there have been several documented instances in which individuals who have endured sexual assault find that they have a heightened sex drive."

"Oh, I wouldn't say mine is heightened. It's more like I just started to feel it and didn't know if it was healthy to want sex at all."

Uncrossing her legs, she stands and grabs a pamphlet from the shelf and hands it to me. I'm mortified to see that it's about sex addiction.

"Read this when you have time, it's not that I don't believe you're telling the truth, I merely want you to be informed on the things to look out for."

"So, it is bad then?" I chew my lip.

"No, Charli, healthy sexual desires are not bad. My intention isn't to raise concern. So long as you engage in consensual encounters there's no harm in embracing your sexuality."

"So, what exactly is a healthy encounter, then?" I fidget, internally scolding myself for having to ask.

"Just ensure you're engaging with trusted, understanding partners who are willing to respect your boundaries. The pamphlet outlines warning signs to look out for."

"Oh, okay that seems simple enough. So, then the next thing. I-I want to work on remembering more."

Her face perks up in a flash, full of excitement. "That's wonderful. I'm thrilled to hear this."

"I figure that I need to start taking control of my life,

the medicine helps with the nightmares, so I feel safer trying to remember more details to try and help the investigation."

"We can begin next week. Take some time to build your mental fortitude up some more and we can tackle the first steps of the memory recovery process."

I rise from my chair as the session time runs out. Doctor Hastings walks me to the lobby.

As Nikolai stands to walk me out, she passes me a knowing look.

"He's very handsome. I completely understand your questions now," she says quietly, patting my shoulder as she turns and greets her next patient.

Nikolai's mouth opens slightly as he looks my way. Clearly her whispers weren't discreet at all. I lower my head and walk past him, running away from the awkwardness filling the air.

I don't talk to Nikolai much for the rest of the day. Fortunately, he understands that my appointments with Doctor Hastings are exhausting, and I haven't even started the memory recovery sessions yet. Those are going to be so much worse. I can feel it. I don't know if I'm truly ready, but I want them to pay for what they did.

We spend the next few days lazing around. Nikolai has either been in his studio or watching TV, occasionally he'll leave to go get art supplies.

His increased efforts to think before speaking, to help me feel more comfortable, have helped drastically. It must be eating at him to not crack inappropriate jokes all day, though. I feel slightly guilty that he's doing so much to accommodate me, but I'm thankful for it too.

I've been nose-deep in books, so the days have flown by. It's no wonder my hormones and emotions have been in overdrive with all the sexual scenes I've read in the last few weeks.

With the conclusion of my latest read, I have finally finished all the books Nikolai bought me. After giving myself a quick pep talk, I've mustered up the courage to ask if he would take me to buy some more.

We've come a long way in our relationship in the past month, but I still don't like frivolously spending his money. After all, he's not my boyfriend. He doesn't *need* to do anything for me, even if he tells me he enjoys it.

He's not in the living room, or the kitchen. He never hangs out in his room, so I assume he must be in his studio. I haven't stepped foot inside the studio the whole time I've lived here. I've never had a reason to.

I open the door, not thinking to knock.

I'm immediately frozen in place, greedily drinking in the sight in front of me.

Nikolai is shirtless, wearing paint splattered gray sweatpants that are barely hanging onto his hips. He's in his element and it's captivating.

I recognize the music permeating the room. He's listening to that same "Sugar" song from the car as he skillfully glides his brush along the canvas. His biceps ripple with his motions. Long fingers firmly grip the sleek black handle. The veins in his hands and toned forearms bulge as he works with avid intent.

"Wow," I breathe out, unable to control my reaction to the heat building inside me.

I've tamped my desire down a lot since that night in my room weeks ago, and the texting fiasco. He hasn't pushed the issue, although we have absolutely had moments of flirtation.

Admiring him now though? Oh, how desperately I find myself wanting him to drag that brush all over my body with the same passion he's giving to the canvas.

Nikolai jumps and sinks into himself as he turns to face me. "Ch-Charli, shit." His face is filled with an unfamiliar distressed expression.

Humiliation? Shame? I'm not entirely sure.

"I'm so sorry! I didn't mean to intrude." Against my will, my eyes hungrily trail over his defined chest and slender waist. Only a fool could look at him like this and not appreciate how beautiful his body is.

"It's not what it looks like, I swear. Please don't hate me." With a few taps on his phone, he stops the music. He's visibly nervous, panicked even. Wringing his hands together, he aims his full attention toward me

I peel my shameless gaze from his body. Scanning the room, I notice what he's painted on the canvas behind him, and various others.

*Me.*

Incredibly beautiful, detailed portraits of me in various poses with soft, but powerful expressions. Swirls and splashes of midnight blues and gold accents as their backdrops. A few with varied shades of red and vibrant pinks.

My eyes grow large, taking in the details of each painting. Nikolai is pale and rigid. He looks like I may as well have caught him committing a murder.

"Nikolai, is this how you see me?" My watery eyes melt into his. "I don't even know what to say. They're—"

"I'm sorry Charli, I know it looks creepy and obsessive, but I promise I'm not some pervert or anything like that. You've got to believe me." Fear coats his words. Every syllable is a plea for understanding.

"Oh, Nicky." I whimper, and he shudders at my use of his nickname. "I'm not angry or creeped out. Though maybe I should be. Hell, any normal person probably would be. But these are so gorgeous. I'm flattered that you see me this way."

"You're...not upset?" His chest deflates, letting out the uneasy breath he had been holding

My courage is bolstered by the strength portrayed in his work.

*If this is how he sees me, I should own it.*

Reaching out slowly, I press my palm against his bare chest, taking in the rapid beating of his heart. He glances down at my hand as his skin warms mine, then back to meet my gaze.

"I'm not mad, I promise. I love the way you see me,

even if I don't see it myself. I know you tell me I'm powerful and gorgeous and all these nice things but seeing it like this is an entirely different experience. But I-I need to ask... Why? Why me?"

His eyes drill into me. "Charli, it's simple. You inspire me. I know you don't understand it, and have no reason to believe me, but you're a fucking gift. You're captivating and so strong. You've mesmerized and amazed me from the second I saw you. I fear sounding like a cliché artist, but you've become my muse. Your existence has reignited my passion, it died years ago with my aunt, but you've resurrected it."

His words break through my protective barrier. Memories of how good he made me feel with his mouth send pure lust flooding through my veins like molten lava. My knees wobble from images of his hard, thick cock standing at attention before me. His moans as I instructed him to kneel and worship me echo through my mind.

*I need him.*

"Nikolai, you're the first man to see me as anything but a weak shell of a woman, fit for nothing more than being used." I breathe in deeply preparing myself for the confession on the tip of my tongue. "You gave me my first, and only orgasms...ever. I haven't been able to stop thinking about it."

He vibrates as I glide my fingers along the sculpted landscape of his chest, grazing over a pebbled nipple, sliding down the ridges of his abs. His cock jumps, fighting against the front of his sweatpants. When he looks at me, with lust blown pupils, I feel braver than ever. Desire like I've never known comes alive inside me.

"You've never had an orgasm before?" A husky, yearning wrapped grumble escapes him.

"No, Nicky. What they did to me was for them, I was merely a puppet for their pleasure. I...honestly, I thought I would never know what the big deal is. I didn't think I could feel true pleasure. Then you showed me what it's like and God, do I want that release again." I trail my fingertips back up, twirling a lock of hair at the back of his neck.

"Just say the word, Sugar and I'll let you use me for all the pleasure you could ever need. You know you're in control here. Take what you want," he rasps, biting his lip.

I can feel the pressure building in his body from the extreme level of control he's exhibiting.

*Screw it. I'm doing this.*

I force myself to imagine the confidence and power he sees in me. Sliding my hand down his front, slipping it into the waistband of his sweatpants and wrapping my fingers around his warm length.

A whimper escapes him, he makes no attempt to stop it.

"God, Nikolai, I want to know what it feels like to orgasm while I'm full of your cock." In a flash, I free him from his sweatpants and lead him toward the couch in his studio. "None of the men that used me were nearly as large or beautiful as you. Ever since that night in my room, I've wondered what it would feel like having you buried deep inside me. I tried to fuck my fingers Monday morning, imagining all the different spots you'd hit that they never could." Another whimper rushes out of him.

He remembers me not wanting him to talk before and is taking it into consideration now. My chest threatens to explode.

*Fuck me.*

Doctor Hastings' words invade my thoughts. Nikolai is the definition of caring and understanding.

I motion for him to lay down. He does as I ask without hesitation and tucks his hands behind his head, undoubtedly remembering that I also didn't want to be touched before.

*Holy shit.*

Even though I have let Nikolai hold me, he's still so mindful, further stoking the flames of my desire.

Fumbling, I drop my panties from under the hem of my dress. His eyes widen and his nostrils flare as I straddle his thighs and stare at his erection.

My stomach drops, self-doubt swirls in my mind. "I'm not really sure what to do. Can you tell me?"

"Just use me to feel good. There's no wrong answer. If you enjoy yourself, then it's right." A bead of precum drips down the length of his cock.

I want to taste it, but I don't have patience for that right now. I need him like I need air.

Wrapping my hand around him, I stroke his length a couple of times, relishing in his warmth before lining the thick tip of him up to my entrance.

His lips part with a low moan as I lower myself slowly onto him. Inch by glorious inch he fills me in a way I've never experienced.

"Oh Nicky, your cock...I'm so full." My ability to breathe has been completely forgotten. My brain can only focus on the perfection of how he fits inside me.

He's rock hard, stretching me so much more than I could have imagined. Soon, the look of disbelief on his face shifts to one of strain. "Are you okay? Am I doing something wrong? You don't have to keep quiet. I need you to tell me how to do this."

He grunts and sucks in a sharp breath. "Charli, you're fucking flawless. But I beg you, please move or I'm going to embarrass myself."

*Oh.*

"Shit, I'm sorry." Blushing furiously, I begin to roll my hips. "Like this?" A breathy moan escapes me from the sensation.

"Just like that, look at you making yourself feel good. You're so gorgeous."

I'm glad nobody else lives here because his praise drives me wild. There's no holding me back. Moaning wildly, I bounce up and down on top of him.

He lays statue still, afraid that he'll make a wrong move, with closed eyes. It's as if he doesn't feel worthy of even looking at me.

"Nikolai, you feel—" *pant* "—so good. God damn."

"Fuuuuuck." He sighs out beneath me, opening his

eyes to take in the view. His hands move tentatively to my thighs, eyes searching for signs of disapproval.

When he grips onto me, I freeze. He rips his hands away as if my skin had scalded him. "Shit I'm sorry." Regret flashes across his features.

"It's okay. Please Nicky, I just wasn't anticipating how warm and firm your touch would be. I love how your hands feel."

In an instant his hands find my thighs again, not wandering, but securing me to him, spurring me on.

I lean forward slightly and drag my fingertips down his chest, slowing my pace. His breath hitches and lets out a deep groan.

"You feel so good. I've never enjoyed a cock before. I want to come so bad." I whine and I continue my torturous ride, growing increasingly needy as I struggle to get myself across the finish line.

Sensing my rising frustration, Nikolai tilts his hips. "Nicky!" I squeak, "You're...so...deep," I gasp out between rough breaths. The ridge of his cock strokes a sensitive spot deep inside me as I haphazardly squirm.

Liquid fire begins coiling inside me, the same heat I felt before the orgasms Nikolai gave me. I grit out a frustrated whimper and keep working to get myself over the edge.

Emboldened by my desperation and driven by his primal need to see my pleasure through, he grabs my ass and pushes my hips in a back-and-forth motion. "Grind your clit against me, my fierce little muse. You're perfect. God, you're so. Fucking. Perfect. Look at you. You're fucking yourself so well. Keep going until you combust."

I stop moving.

His eyes flash with panic. "Oh God Charli, I'm so sorry, was that too much?"

Staring down at him, I'm completely lost in the pure passion of this moment. I take in how different the man under me is from the ones I was ruined by. My emotions take the reins as I lean down and claim his mouth with mine.

Nikolai gasps in surprise at first, then rewards me with a blistering, all-consuming kiss. His soft, warm lips caress mine eagerly as he thrusts up into me. My hands find his hair and pull, drawing a lusty growl from his chest.

Hungrily, I grind myself against him like he showed me. He slides his hands back to my ass as I let go of the last of my trepidation and thoroughly please myself.

His grip tightens, urging me to continue. He moans into my mouth as I press him deeper than ever. The coil in my core tightens until I'm throbbing around him. As I'm about to burst Nikolai pulls his mouth from mine.

Out of breath, he stares up at me as I keep building myself closer to blissful release. "Am I allowed to come? I won't if you say no, I'll hold it back. But please. Can I come for you?"

God damn. Even on the brink of orgasm he won't finish without my permission. I almost explode at the thought that he wants to come for *me* not for him.

As I topple over the edge I wail loudly, frantically

nodding while I grip his hair in my fists. "Come for me, Nicky. You're such a good boy. You've earned it."

With a powerful thrust and a loud strained groan, he barrels deeply into me. His cock pulses as a rush of warmth fills me. I've never seen a man come with such passion and fervor.

Thoroughly drained and sated, I collapse and curl into his chest. His arms slowly wrap around me, and he traces small circles on my shoulder.

"Is this okay?" He whispers into my hair.

I have just enough energy left to nod against him.

He's still inside me, making no effort to make me move, so I don't. "You're magnificent, Charli. I know you don't see how beautiful and impressive you are, but I'll spend eternity reminding you, until you believe it."

His words liquefy my heart.

I had thought this feeling of being held and cherished while melting into a puddle of ecstasy was something I would only read about.

While I'm not ready for a real relationship, I'll be damned if I rob myself of this. The here and now is all that matters, tomorrow I can go back to keeping Nikolai at arm's length.

A soft kiss against the top of my head followed by murmurs of sweet nothings lull me to sleep.

# CHAPTER 18

## *Nikolai*

I can't believe the perfection of the situation I've found myself in. As I lay here with my semi-hard cock still nestled comfortably inside of Charli my heart is on the verge of bursting.

She was exquisite.

We've laid here in a tangle of limbs for a solid hour now. I don't want to wake her, but it's getting late.

I run my fingers through her silky hair and softly kiss her forehead. I know I shouldn't, but I just can't help myself.

She stirs slightly, then pauses.

A tinge of panic stabs me for a second, unsure of how she'll react to the reality of what has transpired. When her tired gaze drifts up to meet mine, an unspoken understanding passes between us.

"I'm sorry to wake you, you were so peaceful. We really should get to bed though," I whisper to her.

She rubs the sleep from her eyes and wipes a bit of

drool from my chest as she sits up.

Her new position pushes me deeper inside her. With a gasp, her gaze drifts down to our connection. "You're…"

"Yeah, I uh. I kind of really enjoy just being inside you. Sorry if it's weird. It'll never happen again if you don't like it."

She makes no attempt to move so I take a few more moments to enjoy her warmth.

My cock begins to harden from our closeness and Charli's heated eyes find mine. She bares down and her pussy tightens around me.

I need to stop this before we get carried away.

"Nikolai," she pleads softly.

Hearing her whimper my name makes me hard as steel.

She's exhausted but undoubtedly wants more. A stronger man may be able to deny her, but when she rocks back on my pulsing cock, I'm a goner.

"Nicky, I'm so tired but you fill me so perfectly. I want to come again. Please?"

"Begging for it is my job, Sugar. You just tell me what you need, and I'll make it happen," I rasp.

She scrapes her nails over my shoulders, dragging them down my arms. "Make me come again, Nicky. You make me feel so good."

"I don't do anything. It's all you." I thrust up into her and she squeaks. "Do I have permission to touch you?"

"Yes. Let me feel those talented hands." The sound of her panting is enough to drive me wild.

Reaching between us I stroke firm circles over her clit with my thumb, grinding deeply into her. She falls forward onto me reeling from the sensation. Her efforts to ride me fall short as she mewls and squirms uncontrollably.

"You're spectacular, Charli. You're a gift and I'm so grateful you're using me to get off. So powerful, taking your pleasure when you want it, my eager little muse. You can have it all, you just need to tell me," I say breathlessly into her ear.

"Nicky, I need you to come again. God It's the best feeling. The warmth, how hard your cock gets as you fill me. It's so good." she demands, face pressed against my thundering heart.

As if I could tell her no.

On command, I erupt and she sits back, pushing my cock as deep as she can. Her nails dig into my chest. Her walls flutter around me as she screams my name, riding out her orgasm.

I'm speechless, staring up at her in astonishment.

She's a goddess and I'm her devout worshipper. She owns me completely—mind, body, and soul. I'm ruined for any other woman. There's no way in hell anyone else could ever live up to her.

She sucks in a deep breath and leans down to place soft kisses on my chest where she's marked me. "Good boy, Nicky."

"I lo—" I choke back the words. "Uh, sorry. I'm just going to go to the bathroom. Stay right here, okay?" I shift her off me and can't help but groan as I watch my release flow out of her. I don't even care that we didn't use a condom, I know we're both clean. This is the most beautiful sight I've ever seen.

"Nikolai, I'm a mess." She hides her face in her hands.

"I'll be right back." I rush down the hall to the main bathroom to wet a cloth with warm water. Relief washes over me when she's still seated as I return.

"May I please clean you up?" I ask, showing her the washcloth.

"You... What? You want to—"

"I want to take care of you, but I want to make sure you're okay with me touching you right now, even if it's through a cloth. Is that alright?"

She nods, shying away from my gaze. I kneel between her thighs and wipe her clean, making sure my movements are gentle, yet effective.

A whisper of a moan leaves Charli's mouth.

My eyes snap to hers.

"Sorry, I don't know what's come over me." She chews her bottom lip.

"Well, I know who came in you."

*Jesus I'm hopeless.*

"Oh God. You're gross. Shut up, perv." She jokingly swats at my shoulder.

I openly gawk at her in disbelief. Charli from even a week ago would have probably slapped me for real and stormed out of the room.

"What? Is there something on my face? Did I not get

all the drool? I can't believe I drooled all over you." Her cheeks flush.

"There's no drool, silly. I'm just admiring the view."

"What on Earth is there to admire?" She huffs. "I'm a mess of wild hair and exhaustion."

"That's what's so beautiful. You look satisfied, glowing like a woman who thoroughly pleased herself. It's a sight to behold."

"I didn't please myself. You did." Her face scrunches adorably.

"Nonsense, I was just there as moral support." I rub her thighs as I stand and pull my pants on.

"I'm pretty sure it's your cum you just cleaned up. You were a lot more than moral support." She folds her arms, trying to look upset.

I see straight through her façade.

I sit down next to her, not touching, but close enough to feel her warmth.. "Everything that happened was done by you, for you. Sure, you can call it sex, but only because I had to be there for it. Just know, if you don't want it to be me again in the future, we can go buy you some toys. Or...if you find someone else that's fine too." I try to hide the hurt in my voice.

"I-I want it to be you, Nikolai. I know it probably wasn't what you're used to. I also don't know when I'll be ready for more, but I really did enjoy it. I uh, I liked how your hands felt and the way you talked me through everything and helped me. I didn't know anything could feel so amazing." She lets out a heavy breath. "Doctor

Hastings told me it was a good idea to try it with a trusted and understanding partner, so that's what I did. I don't want to find anybody else. I just don't want you to wait around for me to be ready for more."

"Charli, I'm not going anywhere. If you ever let me near you intimately again, I'll make the most passionate love to you. I'll run my hands all over your body and tell you how magical you are. You think this was amazing? I'll have you forgetting anyone else who has ever dared to touch you without bringing you to the peak of blissful insanity. But not until you're ready to give me the privilege, if you're ever ready."

"Oh." She breathes out with a shudder.

"Yeah, 'oh' is right." Slowly, I tuck a lock of hair behind her ear. "You're all cleaned up now, Sugar, so go get some rest. Caroline and Uncle Ivan are coming over tomorrow night when they get off work. They'll be here Saturday, too. But I wanted them both to be here tomorrow as well." She gives me a questioning look but doesn't press the issue.

She goes down the hall to her bed and I head to the living room. I work quietly getting everything ready for tomorrow's surprise.

Tonight's development may make it hit a little differently but there's no backing out now.

I pull out my phone and message Caroline and Uncle Ivan in our group chat.

**Me:** *We're still good for tomorrow, right Caroline?*

*Parasite: Yes! I was so shocked when I heard. Charli is going to kiss you.*

*Uncle: Caroline don't be so uncouth.*

*Parasite: What?! It's true. There's no way she won't. Even if she waits for us to leave.*

*Me: I'm not doing this for me, that's childish. I'm doing it because I know it'll make a difference for her.*

*Uncle: At least I raised one decent human...*

*Parasite: Hey! I'm not indecent. I just see how she looks at Nicky. This is going to seal the deal for sure! I'd better be the maid of honor. :)*

*Uncle: Caroline Diana Koval! That's more than enough picking. Nicky, we'll be there as soon as we can tomorrow evening. I'm looking forward to seeing the smile on Charli's face.*

*Me: Me too. More than you know.*

*Uncle: You're a good man, Nikolai. I'm proud of you.*

*Parasite: Hubby materiallll.*

*Me: Okay, okay. See you guys tomorrow. Good night.*

I sleep like a fucking king. When I wake up I'm riding a high like never before. I only hope Charli doesn't have any regrets when she wakes up.

She loves ham and cheese omelets and chocolate chip waffles. So, I'm making both. Some might call it overkill; I don't care in the slightest.

My little muse deserves a revitalizing meal after the

workout she put herself through last night.

Is it the afternoon? Yes.

Is Charli still fast asleep when I peer through the cracked door to her room? Also, yes.

Sliding her curtain open, I decide that letting the sun wake her is probably the safest method. I still won't touch her without some sort of consent, so this is the best option I have.

Charli stirs from the intrusion of sunlight. Her face is illuminated as she sits up. She blinks at me before rubbing her eyes. At the sight of her, my breath stops.

Bathed in sunlight, she's divine.

Her gaze locks on to the plate I'm holding. She literally gestures with grabby hands like an impatient child. I can't stop my laugh before it escapes.

"An omelet *and* waffles? Is this some sort of morning after 'thank you' meal?"

"This is just me taking care of you. Would you like it if I thanked you for the honor of being used by you?" I raise a brow.

Her face ignites with more blush than I've ever seen. "N-no, I uh, I don't need you to thank me. I should be thanking you, if anything."

"Charli, you don't ever need to thank me for making sure all your needs are met. It's literally my pleasure."

She pats the bed next to her and my heart thumps harder as I sit down.

"You don't have to do all of this for me. I appreciate all your hard work and dedication. I really don't deserve any of it though." Her face lights up when she takes a bite of waffle.

"Of course you deserve it. Just know that I do it because I want to, that will never change. Please don't think this is all some ploy, or just temporary... Can I be completely honest with you?" My hand makes a move to reach for hers on its own accord but I'm quick to stop it.

She surprises me by reaching out and linking our fingers together. "Please tell me whatever you need to." She's still eating, but is giving me her attention while she indulges.

"I, uh. I have some kinks, as I'm sure you may have picked up on. It's the primary reason I don't date much. While they aren't extreme, most women I've tried to date don't share my preferences." My voice trembles. I haven't been this vulnerable with anyone in a long time.

"When I say I enjoy taking care of you, I mean it. I'm *very* submissive both inside the bedroom, and out. It's referred to as service submission and it doesn't have to be sexual in nature. Your intensity has had me in a chokehold from day one. Even if we never were sexual, and if we never are again, I'll still find immense amounts of pleasure in taking care of you platonically."

Charli looks me over. Her gaze isn't judgmental, it seems that she's trying to make sense of the information overload I just dumped in her lap. "So, the breakfast in bed isn't because of the sex?"

I bark out another laugh, shaking my head. "No, Charli. I'd have done this if you had a long night either way, sex or not."

"Hmm. So, what other kinks do you have then? You only told me about that one." Her head tilts. "Nothing has seemed too unusual so far anyway."

*I guess this is happening then.*

"Oh, uh. Well, the others are all sexual in nature. I think you've experienced most of them in a minor way at this point. I predominantly like biting and being edged. Pain is a huge turn on for me, too. Bondage was new, but being tied up with your panties really did it for me. I'd like to explore that some more, if you ever want to." I shoot her a playful wink.

She blushes, rewarding me with a roguish smile. "Honestly, I wasn't even sure where that came from. I've obviously never really done anything before you. Well... you know what I mean."

"It was extremely exciting to have that control taken from me as well. The whole situation was honestly one of the best experiences of my life." I gently wipe a bit of melted chocolate off her lip.

"You really liked just pleasing me that much? I was so cruel and told you not to come." She tracks my movement as I slip my thumb into my mouth. Her eyes light up.

"Oh, I loved it. Not letting me come made it so much hotter. I enjoy it when you exercise your control over me." Feeling out her reaction, I lean in and place a soft kiss in the crook of her neck. She lets a soft moan slip out.

I need to leave the room before something else happens between us. I'd stay in bed and get lost in the fray with Charli all day if I could. But, in a couple short hours my uncle and Caroline will be here, and they're delivering my surprise.

"Finish eating, I'll run you a bath so you can get ready for the evening. I have a surprise for you. I'll clean the kitchen up and get everything ready for later while you soak."

I can see the questions in her eyes, but I leave the room before she can ask.

# CHAPTER 19

## *Charli*

I'm thankful for large bathtubs and water that never seems to get cold. Nikolai absolutely blew my mind last night and my muscles ache. As I lay back in the bubbly warmth and soak, I feel flushed all over again.

If I had the faintest idea that sex could be anything close to that incredible, I may have tried to act on my impulses sooner.

Our conversation on my bed this morning wasn't nearly as overwhelming as I'd imagined it would be. Between the work I've been doing to better myself, and Nikolai's efforts to help me feel more comfortable, my confidence levels are at an all-time high.

Something about knowing I hold the power to make him lose himself makes me feel unstoppable. Just a week ago, the thought of openly discussing kinks and sexual encounters would have completely overwhelmed me, but it was tolerable.

I'm proud of myself.

The concept is foreign, but it's growing on me.

I wait to leave my room until I hear Caroline and Ivan arrive.

They're talking to Nikolai at the front door. All three of them turn their attention to me as I approach. Immediately, I become aware that I'm being left out of some sort of secret.

"Go on, Nicky, Caroline has everything just outside." Ivan coaxes him out the front door and blocks my view.

"What's going on?" I'm immediately on edge.

In all reality I barely know any of them, but I'd like to think they're not going to do anything to hurt me.

As Nikolai and Caroline appear, I'm floored. My mouth is agape. "What? What is all this? This can't be...What?"

"Charli, I know you're shocked and confused, just breathe." Nikolai puts the familiar carrier down on the floor and opens the door. Out bounds the same corgi puppy Caroline has been fostering.

He's wearing the denim jacket I picked out, and his midnight blue bowtie. I drop to my knees and cradle him. Caroline is behind Nikolai grinning from ear to ear, arms overflowing with all the goodies Nikolai bought.

"I-I don't understand. I thought he was going to his new home today?" Soft licks on my chin make me giggle.

"He's in his new home." Nikolai crouches next to me and scratches behind the pup's ear.

I turn toward him, in a state of disbelief. I can't control my emotions, or my mouth. "Is this because of last night?"

Caroline whips around to us, a knowing look on her face. "What happened last night, Nicky?"

"Nothing you need to worry about." Shutting her down, Nikolai returns his focus to me. "Charli, I applied to adopt him after the first time Caroline brought him over. When you were at the spa, I filled out the papers. He made you smile for the first time since you'd been here, and I knew he needed to be yours."

"Mine? For real?" Tears blur my vision.

"Yes, Sugar. He's all yours. I know sneaking around and secretly having you shop to buy all the things you wanted for him was a bit deceitful, but I wanted to surprise you."

"Thank you, you're so thoughtful. This is...I don't even know what to say. Just, thank you." I want to hug him, or kiss him. Either would do at the moment.

How do you even begin to properly thank someone for such a generous gift?

"I can hear your gears turning." He reaches out and taps me lightly on my forehead. "Don't stress about it. All you need to think about right now is finding the perfect name for this little cutie." He busies himself by unpacking the baskets full of supplies and toys.

"I want to name him Navy. Like my favorite color. It's a cute name for the world's cutest puppy."

"Well, you've sure thought about that, haven't you, Milaya?" Ivan finally speaks up. "I also apparently need to have words with my nephew about boundaries." His mouth forms a firm line.

"Uncle," Nikolai starts to defend himself. I raise a hand, stopping him.

"It's okay, Ivan. Nothing has happened that I didn't allow or want. Please don't be upset with Nikolai. My boundaries are being respected for once in my life."

"You're not feeling pressured in any way?" Ivan crosses his arms in a protective, fatherly manner. "He may be my nephew, and I love him dearly, but I'm not too old to put him in his place if I need to."

Chuckling, I shake my head. Ivan nods back to me and lets out a rough grunt. Nikolai shrugs the whole situation off and continues his organization of the various toys and treats.

Caroline comes over to me, still wearing a mischievous grin. "I knew you'd love him. I called it!"

"Whoa, nobody said anything about love, Parasite. Thank you for bringing Navy to us, but I think it's time for us to settle down for the evening. We'll see you tomorrow. Charli needs to spend some quality time with her new best friend."

Surprisingly, neither Ivan nor Caroline argues back, they dip their chins and leave.

"Sorry about saying anything. I didn't mean to ruin a nice surprise. I wasn't thinking and just said the first thing that came to mind." My mouth won't stop spewing out words.

Funny how our roles have swapped.

"Charli, it's alright. Nobody is upset, and you didn't

ruin anything. Uncle Ivan and Caroline weren't planning on staying long anyway. I promise they're not mad." Brows wrinkled with worry; he looks me in the eye. "We're okay, right? You're not upset that I kept this from you?"

"Are you kidding? This is the kindest and most amazing thing ever. Can, um, can I kiss your cheek?"

Momentary shock flashes across his face, he nods with a tender smile. I step up on my toes, hesitating for a split second before pressing my lips against his warm skin. The scratchiness of his stubble tingles against my lips and he leans into me ever so slightly.

"Thank you again, I love him so much." I smile up at him softly.

"Can I please sit with you while you play with him?" he asks, his voice light.

"Of course, you're his dad now."

My announcement seems to catch him off guard. He wavers for a moment before taking a seat next to me on the floor. "I'm his...dad?"

Hearing the slight excitement in his voice fills my body with flutters. "Yeah, you adopted him after all."

"But he's yours Charli. You're his doggie mama." He boops Navy's nose. The baby voice he uses could melt steel. My insides are officially mush.

"Well, you're his doggie dad. I insist."

"Did we just become doggie co-parents?" His eyes sparkle with his question.

Too enchanted to resist my urges, I lean over and

brush my lips over his. Tingly jolts of electricity course through me.

A moment of surprise passes between us before Nikolai speaks up, "Wow. Uh, okay. I'm officially labeling the last twenty-four hours as the best of my life." The corners of his eyes crinkle from the intoxicated smile on his face filled with genuine happiness.

I love how readable he is. His compassion has never ceased to amaze me. At no point in my messed up life did I think I'd know anyone who would simply notice how happy something makes me, immediately decide I need that thing, and get it for me without a second thought.

Not until I knew Nikolai, anyway.

"Do you think we can eat dinner in my room?" I ask, trying not to sound too emotional.

"Oh, sure, did you want me to bring my laptop, and we can have another movie night in bed? I promise I'll leave this time. No more surprise sleepovers." He rubs the back of his neck.

"Change into your pajamas, bring the laptop...and I want you to stay." My voice falters slightly, not quite giving off the confidence I was aiming for.

"Are you sure?" His face is soft as he chews his lip.

"Nikolai, stay with me tonight. I want us all to sleep in my bed for Navy's first night home. We can alternate after. But I don't want to hog him all to myself. He needs to love you too."

"Oh. Right. That makes sense." Dim, downcast eyes broadcast his disappointment.

I place my hand on his arm. "Hey, I want you there. If I didn't, I wouldn't have offered, okay? Truthfully, I enjoyed waking up in your arms before. I won't be mad if it happens again."

The gigantic smile on his face is worth every ounce of panic my admittance caused me.

*Damn it, I'm falling for him.*

Navy is curled up between us in the middle of my bed. We're devouring tacos as we watch another Captain America movie. Tears build behind my eyes as my mind runs wild.

Nikolai, ever observant, pauses the movie and turns toward me. "Hey, are you okay? What can I do? Or did I do something to upset you?" His brows crease.

"No, it's fine, I'm fine. I just—" My next words get caught in my throat. "I still can't believe any of this. My life has changed so much in the past month. It's a lot to take in." A heavy sob breaks free. "Sorry, I guess I should bring this up to Doctor Hastings on Monday." Wiping my tears away I pull Navy to my chest. He stirs briefly before falling asleep in my arms.

"Charli, you can talk to me about your feelings. I just want to be here for you. Obviously, I'm not a therapist, but I have ears. Sometimes just getting it all out there can be very therapeutic."

"Why are you so nice to me? I was so horrible to you

for weeks!" I shriek, drowning in tears. "I was so unfair to you because of *them*. You didn't deserve any of that. Even now, I still feel uneasy with you sometimes. All you've ever done is try to be there for me and I can't just let you!" Navy whines in my arms, awoken by my frantic rambling. "Please say something. I feel like I'm crazy."

"Charli, I'm a patient man. It's that simple, really. Sure, it helps that I'm a bit of a masochist... Well, more than a bit." He places his laptop on the stand next to the bed and turns his full attention to me. "Would slapping me across the face again help?"

I'm not entirely sure whether he's joking or not. My hardened stare seems to go straight through him and he flinches. "Okay, okay, sorry. For real though, I *am* patient, and you deserve patience and grace while you heal. I watched Caroline go through a horrible healing period after we lost Auntie T. You're honestly not even close to as terrible as she was."

"How is that even possible?" The dumbfounded grimace on my face elicits a small chuckle from him.

"Charli, she's a very emotionally immature person, she was also barely nineteen at the time, her world got knocked off its axis and she took a while to readjust. Her mother was her best friend, and the tragedy of her sudden loss shattered Caroline."

"So, you're saying you have experience dealing with emotional outbursts?"

"Yeah, you could say that. Have you met Caroline?" Mischief flickers in his eyes.

"She can be a lot, that's for sure. Nothing can excuse how I've treated you though. So, just know that I'm sorry. I'm trying my best to adjust to life and I feel like I'm getting better, it's just taking longer than I'd like."

"Take all the time you need. I told you before, I'm not going anywhere. I've been through a lot, and dealt with worse things from people who genuinely didn't deserve my patience. You do." The energy radiating off him is intense. I can sense how badly he wants to hold me and reassure me.

I want it, too.

"Nikolai, I know you hold back a lot on my account. I can see it every day. Touch me. Whenever you want. Don't hold back anymore, okay? Any time you want to show me affection or comfort me with a pat on the back, or a squeeze of the shoulder, hell, even forehead or cheek kisses." My eyes connect with his. "I-I like the way it keeps me in the moment, reminding me I'm not alone anymore."

His hand gently grips my thigh as he leans in and places a soft kiss on my temple. He doesn't speak, thankfully. Words would only interfere with the energy buzzing through the air. I'm not entirely sure what's transpiring between us, but I've decided that I'm done trying to fight it.

Someday I'll ask about his past. I've sensed from the beginning that he's damaged, too. I want to repay his kindness and be there for him as much as he needs.

When I turn my face toward him, the tips of our noses

brush against each other. We stare lazily into one another's heavily lidded eyes.

In a breath our mouths connect. Nikolai's hand finds the back of my neck as I lean into him. His lips are full and soft and they meld with mine perfectly.

Gently, he drags the tip of his tongue over the seam of my mouth. As my lips part for him, he deepens our kiss. Our tongues dance together sensually. My mind whirls with all the new sensations.

His free arm wraps around my back and pulls me into his lap. I moan into his mouth, pressing myself into his hardness.

He breaks our kiss. "Fuck, sorry I didn't mean for all this to happen. It isn't too much, is it?"

"God no, Nicky. That was... Wow." I'm out of breath, aching for more friction.

Nikolai lifts me off his lap, slides down the bed and wraps us in the covers. "We should get some sleep. It's late and we've got an exciting day planned tomorrow. I'd love nothing more than to keep exploring this seductress you've unleashed. I can only hope there'll be plenty of opportunities for that later."

"You don't want more after that kiss? Are you even human?" I whine.

"Charli, trust me, I want to bury myself inside you so bad. But I need you to be ready for the way I'm going to fuck you when I finally get the honor."

I pout and roll over facing away from him.

Adjusting himself, he sighs and wraps his arm around

me. "What do you need? Tell me." His lips press against the back of my neck.

"I-I don't know. Just hold me."

"As you wish.." He pulls me securely against him as I snuggle Navy in close, and we lose ourselves in the quiet of the night.

# CHAPTER 20

## *Charli*

Nikolai stirs behind me. His hands trail lightly across my stomach as he rolls over and gets up from the bed. Navy wriggles in my arms as Nikolai makes his way around to my side. He bends down and scoops Navy up, nuzzling him and cooing adorably. His voice, thick with sleep, makes me feel tingly.

"Where are you taking him?" I grumble, half awake.

"I'm sure he's got to go pee. I'm surprised you didn't notice when I took him out in the middle of the night." His tone is light-hearted, thankfully.

"Oh my god, I'm the worst dog mom ever!" I cover my face with my hands. "I didn't even think about potty breaks."

"It's not a big deal, he's pretty much housebroken. He's five months old and Caroline has done a lot of work with him in the last few weeks. Just enjoy him. I'll take care of the important stuff." He's already heading out into the hall.

Before leaving my view, he turns back to me. "You should probably get dressed though. Our day will be starting soon."

Huffing as I get out of bed, I open my closet. I smile when I find a dress to wear for our day out. Naturally, it's another midnight blue sundress. The sleeves drop off my shoulders and the scoop neck shows off a slight peek of cleavage. The bottom of the skirt skates just above my knee.

I feel like I could take on the world.

As I stroll into the bathroom, I'm greeted by the patter of little paws on the floor.

Navy is my shadow already. His presence alone calms me.

Sleeping with him in my arms was extremely comforting. Paired with Nikolai's affection, it was almost a system overload. My heart could have exploded from all the emotions welling up inside me last night. On the long list of ways to die, that's pretty much the best way I can think of.

I put Navy on my bathroom counter. He paws at things and wiggles his butt at me while I brush my hair and pull it back. Once it's securely in place—in the half-up, half-down style I've decided on for the day—I bend down to give him some kisses.

Caroline showed me how to do some basic makeup after our spa day, but I haven't bothered trying it on my own. I haven't particularly had a reason to trouble myself with looking nice until now.

There's no time like the present I suppose.

Today's objective is to not look like a two-year-old who got into her mom's bag.

Three attempts, and several choice words later, I decide it's as good as I'm going to get it. With all things considered, I'm pleased with the result. Getting to this point only took me about thirty minutes. My heated battle with an eyeliner pen determines that liquid liner is my arch nemesis.

Navy is napping on my countertop as I apply my finishing touches. A soft knock on the bathroom door makes him perk up. "You can come in," I answer.

Nikolai's eyes bulge out of his head as he opens the door. He makes no effort to hide his reaction as his gaze sweeps hungrily over me. "You're devastatingly beautiful. I could drown in you and not even try to come up for air." He chews his lip, staring in a daze before blinking it away.

I'm vibrantly flushed from the intensity of his reaction.

"Sorry, they'll be here in a few minutes. I was just checking in on you. We're all going to ride with Uncle Ivan today." He picks Navy up and shuffles out of the room.

Nikolai has Navy loaded up in his carrier as I approach the front door. I lift a curious brow toward him.

"You didn't think we were going to have our first family day without the little man, did you? Don't worry, he's got a spa day planned after we get breakfast and go to the park for a bit."

"We're really going to spend the whole day together, all of us?" The concept seems alien. I doubt I've ever had a family day before. I'm not completely sure what to expect.

"Charli, that's the whole point. We're all just going to enjoy each other's company. Nobody needs to stress about hosting if we're out and about. It'll be fun, I promise."

I don't understand how he can make such a promise, it's not as if the universe will go out of its way to ensure we have a great time.

Nikolai opens the car door for me, then makes his way around to his seat behind Ivan. He places Navy's carrier on the seat between us, giving my thigh a soft squeeze of reassurance before buckling himself in.

"Milaya, you look well. Nicky hasn't caused any more trouble for you, I presume?" Ivan's eyes meet mine, a hint of teasing flickers in his gaze.

Nikolai rolls his eyes and sighs.

"No, he's growing on me, actually." It's an innocent enough statement, but Caroline grins back at us with a playful titter.

I suddenly feel like this is going to be a long, annoying day.

We stop at a drive-thru to get coffee and muffins for

breakfast, then head to a large recreational park. The entire area is fenced in.

Children of all ages are running around on the old wooden playground, swinging happily and squealing with joy as they whirl down corkscrew shaped slides.

Parents are scattered nearby on benches and picnic tables, most have their faces buried in their phones.

It's a clear, sunny morning. The slight breeze isn't chilly, but it keeps the late spring air from feeling too warm. I breathe in the scent of the world. Everything seems so vivid and alive.

"The park is off-leash dog friendly, so our little guy can run his heart out before we take him to the groomer." Nikolai sets the carrier down, opens the latch and Navy leaps out like a bunny rabbit. His little legs bounce him around at our feet.

"Mister Ivan! Oh my goshhh is that doggie here with you?" A small girl with copper-colored springy hair skips over to us. Her pale pink overalls are grass stained, and paint splattered.

"Hello, Abigail. Yes, this is Navy." Ivan beams at her.

"Can I pet him?" Her half toothless smile is shy. She tucks her arms behind her back and tips her head up to Nikolai.

My entire body turns to jelly as he kneels, takes Navy in one arm, the little girl in the other and sits with them both.

Abigail immediately squeals with pure childish glee as Navy licks her face. Nikolai sports the biggest smile as he tries to contain the chaos unfolding in his arms. The sight of him with this little girl and Navy sends a strange zing of longing through me. He looks up and our eyes connect for the faintest moment.

"I see those hearts in your eyes," Caroline whispers beside me.

"I don't know what you're talking about," I quip back.

"Come sit with me, out of earshot." She hooks a thumb over her shoulder at Ivan, who is busy watching Nikolai and talking to Abigail, who is apparently one of his students, and he's one of her favorite teachers.

We sit down at a small table with a large umbrella overhead. Caroline pins me with a serious look. "Listen, I know you've been through a lot, and I know you have a lot to figure out. Trust me, Nikolai will be there through anything you can throw at him. That man is the definition of devoted. Once he's sold on something he sticks with it."

"I-I don't know if I'll ever be able to properly reciprocate. I don't want him to get hurt by getting caught up in my mess."

"Li, it's simple, just don't hurt him then. He'll take whatever you give him, and he'll cherish it forever. I've seen him love with all he has and get nothing in return. I can tell you're already giving him...something though. He's happier than I've seen him in a while."

"Well, I did give him a couple of orgasms, so that's probably part of it."

*Shit, why did I say that?*

Caroline's jaw has come completely unhinged across the table from me. The state of utter shock she's in has rendered her speechless for the first time since I met her.

"YOU WHAT?! Girl! Wait, you fucked him? Li! Oh my god! I knew there was some sizzling chemistry between you two, but I didn't think you did the horizontal tango!" Unfortunately, she's found her voice.

"The what?!" I whisper-yell back at her, shielding my face with my hands in a weak attempt at hiding my humiliation.

"The sideways salsa. Good, old-fashioned, trip to pound town." She wiggles her brows.

I pinch the bridge of my nose. "I didn't mean to tell you. Please stop freaking out. I don't plan on letting it happen again."

"Did I hear my daughter's shrill scream correctly, Charli?" I grow pale at the sound of Ivan's voice behind me. Caroline, as surprised as I am, flinches and shrinks.

"Y-yes." The hardest word I've ever had to mutter.

"And? Was it your idea? Did you consent freely?" He raises his brows.

"Dad, don't make it sound like Nicky is some creep who would force himself on anyone," Caroline cuts in.

"I didn't mean it that way, and you know it. I love Nicky dearly, and I know what kind of man he is. I also know that Charli is delicate and even if Nikolai didn't intend to, he may have unintentionally influenced her decision."

"I—He didn't pressure me."

*Did he?*

"I was in control of it all. I swear." I straighten my spine.

"Very well then, just be careful with my boy. He's delicate too." He turns and strides back toward Nikolai and Abigail.

She's completely entranced by him as he braids her curls. My stomach swoops at the sight.

"Dad will be okay. He's just fatherly to everyone like that. Always the overbearing protector. I think Nicky learned it from him to be honest. We should go swing." Caroline stands from the table.

I nod in silent agreement.

As we make our way to the line of empty swings. My eyes drift to Nikolai as Ivan approaches him. Dread tickles the back of my neck as my hair stands on end. I can only hope Ivan shows him some mercy.

# CHAPTER 21

## Nikolai

Fuck my life. That's all I can say at this point. As soon as I heard Caroline announce to the entire state that Charli and I had sex, I saw my uncle go rigid. I screamed internally as he marched over, to hear it directly from the horse's mouth no doubt.

I considered faking an emergency to avoid this shit-show. I didn't though. I sat here, braiding Abigail's hair and trying not to panic.

I can tell by the tension, and the tightly drawn look on Charli's face that she didn't lie to him.

The fire burning in my stomach dwindles. If she's brave enough to be honest, I can be too.

I know he's going to give me hell for overstepping. Charli is worth the lecture though. Her happiness is above all else on my list of shit to care about.

Abigail rambles on obliviously about painting and her favorite colors, which are apparently *all* the colors. She's an adorable distraction from my looming panic.

Once my uncle is satisfied with his interrogation of Charli, he turns and stalks my way. The calmness in his demeanor is unnerving.

"Abigail, I need to talk to Nikolai alone for a minute. Can you please go play with some friends?"

"Okay Mister Ivan. Thank you for letting me pet the doggie. Thank you for braiding my hair!" She gives me a hug and sprints back to the swing set.

"Nephew..."

*Fuck, that tone isn't good.*

"I'm not going to make excuses, Uncle. Charli is—"

"A fragile soul, who I entrusted you with?" He stands firm.

"She's not as fragile as you make her out to be. She's come a long way. I know you think my dick is doing the thinking, but I promise I'm not being a complete idiot."

*Only mostly.*

"Nikolai, you're a kind and wonderful man. I know this. I've seen it firsthand. However, you have your own issues and...quirks. Do you think involving Charli in that is in her best interest?"

I know by his expression he's talking about my submission kink and supposed savior complex. It hurts to have it thrown in my face right now, as if I'm not in control of my own emotions.

"Charli hasn't seemed to mind. Sure, she didn't even want to breathe my air at first, but we've worked through a lot of those issues. We're together every day, Uncle. For over a month our lives have been forcibly intertwined.

We each have our own spaces and hobbies, so it's not twenty-four-seven, but we've worked through a lot of the initial roadblocks and have been spending quality time together," I rattle off my defense.

He stands with his arms crossed waiting for me to finish.

"I'm being patient, I'm being as chivalrous as I can. I haven't done a single thing she hasn't told me to. Hell, I'd like to think I've gone above and beyond caring for her. She's special to me. I've already told her that, even in the event we're never intimate again, absolutely nothing will change in the way that I treat her."

"Nicky, you're too attached already. There's no way any sort of strictly platonic relationship between you two would ever be healthy. Have you opened up to her about your past?" His voice has softened slightly.

"I could never touch her again and still find happiness in her healing. Her peace of mind is the only thing that matters at the end of the day." I blow out a cleansing breath, reminding myself that he's just trying to keep both of us from getting hurt. "My past isn't important. She's not Lilah." Even her name tastes rotten in my mouth.

What he doesn't understand is that Charli could break me, and I'd thank her for it, then beg her to do it again. My happiness comes from hers. We're entwined, and I wouldn't have it any other way. Her broken pieces fit perfectly with mine.

Lilah was like polished stone, smooth and nice to look

at, but ultimately nothing special beyond that shiny surface. She had expectations, and I didn't meet them. That didn't stop her from using me to fill a void until someone wealthier and more 'her type' came along.

"I love you, Nicky. Charli is a sweet girl, and I care about her wellbeing. Just give her time to heal without confusing her more." His eyes lose their edge.

"She's not confused. She talked to her psychiatrist about it and everything, before she acted on her feelings. She's not a child. I think she deserves to live a little. If she ends up deciding that using me to regain some sense of power was a mistake, so be it. It's her right to make mistakes. For the first time ever in her adult life, she's allowed to make choices. I'll be damned if I'm going to stop her from taking control of her life."

"Is that what you're going to call it?" He tucks his hands in his pockets.

"Yes. I won't stop her. If crushing me is what she needs, I'm prepared for it. Have you stopped for a second and taken into consideration that this thing growing between us could work out, though?"

"You're right. I'm sorry. I just care and don't want anyone to get hurt. You've been through the wringer with women and her situation speaks for itself." His voice warms and he reaches his arms out toward me for a hug. I wrap him up and squeeze. "Easy now, I'm not getting any younger, and you're not getting any weaker."

"Sorry. I love you, Uncle. I know you mean well. You wouldn't be so hard on me if you didn't care."

"You and Caroline are all I have, Nicky. Now Charli is part of that, too." He swallows hard, holding back tears.

"I know, I care about all of you too. Caroline has her moments though." A chuckle rumbles through me.

"Children." His sigh is filled with adoration as he feigns annoyance.

"You'd be bored without us shaking things up. But I've got to admit, you kind of shook *my* life up first with the surprise roommate and all." I pat him on the shoulder.

"Yeah, yeah. Try and blame it on me all you want. I love you anyway, kid. Just be careful with Charli, okay?"

"I swear on my life I'll protect her. Now, let's go get the girls, take Navy to the groomer, and get some lunch. All this anxiety has me starving."

Sliding into the pale blue vinyl booth next to Charli, she does her best to smile at me. There's an air of awkwardness surrounding us now that everyone knows Charli and I have been 'involved' as Uncle Ivan refers to it. Fortunately, the popular seafood diner is surprisingly slow for a Saturday afternoon.

As I flip through my menu, I feel the tension radiating off Charli next to me. She gave me permission to touch her, but I'm still nervous to act on it. The need to calm her overshadows my internal panic and I drop my hand under the table to gently squeeze her knee.

A quick jolt and short freeze on her part have me second guessing my decision at first, until she lays her hand on top of mine and relaxes. My heart swells, I feel about twenty pounds lighter. Even these small steps feel like cresting the final peak of a treacherous climb up a never-ending mountain.

"What are salmon croquettes?" Charli leans over to me and whispers, as our waitress arrives to take our orders.

"Oh, the ones here are pretty good, actually. They're salmon with chopped bell peppers, breadcrumbs, eggs, cilantro, and some other seasonings. They mix it all together, shape it into patties and pan fry them. They're crispy, flaky and well-seasoned."

"I liked salmon sushi, maybe I'll like these too?" Her eyes sparkle with excitement.

"You can get whatever you want, Sugar. If you don't like what you order, I'll buy you something else."

"That seems so wasteful," she grumbles.

"Don't even worry, Girlie. Nicky will eat anything you don't like. He's like a garbage disposal," Caroline quips from across the table.

"She'll take the croquettes, thanks!" I give Caroline the finger once the waitress leaves.

She reaches across the table and twists it. I pinch her in retaliation.

"Could you two not act like toddlers everywhere we go? Charli, I'm sorry that this is the family you've stumbled into, dear." My uncle scowls.

"Oh, I enjoy it though, Ivan. It feels like a real family. I didn't think I'd ever get to experience anything like this." Charli stirs her water with her straw and smiles.

"I know someone who's very glad you stumbled into our family." Caroline pokes at me.

Charli chokes on her water.

"Jesus Christ, Parasite. You don't possess an iota of politeness, do you?" I snap.

"Rich, coming from the man who put his dick in her. How polite of you." She has the nerve to rest her chin on her hand and bat her eyelashes at me.

Charli groans, her face a vibrant shade of pink.

"Caroline, what is wrong with you? Act like an adult for once." My uncle is red in the face.

If he makes it through this lunch, I'll be amazed.

"You know I'm just picking. I'm honestly happy someone around here is getting laid. It's been dry as hell for me." She leans back, crunching on ice.

I swear I hear my uncle counting backwards under his breath.

"It was *one* time!" We all snap our attention to Charli as she wails. "Once! I don't know what made me even want it! He was just *there,* and I saw the paintings and I felt good about myself. Confident, powerful even. I don't understand what the big deal is. We're adults and I may not be able to remember much, but I still have adult wants and needs."

"I need to go to the restroom, Caroline please let me out of this goddamned booth." I've never heard my uncle so frenzied.

"Holy shit, Dad. You swore! What is happening?" Caroline's jaw goes slack.

"You three are going to put me in an early grave, that's what. Can we please have a civilized conversation when I return? I'll take my time so you...you can all get this nonsense out of your systems." He rushes from our table at a speed that is almost impossible.

"This is going well," I huff.

"I mean, I wasn't expecting to learn that you guys played hide the pickle. It's been a very enlightening morning so far."

The sound of a throat clearing brings us back to reality. Our waitress is standing with an uncomfortable look on her face. Our plates full of food steam on the tray she's precariously balancing on her open hand.

I reflexively rub the back of my neck and look at Charli, whose gaze is glued to a spot on the table.

"Ohhh! This all looks delicious. God, I love this place. Thank you!" Ever outgoing, Caroline takes our food from her.

"If you need anything else, just let me know." Her smile is strained. She undoubtedly heard enough of our conversation to warrant a fifty percent tip, at least.

I'm sure she's just as traumatized as Uncle Ivan. Fortunately, he's just now returning from his trip to the "restroom" though I'm pretty confident he went outside to get some air.

Charli's face brightens as she bites into her croquette.

A faint hum of satisfaction escapes her with a sigh. Fuck I love seeing her relaxed and happy.

My adoration for her must be written all over my stupid ass face judging by the smug look plastered on Caroline's.

I pin her with a glare, and she smirks into her chowder at me. She pulls her phone out of her pocket and within seconds my own phone vibrates.


**Parasite:** *Oh boy, you've got it baaaaaaad. How long 'til you propose?*

**Me:** *Shut up. You're out of your mind.*

**Parasite:** *Oh please, I've seen you when you THINK you're in love, that was nothing compared to how twitterpated you are over Li.*

**Me:** *Twitterpated? You've officially lost what miniscule bit of sanity I thought you still had.*

**Parasite:** *It's a real word! Your picture is next to it in the dictionary now. I've made the necessary calls.*

**Me:** *You're such a pest.*


"Can we please not text at the table?" A crinkled scowl consumes my uncle's face.

"Yes, Dad. Sorry. I was just telling Nicky about the new Captain America movie in theaters and asking if he wants to go tonight."

Charli perks up next to me. "Oh! He does love Captain America. Can we go? I've never been to a movie theater before."

Well, it looks like I have plans for tonight then.

Captain America, and the company of the most incredible woman in the world sounds like a dream.

"Hell yes, we're going. I'll reserve the tickets now." I grin, almost too cheerfully.

"That's going to run too late for my old bones, I'll let you kids have your movie night." My uncle relaxes back in his seat, popping a hush puppy into his mouth.

"I know you don't like being out late. We can go earlier if you'd like?" I offer.

"It's quite alright. I'm already exhausted from dealing with all of you, and it's only lunch time. I still need to survive the next few hours." He sighs.

Charli lets out the first squeak of a giggle before stopping herself. Blush blooms over her cheeks.

"You can laugh at his discomfort. Dad knew what he was signing up for when he decided to spend the day with all of us. Usually, Nicky and I are bad enough, you've just helped ramp up the intensity." Caroline chuckles impishly.

"I wasn't expecting such salacious revelations," he grumbles.

"Sorry, I didn't mean to make everything awkward." Charli's blush deepens.

"You didn't, if anything Parasite over there did by running her loud ass mouth." I point across the table.

"Hey! It's not my fault she just casually told me she rode you like a prized thoroughbred," Caroline argues back at me.

"Oh my god I did *not* say that!" Charli's hands cover her face as she shrivels into her seat.

"I thought we agreed to move past discussing this inappropriate topic?" The veins in my uncle's temple look like they could burst at any second.

I undeniably need to tip the shit out of our waitress, who is awkwardly standing at our table side. The pitcher of water in her hand almost spills.

"Can we just get out of here? The groomer sent me a text that Navy is all done with his bath and nail trim." I slump in my seat.

"Please. For the love of God." Charli groans.

I pay our check and slide the waitress a one-hundred dollar bill for her troubles.

# CHAPTER 22

## *Charli*

Navy smells like blueberries. I just want to snuggle him forever. He's soft and sleepy and all fluffed up from his bath. He's such a perfect little angel.

Yet another thing I'll never be able to repay Nikolai for.

I'm starting to believe that he legitimately doesn't want to be repaid though.

This still doesn't feel real. It's been over a month since I've been free. There's no update from Detective Hastings on the investigation, or attempts to locate the place I escaped, but I know that will start changing soon.

Tomorrow I'm taking the first terrifying steps to work with Doctor Hastings on recovering memories of that day.

That same uneasy feeling, as if I was being watched, washed over me while we were out at the park. I think I did a decent job hiding my reaction. Nobody seemed to notice my discomfort anyway. They were a bit distracted though, to be fair.

Now that we're back home I'm far more relaxed than I was when we were out. We're in the living room playing with Navy. Nikolai is seated next to me on the floor.

I'm grateful he handled my slip-up so well. I've sworn to everyone that nothing will happen between us again, but I can feel it burning deep within my bones that something absolutely will. My guard is still up, but every day I feel the walls crumble more and more.

Ivan stands from his spot on the couch to leave and Caroline gets up, too. "I actually don't feel super great. I think I'm going to go home and rest. You two enjoy the movie without me. I don't really care for superhero stuff anyway. So, I'm not that sad about it." She shrugs.

"Oh, do you still want to go, Nikolai?" I ask, trying to keep my voice neutral, in hopes that our plans aren't completely ruined.

"Y-yeah, as long as you're comfortable with it." His hesitation makes my stomach drop.

"Why? Are the seats bad? I was looking forward to my first movie theater experience."

Caroline's playful chuckle echoes through the house as she walks out the door.

"Charli, my cousin thinks she's creative. I'm willing to bet she never intended to go to the movies with us at all tonight."

"Why would she even offer then?" My face twists with confusion.

His jaw is tight as he sighs. "She's trying to be quirky

and play matchmaker. By 'tricking' us into going on a date."

*Oh.*

Do I want this to be a date? Does he?

There's only one way to know for sure. This is my week to take on brave new endeavors, after all.

"So...are we going on a date?"

His mouth forms a perfect "o". "D-do. Uh, would you, uhm." He pauses and inhales through his nose. "Would you like it to be a date?" he spouts the question out so quickly I'd have missed it if I wasn't expectantly zeroed in on the conversation.

"I've never been on a date before. I'd like to, but I might mess it up," I mumble, subconsciously fiddling with my hair.

"Charli, you couldn't possibly mess anything up if you tried." He seems to have rediscovered his confidence as he brushes a loose lock of hair behind my ear.

My body burns under his touch. I manage to offer him a tight smile through the nerves.

"Let me take Navy out, you go freshen up. When you're ready we'll head to the theater." He kisses my temple before scooping Navy up.

Pacing back and forth in my room. I'm in a full-fledged panic. I need input. I know it's probably the dumbest idea on the planet, but I have nobody else to ask, so Caroline will have to do.

**Me:** *HELP!*

**Caroline:** *Are you okay? Is he already messing up? Boys.*

**Me:** *No! I've never been on a date before. I don't know what to do. How should I dress? What do I do with my hair?*

**Caroline:** *Well, that depends. Do you want to get freaky in the theater? Or are you going to keep it PG?*

**Me:** *WHAT?!*

I almost drop my phone.

**Caroline:** *Okay, PG it is then. Just wear a cute dress either way but wear panties if you're not trying to get your rocks off.*

**Me:** *There's absolutely no way that would ever happen.*

**Caroline:** *It totally would if you don't wear any panties and tell him. No man can resist. I promise. ;)*

**Me:** *You really are terrible. I told you nothing is happening between us ever again.*

**Caroline:** *I know what you told me. But I also know even you don't believe that line of BS. You're both adults. Do some freaky adult shit together!*

**Me:** *...*

**Caroline:** *Love you too, Girlie. You're welcome!*

After putting on a slightly nicer dress and touching up my makeup, I head back to the living room where Nikolai is waiting for me. He's changed into some nice fitting jeans. Tucked into them is a deep blue button-down shirt. The top few buttons are undone, showcasing the faintest hint of his chest hair. His sleeves are rolled to his elbows.

*Damn it.*

This is a new, more cleaned up, version of Nikolai. It's still subtle, but I can't even begin to hide my attraction.

"Hey." He looks down at me as I approach him.

"H-hi. I hope I look okay. I tried to ask Caroline for advice, but she just told me not to wear panties." Shit, word vomit.

Nikolai's eyes flash with pure lust.

He leans into me, grazes his lips over my ear and whispers in a husky tone, "Well?"

"W-well what?" Goosebumps prickle my skin.

"Are you wearing panties, or are you wanting to get finger fucked in the theater?"

*Holy shit.*

It's almost comical. I've read those lines in romance novels when the woman says she can feel herself soaking her panties. I've never understood the concept when reading it. But right now, mine are literally drenched.

Burning need takes over as I press forward into his chest. He kisses my neck, inhaling my scent as he squeezes my ass.

"I feel like I need to change my answer," I say on a moan.

"No, I can work with either option. If it comes to that." With a swift kiss to my cheek, he walks me out of the house, opening my door for me when we make it to the car.

He holds my hand the entire drive.

We make quick work of the line at the concession stand and head to our assigned seats with giant tubs of popcorn, boxes of gummy candies and two huge frozen sodas. Our seats are in the back of the theater, away from everyone else.

My stomach swoops. He didn't want me to feel overwhelmed by the crowd, so he made the conscious effort to make sure we were away from it. My heart overflows with silent gratitude.

Nikolai is completely captivated by the movie. His gaze hasn't left the screen in at least fifteen minutes. I sneak the occasional glance at him, admiring the way his face looks highlighted by the colors bursting from the screen. His attention shifts to me and his arm comes up around my shoulders, pulling me into his side.

"Are you okay, Sugar?" I can just hear his hushed voice in my ear. Soft kisses pepper my cheek as I nod to him. "Thank you for coming out with me. I'm so lucky to have you in my life."

His words make my heart race. I feel myself melting into his embrace. His crisp, earthy scent fills my senses. "I'm fortunate to be in your life, too." I snuggle in closer.

His arm slides down behind me, wrapping me up. I turn in my seat so I can cuddle into his chest. My hand wanders, dancing along the ridges of his stomach.

We snuggle through the remainder of the showing. Enjoying each other's casual affection, soft occasional kisses, gentle caresses. It's all so sweet and romantic. I can't imagine a more perfect time.

I sigh deeply, knowing I could have this any time at home on the couch, if I'd only let it. Damn me for being so unapproachable.

Our drive home is a blur. Nikolai rambles on, still sharing his excitement over the ending, and I smile and nod, letting him enjoy it.

He can, and will, go on and on about anything if he cares enough about it. I used to take it for granted, but after years of isolation his excitement over the little things in life is contagious.

Navy is fast asleep in his bed when we get home.

"Nikolai. Will you sleep with me tonight?" I bite my lip and give him my best pleading look.

"Yes." His answer is immediate, bubbling over with enthusiasm.

I playfully giggle at his eagerness. "I just really want you to hold me again. I sleep so well when you're there. On second thought, maybe it's Navy." I grin teasingly as he pouts.

"I just so happen to enjoy holding you through the night. So, it's a win-win." He pulls me into his chest and kisses my forehead, turning my heart to goo.

We're curled up in my bed in no time. With Nikolai's warmth surrounding me from behind, and Navy snuggled up close to my chest, my mind is at peace as I fall asleep.

I wake up in a small panic. My sudden jolt disturbs Nikolai, who is still clung on to me from behind. "Are you alright?" He asks, voice is rough with sleep.

He stretches, yawns, and brushes my hair out of my face as I roll to look at him. "Yeah, I'm sorry. I'm really trying to not freak out over you being in my space. Sometimes I forget that I'm safe here."

"Hey, there's no timeline for how quickly you feel comfortable. I'm honestly amazed at how much you've relaxed and opened up in such a short time." He cups my face with his large, warm hand, brushing his thumb softly over my cheek.

The warmth of his palm soothes my frayed nerves. "It feels like I'm still so far from being able to fully trust and be comfortable though." My voice is thickly coated with frustration.

"Charli, I promise you that it doesn't matter to me how long it takes. You really do deserve so much more than just patience and understanding, it's the least I can do for you." He kisses the tip of my nose.

I swallow my emotions.

*I can't cry, I need to be stronger than this.*

"Why? You don't owe me anything. Nobody does." A stray tear breaks free despite my best efforts.

"Charli." His voice is strained. His Adams Apple bobs as he swallows, holding back his own emotions. "I don't need to owe you anything. I'm here because I want to be, not because I feel obligated to. Sure, I'd help just about anyone who needed it, but that's not the only reason I'm here for you." His soft lips kiss my tears away. "I'll be able to show you someday how much I care about you. When you're ready for it. Until then, I'm here as much as you want me to be. Just say the word."

"Thank you. I really mean it. I was so scared to come live here once I realized you were, well, you. I know you say it's no big deal, the way I treated you... But I'm so sorry for letting *them* cloud my judgement in the beginning. Even if I didn't know that's what was happening." My chin quivers.

I'm terrified of the future, but his energy is calming and reassuring.

"Don't beat yourself up over it, okay? You're working so hard on yourself and I'm just thankful I get to be here to see it. Watching your metamorphosis is a beautiful thing." He presses another soft kiss to the tip of my nose.

"Can we talk about you? Ivan and Caroline have both mentioned that you went through... something but won't elaborate."

His jaw clenches. "Charli, it's not as bad as they make it seem. I was with a woman, Lilah. She led me to believe that I was her everything. I'm a romantic at heart, and it made me blind to her deceit. All I've ever wanted was a life changing love like what my aunt and uncle shared." He takes my hand kissing my knuckles. "I was with her for about two years, shortly after I found success. When Auntie T died, she left me high and dry for a 'better' man. I was alone, my family was falling apart around me and the person I thought I could count on discarded me. I fell into a deep depression and swore off love. Eventually, I pulled myself out of the ditch she left me in and I'm better for it now."

He won't meet my gaze, so I place my hand on his face and turn him toward me. "You didn't deserve any of that. If you were even half the man to her as you've been to me, she can rot in Hell for what she did to you." A tear streaks down his cheek

I've never seen him cry, the sight hurts my soul.

"I'm far from perfect. I had given up on happiness for myself a few years ago. I resigned to a life of solitude and haven't been this close to someone in so long." He kisses the palm of my hand before pulling me into a close, warm embrace.

"You're smothering me." My voice is muffled by his chest. He huffs out an abrupt laugh before letting me go.

"Thank you for listening, my muse." He places a final, tender kiss to my forehead before unwrapping himself from the covers and getting up.

Navy is sleeping at the foot of the bed. Nikolai cradles him and strolls out of the room. I roll onto my back and stare at the ceiling, contemplating my entire existence.

Tomorrow's therapy session is going to wreak havoc on my mental state. Maybe Nikolai will let me stay in bed for the rest of the day.

That would be amazing.

# CHAPTER 23

## *Charli*

Nikolai does, in fact, let me lay around in bed all day, it's exactly what I needed. I've heard of the concept of 'lazy Sundays' but never thought I'd get the chance to enjoy one. Nikolai is attentive, but not over-bearing and honestly, I enjoy his check-ins.

Despite the way he cares for me all day, I made him sleep in his own room tonight. I don't want to develop some sort of dependency on him to sleep well. I also let him take Navy to his room.

My sleep is tormented by horrendous nightmares, de-spite my medication. I can officially admit to the fact that either Nikolai or Navy's presence helped me sleep better the last few nights.

It may have been both, I don't truthfully know.

I don't want that to be the case, but I can't do a damned thing about it right now, which is infuriating.

"Good morning, Sugar. How are you feeling about today?" Nikolai has a hot cup of coffee extended toward me as I shuffle into the kitchen.

"Well, I slept like shit, I feel like shit, I'm stressed beyond belief. What could possibly go wrong?"

"I'm sorry you didn't sleep well. You can have Navy every night, you know. I adopted him for you."

"But you love him too. It's not fair if I hog all his attention."

"Charli, I do love him, and I love all the time I get to spend with him, but I love how much you love him even more. We spend plenty of time together." He places a quick kiss on my forehead, pausing for a moment when I jump at the contact.

His face is soft as he pulls back. "Sorry, I know you gave me permission to be affectionate with you, but I hope I'm not doing too much. I can be very touchy-feely so just tell me to stop if I need to."

"It can be a lot sometimes, but I like it. I just have a reaction every now and then that has nothing to do with you. I can't help it, but I'm trying to do better," I say, hoping the words seem genuine.

"I'm just letting you know that I can, and will, tone it down if you want me to." His brows are still pinched together.

Without much thought I lean up onto my tip toes and kiss him. His hands extricate themselves from the pockets they'd been banished to and find my waist. Nikolai's touches are tender, never overwhelming. One hand lightly grips my hip, the other rests on the small of my back as he leans into me.

A soft rumble rolls through his chest as I press myself against him. "Charli, we really need to get going to your appointment." It's as much a plea as it is a statement.

"Sorry I'm not sure what happened there." I shy away from him.

Nikolai puts Navy in his brand-new outdoor dog run before we leave. My whole body vibrates with anxious energy.

The truth is, I kissed Nikolai out of need. The need to remind myself that not every man is bad.

The moments I'm about to relive with Doctor Hastings are going to challenge that knowledge. I know I need to go through this step of my therapy, but I'm terrified. The information I have already remembered, paired with anything new we unearth in these sessions, is important, but so is my healing.

I'm just now able to let Nikolai touch me and show me what it feels like to be cherished and cared for, even in minor ways. I don't want to compromise the progress I've made. This is important, I can do this.

"Charli, you look well. Have a seat, I'll get the aromatherapy started and we can take a moment to debrief before diving in."

Doctor Hastings looks flawless again today, with a burgundy blouse tucked into fitted beige slacks. The heels she has on are shiny and pitch black. Her office has the same fresh, clean smell until the scents of lavender and herbs fill the air.

"Good morning. I do want to talk about what I have remembered so far, as well as some paranoia I've been experiencing." I shift uncomfortably in my seat.

"Well, in that case, let's begin with the topic of paranoia. What have you been experiencing?" She tips her head.

"When we're out in public, especially open spaces, I swear it feels like someone is watching me." I take a long drink from my complimentary glass of icy sparkling water. "There's always this sensation of eyes on me. When I look, I don't see anybody. But I *feel* them. I know that must sound crazy."

"Charli, nothing sounds crazy. You're likely feeling a minor bit of social anxiety. You must take into consideration how long you were isolated. Large crowds are bound to be overwhelming. In due time you'll readjust, but there is absolutely no need to rush. If you feel uncomfortable in any situation it is your right to remove yourself."

"I know. I just don't want to miss out on things because I'm stuck in my head. I'm trying so hard to move on with my life." My lower lip wobbles.

"That is a completely valid feeling as well. Time will make everything less intimidating. Please just mind your limits. Trying to do too much, too soon could prove to be detrimental." Her voice is soft, reassuring.

"Speaking of my limits. I, well... I have opened myself

up to my roommate more. I gave him permission to touch me and show me affection. I even had him take me on a movie date. It was nice, I only slightly freaked out." I smile, imagining him here with me now, hand on my knee, squeezing softly.

"That's so wonderful to hear. I must ask, though. He isn't overstepping in any way, is he?" she asks tentatively.

"Oh, no. Not at all. I mean, we did have sex, but it was all my idea. He was just there to 'use' as he put it." The look of surprise on Doctor Hastings' face makes me flush with embarrassment. "Sorry. God, that was so inappropriate."

"It wasn't inappropriate, merely an unexpected admission. Very interesting development." She taps her pen to her chin as she mulls over the information. "There was no coercion on his part?"

"No! God, why does everyone seem to think that?" My voice comes out louder than I intended. I'm not sorry about it though.

"I didn't assume there was, I was merely ensuring you're in a safe space. I'm not familiar with your living arrangements. Is it safe to assume you're staying with the man who walked you out of here last week?"

"Yes, that's Nikolai. I hated him at first. Then some memories came back to me, and I gathered that it wasn't *him* I hated. I realized that I'm actually attracted to him and didn't really understand how I could even feel like that for anyone, especially this soon. Anyway, I'm rambling." I bite my lip, and gulp down more water.

"What do you mean when you say you didn't hate *him*? What helped you draw that conclusion?" Her head tilts as a quizzical look crosses her face.

"Well, that's going to bring us into part two of today's meeting. I had a flashback of one of the men, Frank. One of his more distinguishing features was his long scraggly black hair. Nikolai's used to be a similar length, but he cut it after I told him about Frank. I think the similarity was enough that my subconscious revolted and thought of Frank every time I saw Nikolai."

"I'd say that would be a very fair assessment of the situation. Has the feeling of unease settled since Nikolai cut his hair?"

"Yes, it definitely has. I don't find him appalling at all anymore, which poses a new problem for me." Familiar heat rises to my cheeks.

"What issue may that be?" A knowing look lights up her face.

A shy smile pulls at my lips. "I find him *extremely* attractive, and I don't know what to do about it. He adopted me a puppy because it made me smile for God's sake! How could I not start developing feelings for him?" I bury my face in my hands, just now admitting to myself that I have feelings for Nikolai.

*Oh shit.*

"I'm no love guru, nor am I here to be a relationship counselor. However, it seems that he's a decent man who cares about you. What would be the harm in allowing something more serious to transpire between the two of you? It seems that your body has already made its decision." A hint of a chuckle passes her lips before she contains it and transforms back into the picture of professionalism.

"What if all the things I remember here make me hate him all over again? I can't possibly let him in just to shove him back away with force."

"Would you though? Do you honestly believe that you'd push him away?"

"I don't know. I constantly crave his attention and want to spend all my time with him. I don't know what I'm doing, but he's so sweet and attentive and loving I'd hate to ruin it." Tears sting my eyes. My nose burns.

"There's nothing wrong with seeking out others for companionship, Charli. Now, in the spirit of complete transparency, I'm elated that you're already comfortable enough with anyone to even consider dating or affection on a casual level. While I won't tell you to force anything, I would like to encourage you to continue being courageous." So much warmth fills her words as she lets her doctoral mask slip ever so slightly again.

"Okay, you're right. I said I was going to take my life back and stop running, it's time to do it!" I straighten in my seat.

"Wonderful. With that settled, let's begin with the guided meditation session. Lay back, breathe in time with the beat of the music when I press play, and envelop yourself in the security of this room. Try and imagine yourself back in that place, the night of your escape."

I do as she says, instantly transported back to that damp, dirty room.

"What are you sensing Charli? Where are you?" Her voice seems so far away, while also feeling as though it's wrapped snugly around me.

"I'm in the dark, only lit dimly by the TV mounted on the wall. It's musty and cold. One of them just left."

The rhythm of the leaky pipe pelting the floor with stray drops of water fills my mind. "Light is shining through the door seam. That never happens. The door to this dungeon I'm kept in is sturdy and soundproof. This whole room is soundproof."

"Wonderful Charli, you're doing a phenomenal job. Keep going."

*I rise to my feet from the shriveled ball I had curled into. Frank didn't bother to take a picture this time. He's been drinking so his visit was shorter than normal.*

*Trembling, I move slowly to the door. My hand reaches for the handle as if it'll bite me. I've tried time and time again to open the door after they leave, in hopes that they forget to lock it.*

"The door is open! Oh my God, this is my chance. I might get out of here alive after all." My body shakes violently. The lines between then and now begin to blur.

*The heavy door peels open. For the first time in as long as I can remember, I see something other than the four walls*

*I've indefinitely called home.*

"It's just a plain hallway, but there's a staircase with a door at the top."

*Ascending the stairs as quietly as possible, I try the doorknob at the top of the steps. A sob fights to escape as I realize it's unlocked.*

*Cracking the door open the slightest amount, I scope out the room on the other side. Cloaked in near darkness I'm able to faintly make out a small kitchen. The wooden walls point to this being a cabin.*

"The walls are logs. Just wooden logs and an old iron stove. It's a kitchen. Beer cans, bottles of whisky and dirty dishes line the counters."

"Wonderful Charli. I'm amazed with the progress we've made today. However, it appears our time is up." Doctor Hastings turns off the white noise that has been serving as my tether to reality as I sit up.

"Here, take some deep breaths and have a couple tissues. You did extraordinarily well." She pats my shoulder as I dab my damp cheeks.

"I didn't really do anything though. None of this will help the investigation."

"I can assure you it will. Contact Theo— I mean, Detective Hastings. Offer him any detail about the men and that house that you can. It doesn't have to be today but do try to help him as much as possible. He's determined to find the men that did this to you."

"I will, but I need time to decompress. This was a lot to go through."

"Unfortunately, this will only prove more difficult next time. We will be walking through your escape process, in an effort to gather information about the location in which you were being held. Don't give it much thought for now though. Relax for the rest of your week and come back next Monday ready to get some answers." She guides me back to the familiar lobby where Nikolai is waiting. His knee frantically bounces until he sees me.

He leaps up from his chair and steps quickly to my side. "Charli, Are you alright? You've been crying. Please don't cry, gorgeous." His hands meet my shoulders before wrapping around me in a comforting hug.

"She was extremely brave today. Do be sure to comfort her as she unpacks everything from our session." Doctor Hastings turns on her heel and disappears behind the large door to her back office.

"Let's get you home, little muse." We step out the door, into the fresh spring air.

"What's all with the nicknames?" I ask a bit more crudely than intended.

"What? I think they're fitting and cute, just like you." He pinches my cheek.

I instinctively slap him across the face. Instant regret fills me.

*Damn it. I need to stop doing that.*

"Fuck, Charli. I'm trying to lighten the mood. But

you're making it very… *hard."* Nikolai pulls me against him, and my jaw goes slack.

I flush at the proof of his arousal pressing into me.

"You were serious? You like being slapped?" I gape up at him.

"I like a woman who isn't afraid to put me in my place. The pain is an added perk." He grinds against me and groans into my neck. "Why do we have to be in a public parking lot?" He opens my door for me, then rounds the car to take his spot in the driver's seat.

"Sorry? I didn't really plan on turning you on." I watch as he readjusts himself in his jeans next to me.

"I'm always turned on for you. Just tell me I'm not allowed to be. Or tell me to come in my pants. Whatever you want, I'll do it." His voice drips with arousal.

"You would do that?" As if my eyes weren't already huge, they manage to widen even further.

He buckles his seatbelt, pinning me with a hungry stare. "Charli, I mean what I say. You have the power. You control my pleasure. What do *you* want?"

"C-can you—"

Cutting me off, he tucks a finger under my chin, forcing me to meet his smoldering eyes. "Don't ask me, tell me."

"Well, I don't know what you're okay with. We haven't really covered a lot of bullet points."

"I'm sure I can handle whatever you throw at me."

"I want to touch you while you drive, but don't come until we get home. I…want to watch you come for me."

I fidget with the hem of my dress.

He mumbles something under his breath that sounded a lot like "Holy shit." But I can't be sure. However, I *am* sure that this is exactly what I need right now.

It's a strange thing, being in complete control of someone's pleasure. After having my own control taken away for years, it's cathartic. I've also never touched Nikolai like this. The time in his studio barely counts. Right now, as he drives, I have the freedom to stroke and play with him however I want.

Nerves and inexperience have my hand trembling as I reach over and free him from his jeans. The hitch in his breath as I wrap my hand around him, coupled with his throaty groan of approval as I squeeze, send waves of heat straight to my core.

He's thick and throbbing under my touch, trying his best to stay focused on the road.

This is dangerous and I love it.

# CHAPTER 24

## Nikolai

*Don't crash, don't crash, don't crash.*

Charli's small, soft hand is timidly acquainting itself with my aching cock. I'm not looking at her, but I know she's looking at me.

You'd never guess she was rolling my balls around in her palm if I wasn't groaning and panting from her touch.

I'm so glad the drive home isn't long. I'm eager to come for her. God, I hope she lets me do it as soon as we're in the door. Hell, I'll do it in the car if she wants, I can get it detailed.

Warm fingertips trail up the underside of my shaft. I bite down on my lip to suppress a moan as my hips jerk. She wraps her hand around the head of my cock and squeezes a drop of precum free. I watch intently out of the corner of my eye as she examines it.

When she dips her finger into her mouth I damn near

swerve off the road.

She hums softly. "Sorry. Was that weird?"

*Damn it, she's so precious.*

"No, that was fucking hot." I rasp.

"I just wanted to know what cum tastes like. It's always described so differently in every book."

"Well, that was precum. So, it's going to taste a bit different, I imagine. Not that I can really speak from experience."

"I'll taste it later then." Her head tilt is deceivingly innocent for such a lewd statement. "Is it strange to be sort of excited?"

"Fucking hell, Charli. You can taste me all you want." I'm grateful we're pulling into the driveway. One more minute in this car would end me. "Where do you want to do this?"

"Oh, I guess I didn't really think about that. It'll be messy. So maybe somewhere easy to clean?"

I hop out of the car and open her door with my dick still out, thankful for my privacy hedges and long driveway. Charli lets out a heady chuckle as I drag her into the house, straight to her bathroom.

"Oh, this is a great spot for it. Are you going to need any help?"

"Just get in position, however you want and say the word. You've edged me so fucking perfectly it won't take more than an order. But you can use your hand...or mouth if you want." I'm probably being a bit pushier than I should, but she doesn't seem to care.

*Interesting.*

She sits on the edge of her bathtub and takes her shirt off.

If I wasn't about to come for her before, I damned sure would be now. The heat of my gaze on her chest doesn't seem to bother her either. I've never been so fucking hard.

Charli looks directly into my wild eyes. "Come all over me instead." She opens her mouth, sticking her eager tongue out for me.

*Call the fucking coroner, I'm not going to make it.*

One pump of my cock at her command and my knees buckle as the hot streams of my cum land across her face and black lace-covered chest. The scene is picturesque, an erotic masterpiece.

She lets out a surprised squeak at the sensation but is otherwise unbothered. "Wow, uh, this is more than I expected." She surveys the mess I've made of her, staring at my cum pooling between her luscious breasts.

"Are you okay? I'll clean you up, one second." I pant, steadying myself.

She licks her lips clean, humming as she savors the taste and my cock begins to stir again at the sight. Subtly, I tuck myself back into my jeans. This is for her, even if it's the hottest thing I've experienced in a long time. I won't show her that I enjoyed it as much as I did.

I wet a cloth with warm water and gently wipe her face, gazing into her sparkling, expressive eyes.

"I don't mind the taste. I was afraid it would be gross

or something. It's not exactly what I would call delicious, but I like it enough to do it again." She slips me the sweetest smile as I finish cleaning her face.

I don't hesitate to lean in and steal a quick kiss, unbothered by the faint taste of me that still lingers on her lips. "Can I clean the rest of you, or is that too much?"

"I think I'll just shower if I'm being honest. It's a bigger mess than I expected. You really let me have it." Her red cheeks and soft chuckle make my stomach flip.

"Right, that makes sense, I'll go get Navy from outside and we can curl up on the couch if you want. I know you've had a rough day."

"Nikolai, I don't know what I'd do without you." She sighs dreamily. My heart skips a few beats, threatening to implode.

*Be cool, you idiot.*

Before I can embarrass myself, I smile, nod, and get the hell out of the bathroom.

Charli showers for a while, I want to check in and make sure she's alright but resist the urge.

Once I hear her shower shut off, I scoop out two bowls of ice cream. One vanilla for me. One with vanilla and chocolate for her.

Shuffling footsteps make their way toward the living room. Charli plops down on the other end of the couch, immediately snatching up the bowl of ice cream.

"Is this peanut butter?" Her eyes are huge, bursting with pure delight.

"Yeah, if you heat it up for a few seconds, it melts down and becomes pourable. Makes for a delicious ice cream topper." I try to sound as nonchalant as possible, but it's no use.

"Nikolai, I swear you're too good to me." she groans around her first bite.

"You deserve the absolute best. I keep telling you."

"So, what are your plans for the week? I need to reach out to Detective Hastings at some point. Other than that, I think a few good books are going to be my happy place. But I was wondering if we could take Navy to the park again."

"Of course we can, I don't have any plans, outside of trying to paint some more. I do need to get in touch with my portfolio manager, but that's not a pressing issue." I take a bite of my ice cream.

"What's a portfolio manager? For your art?" She scrunches her brows together.

"No, I have a person that I pay to manage my investment portfolio. I invested a large portion of my initial earnings when I first had my break. I'm a realist and knew I didn't want to be some super famous artist, but I also liked the money. So, I was smart and hired someone to manage a stock portfolio and silently invest in a few businesses around the area."

"So, you really are rich then?" She looks like she's just now considering that I'm not putting on a show. It stings a bit, but I fully understand her disbelief.

"Yes, I know I don't exude wealth, but that's because I'm just not that kind of guy. My mother and uncle moved to this country when they were young teenagers. They both worked very hard to acclimate and build themselves up. I never knew my grandparents, since they passed before I was born, and, well, you know the deal with my mom."

"I'm sorry, I wasn't trying to be judgmental. I just want to understand." She squirms in her seat.

"It's alright. I never planned on 'making it' as they say. I enjoyed my humble life living with my aunt and uncle and just painting to express myself. When the opportunity arose to secure financial freedom, I had to take it. I just knew I didn't want to keep doing it. So, I invested a good chunk of money. Eventually those investments paid off and I had enough to buy this land and build my dream home. Now, my money makes me more money. At this point, I have more than I'll ever need. So, I invest in startups and donate to charities regularly. The extra zeroes in my bank account aren't going anywhere any time soon." I smile softly at her.

"So, why didn't Ivan and Caroline move in here, or have you build them houses too? It seems like you could afford it." She wipes a stray smear of peanut butter from the corner of her mouth.

"You've met my uncle, right? Believe me, I tried. He still hates it when I pay for dinner. They each let me buy them a car, since they needed reliable transportation, but that's as far as I was allowed to help."

"So, I'm really not a financial burden to you?"

*Oh, this sweet soul.*

"Charli, you're not any type of burden. You're a gift. I love taking care of you, in every way."

"But what if I want to work at the shelter like Caroline suggested? I don't want to just be dependent on you forever." She presses.

"I'll buy you your very own shelter to run if you want. Shit, I'll buy the land and let you design the facilities yourself." I slide over next to her, placing Navy in my lap. "I love animals. Clearly you do, too. I think it would be really rewarding."

"That's got to be expensive. It's way too much." She shrivels into herself.

I press my palm to her cheek, meeting her gaze. "Charli, nothing you could ever want would be too much. If you want it, I'll make it happen or die trying."

"What if I just want to start over? Can we do that?" She leans into my touch, nestling her face into my hand.

"Start over, how? Say the word and I'll start making it happen." I brush my thumb over her cheek.

"Ugh, I don't even know. I-I just want to help find the monsters that hurt me, but I also don't. I feel like the fact that my brain locked away everything from before is a sign. Maybe I should leave the shitty past I had behind me." Her voice trembles as she steadies her emotions.

"If you don't want to remember, don't. Whoever you were before is of no importance now. We've already established you had nobody, but now you do. I know Uncle Ivan is a stern old man, and Caroline is irksome on her best days, but we're family and we love each other. That love will gladly extend to you, should you desire." The yearning in her eyes is going to undo me. I can't handle how disheartened she looks.

Sensing her upset, or maybe just looking for peanut butter, Navy slobbers all over her face. Charli snaps out of the trance she was in and hugs him.

I scratch behind his ear. "See, Navy agrees. You're worthy of being loved and appreciated. Don't ever let anything make you think otherwise."

"You're so amazing, Nikolai." She pauses for a moment, chewing over her next words. "What are we?"

*Well fuck.*

"Uh. I'd like to think we're friends now, at the very least."

"Friends don't do the things we do." Her tone leaves no room to debate.

I still try.

"Friends... with benefits?" I shift awkwardly.

"You want to just be friends with benefits? Was our date nothing to you? Or was it just to make me happy?" She's on the verge of tears.

*Shit.*

"Charli, I want whatever you want. I just... I don't want to assume anything. I don't want you to feel like we *have* to be anything. If you want to keep it casual and free that's fine with me. If you want an official label, that's incredible, too. Please don't cry. I'm just trying to tread carefully. I'd have made you mine the day we met if you would have allowed it." I'm spouting my words out as quickly as I can to avoid the fast-approaching fallout.

"Y-you would have asked me out on day one?" She rears her head back, eyes bulging.

"Charli, I'd have probably proposed by the end of the first week." It's not an exaggeration, not even close.

"Wow." She tenses.

"Shit that was too honest, wasn't it? This is why I didn't want to say anything. I just want you to be the happiest woman in the universe." I kiss her hand, and she falls into me with Navy cradled against her chest between us.

"Maybe we don't need an official title, but I just don't want you to go anywhere on me. I was so alone forever, I didn't know what it was like to be cared for." Large hot tears soak into my shirt as she sobs.

"My little muse, there's nothing that would ever make me leave you, I promise." I press a soft kiss against her hair and pull her into me. Navy squirms free from her hold and plops down on the cushion next to us.

I hold her as she cries herself to sleep, just as I did weeks ago. This time, when I put her to bed, I stay.

As she snores softly, I whisper affirmations to her. I only hope they engrain themselves into her subconscious.

"You're loved. You matter. You're so brave. You're amazing and inspiring. You'll never be alone again. I'll keep you safe, no matter what."

# CHAPTER 25

## *Charli*

God damn it, I did it again. I can only hope that one day I won't break down into tears at the first hint of an emotional discussion.

By one day, I mean some day this week. I *need* to have this conversation with Nikolai. Getting my jumbled emotions under control will have to be the first step, though.

My head hurts from the violent sobbing. I roll over as slowly as I can, trying to avoid waking Nikolai or Navy. When I bury my face into Nikolai's bare chest, he pulls me in tightly.

"Well, good morning, gorgeous." His raspy morning voice thunders in his chest. "This is new." He squeezes me and rubs his chin against the top of my head.

"Is this alright?" My voice is muffled by his chest.

"It's perfect." He rubs my back and maneuvers so our legs tangle. His warmth wraps around me, soothing me back to sleep.

We sleep like that forever, that's what it feels like any-way. Occasionally stirring to reposition and place soft kisses on random parts of one another. Surely, such an idyllic morning could have never been meant for me, yet here I am. I feel lighter, freer and completely at peace as we lay here. The silence between us is comforting.

My mind swirls with thoughts of Nikolai rambling on, spouting random bits of information, how it used to secretly ease my nerves when I was on the edge of panic. "Why don't you tell me random facts anymore."

"What?" He peels an eye open. My words effectively pulled him from a deep sleep. "Oh, yeah. That's more of an anxious habit. When I'm nervous or just don't know what to do I get fidgety and random bullshit flies out of my mouth." A deep chuckle rumbles through him, vibrating my cheek.

"Oh, I liked hearing about them. The Mona Lisa's mailbox is ridiculous to think about."

Nikolai shifts so he can look me directly in the eye. "You remember that? I thought you were ignoring me."

"Of course I remember. I couldn't ignore you, no matter how hard I tried. You've been this undeniable presence since I got here. Even when I thought I hated you, I wanted to be near you. It was really confusing."

"Fuck " he groans out before our mouths connect. "I love it when you hate me, but I love it even more when you don't," he mumbles against my lips.

*Well, I guess it's now or never.*

I pull back and look into his sparkling green eyes. "I

don't hate you at all. I've actually really grown to like you. I, uh, came to the realization during my therapy yesterday." My voice is shaky, I feel my hands trembling against Nikolai's chest. He stays quiet and lets me say my piece. "I *like* you, Nikolai. That's what made me so emotional last night. I'm not used to...feelings. But I recently became aware that I have developed strong, undeniable feelings for you." I breathe deeply. "I don't want to be 'just friends' or 'friends with benefits' or anything like that. Unless that's all that you want, then I'll just cope."

"Charli, I don't want you to 'cope' and I don't want to be just friends, or anything of the sort, either. I want you. You're my whole world." He pauses to brush my hair off my face. "I have been admiring you from a distance, so I don't scare you off. I know I've done a shitty job of hiding my feelings. I had the best intentions though."

I chuckle softly. "That was smart, to be fair. I have been very cold and unpredictable at best."

"You were protecting yourself. I was just trying to make sure you had time to heal. But I want you to know that whenever you're ready for it, I'd like to be yours. Just going to rip that Band-Aid off now. But don't feel pressured." His lips press against my forehead.

I lean into the kiss; a soft smile pulls at my lips. "I don't feel pressured about anything with you. I'm ready to let myself accept everything you have to offer. I'm done living in fear."

"Are you saying what I think you're saying right now?" The jolt of excitement has awoken him entirely.

He looks at me like a child who has just been given a giant present.

"Yes. I'm all yours if you want me, Nicky."

"Of course I want you. Have you met you?" He kisses me quickly and beams brightly as he pulls back. "We need to celebrate! We're also going to have to tell the family. Oh! I'll take us all out to sushi." He sits up, speaking rapidly with glee and excitement painting every word.

"You're adorable when you're excited. Do you know that?" I can't help the giddy smile on my face. I thought this conversation would be vastly different.

"Am I being too much? I feel like all my dreams just came true. I'm sorry if it's overwhelming." A wince pulls at his features.

"No, it's not overwhelming. The whole situation kind of is, but you're not, I promise." I kiss his cheek. "Now go make me breakfast while I get ready. I'm absolutely famished."

"Anything specific you'd like to request?" Glimmers of joy still sparkle in his eyes.

"Hmm. I don't know, everything you make is delicious. Maybe an omelet? No, wait, waffles!"

"How about both again?"

"Yes please, that sounds heavenly." I sigh dreamily.

He chuckles as he stands from the bed. I watch him leave the room with Navy before rolling onto my back. I stare at the ceiling, mulling over everything that has happened to me in the last several weeks.

Am I moving too fast? I don't think so. I can only hope Ivan and Caroline don't disagree. They're already more of a family to me than any of my actual relatives have ever been.

Nikolai returns a few minutes later, empty handed and slips away into my bathroom. Seconds later I hear my bathtub filling. My chest warms as he steps back into my room with a timid look on his face.

"I'm running you a bath. I was wondering if we could enjoy it together before breakfast. You can get in first, and I won't look, or do anything you don't want. I, uh—" He scratches at the back of his neck. "—never mind. I'll leave you to enjoy it alone."

My silence has clearly been interpreted as disapproval. *Say something, He's spiraling.*

"Nikolai, I think I'd like that. Will you let me get situated first though?" I ask with a slight tremble in my voice.

Relief and a hint of excitement light up his face. "Of course, just let me know when it's alright to come in."

My bathroom smells divine as I step inside. Citrus and a touch of mint with herbal notes permeate the air. I lower myself into the sea of bubbles, submerging so that nothing below my shoulders is visible before giving Nikolai the go-ahead to join me. If I wasn't in a steamy bath, I'd be shivering from the nervous tension.

I've never been fully naked around Nikolai. To say that making this the first time, while in such an intimate situation was insane would be a monumental understatement.

Ever confident in his body, Nikolai enters the room and makes quick work of liberating himself from his clothes.

*Keep your eyes on his face, Li.*

Before lowering himself across from me, he starts soft music on his phone. The room feels smaller than ever as my pulse quickens. I'm abundantly aware of my body's reaction to him.

He settles on the opposite side of my large soaking tub and gives me a warm smile. "Can I wash your hair? I just want to pamper you. I won't if it's going to be overwhelming. You call the shots, as always."

"Wouldn't I need to be facing away from you?" I can ignore my building arousal easier if I don't have to look at him.

"Yeah, it would be easier if you sit between my legs, but I wasn't sure if that would make you uncomfortable." There's no sign of tension or desire coming from him. He's genuinely here to care for me.

*Be brave.*

I'm not going to make progress unless I do things that push my limits. Right?

Without a word, I lift myself up slightly, putting my bare breasts on full display. I'm completely aware that this is also the first time Nikolai has seen them, to my knowledge anyway.

His eyes drop for a fraction of a second and an endearing pink flush lights up his face. He tosses his gaze to the wall and swallows hard. "I'm sorry for looking without permission."

"You're forgiven. I didn't give you any warning." Spinning myself carefully, so I don't spill any of the water, I settle between his legs. "Okay, you can look again."

"Charli." He whispers nervously behind me. "Tell me what's okay, I won't do anything you're not comfortable with."

"*I* don't even know what's okay," I admit. "Let's just start with my hair."

"As you wish. Lean back for me. I have a cup here, so you don't have to fully lay down." He shifts so I can lay against him.

Leaning back into his chest, I look up into his eyes. There's no heat in them and I can't completely understand the expression on his face, it's not one I've seen before now. Admiration maybe?

Warm water cascades over my forehead as Nikolai massages my scalp. A blissful hum breaks free from my throat. I press closer into him as he continues to work the shampoo into a luxurious lather. As his fingers press firmly and scrub small circles all around, my now-exposed chest is the furthest thing from my mind.

"You have such silky, thick hair. I've honestly wanted to do this for so long. Thank you." His voice is low and warm.

"You're thanking me? This is the most amazing experience of my life. Forget about the spa."

His soft chuckle makes my body bounce slightly

against him. Panic flashes across his face as his previously concealed erection presses into my back..

"Charli, I'm sorry," a rapid-fire apology tumbles from his mouth. "Just because I'm hard doesn't mean I'm trying to gain anything from this. Being close to you and caring for you is just such a gift that I can't help my body's response."

He removes a hand from my head to reposition himself. Before he has the chance, I grab his wrist directing him back to my hair.

"I trust you, Nikolai. I'm not upset. Honestly, I kind of like it. It's silly."

"What makes you feel that way?" His head tilts.

"I don't know. I can only imagine how weird it is for you that I like just feeling when you're turned on."

"Charli, once again, I'm *always* turned on for you. If it pleases you, you can feel it whenever you want," he murmurs with a playful half-grin.

"No, it's not *feeling* it. Not really, anyway. It's more so the fact that you're choosing to be aroused by me. I don't feel like...like I'm just 'good enough' because I'm your only option."

He scoffs. He *audibly* scoffs.

*What the hell?*

"I'd choose you every single time. You're so much more than 'good enough'. I don't believe in fate and all that bullshit, but you're here against all odds. I'll be damned if you aren't the perfect person for me. You check me on my shit, you don't run away from my awkward rambling. You're *just* mean enough to boss me around exactly how I like." He winks teasingly. "Above all else, you're the most inspirational and determined person I have ever met. I can't get enough of you. All the crumbs I've treasured the past several weeks have reignited my own passion for life. I needed you, and I'll do everything in my power to be what you need, too."

"Nikolai, you can't say all of that and not kiss me." I pout.

He presses his mouth to mine, upside-down. It's a bit awkward, but I feel his sincerity just the same.

Too soon, he pulls back and busies himself rinsing my hair. "I don't want to get carried away. We'll never leave this tub if you let me get lost in you. Let me finish your hair, then I'll make us breakfast while you get ready for the day."

My mind races as he rinses the shampoo out. Emotions bubble up, self-doubt creeps in itching the back of my mind.

"Nikolai, seriously... I don't know what I did to be worthy of someone like you." My eyes drop and I sit up to face him, covering my chest with my arms.

"Hey." He takes my face in his hands. "I promise you that you're more than I could have ever hoped for. Now, let's get out of this tub before we get too wrinkly." He places a kiss on my cheek, rises out of the tub and grabs my robe. He extends it to me while turning away to give me privacy.

The way he understands my feelings will never cease

to amaze me. The fact that he can sense that I'm still not comfortable showing him all of me, despite the fact that I've *given* him all of me, makes my chest squeeze.

As I wrap myself up, I can't help but admire the expanse of his back. He isn't a large man, but he's tall, muscular and defined. His wavy hair is damp at the ends and falls just behind his ears.

He truly does look like Bucky in that first Captain America movie. He doesn't seem to see it, but with his glasses off like this, if his face was a bit squarer, the resemblance is there.

"You getting a good look?" The playful tone of his voice makes me giggle.

"Sorry, I shouldn't stare."

"I'll put on a whole performance if you want." A lazy smirk crosses his face as he turns to me, still *very* nude.

"You know, Caroline did mention you're a dancer, but I've only seen your kitchen moves," I poke back.

"Don't take her words to heart. I'm not a dancer, but I do like to dance around when I'm cooking, so what you've seen is about what you get." He wraps a towel around his waist, much to my disappointment. "Speaking of Caroline. I'm going to text her and my uncle to let them know family dinner is being moved up. Go ahead and get ready, we're going tonight."

"Tonight?" I gulp; the burn of anxiety fries my nerves. "Not wasting any time then, huh?"

"Trust me, if we wait there will be a riot. Uncle Ivan would be disappointed that he didn't know as soon as possible, and Caroline would be upset that I didn't immediately text her to let her know her 'plans' worked." His eyes roll with such force even I can feel it.

"Her plans?" My brows scrunch.

"She likes to think she's playing matchmaker. Hence the date night she orchestrated, and the not-so-subtle hints about me being an expert dancer and I'm sure she's said things to you to try and convince you I'm some sort of 'dream guy'."

I'll be damned if he thinks his hand quotes and sarcasm are going to go overlooked.

"You *are* a dream guy. Stop it. Sure, she's told me things about you, but none of them have been untrue, or even exaggerations. I've gotten everything she's told me, and then some. Don't sell yourself short." I cross my arms.

"I'm glad I've lived up to everything then." The tips of his ears redden. "I'm going to go get dressed and let Navy back inside. Poor little guy probably feels left out."

"Okay, I'll get ready for the reckoning." I give him a playful smile and begin brushing my hair. He kisses my cheek one final time before leaving the room.

Let's get this over with.

# CHAPTER 26

## *Nikolai*

If I never live to see another day, so be it. Charli's soft, naked body pressed against me as I pampered her was far more euphoric than anything I could have ever imagined. In the last twenty-four hours alone so much has changed between us.

She's a whole new woman, it seems. I can't quite wrap my head around it, but I don't even care to try. She's made so much progress, so quickly I can only assume that she's set that beautiful mind of hers to moving on with her life. Regardless, I'm here to support her through it, however she needs.

*As her boyfriend.*

The fuzzy, tingly sensations passing through my body feel strange. I don't know the last person I had genuine feelings for. But damn do I have them for the firecracker in the other room. I hope my family accepts our relationship. Well, mostly my uncle.

If he doesn't, it'll fucking hurt. I'm not the type of

man who does well with ultimatums or tough decisions, which is why it's so great that Charli is so open and willing to be direct with her wants and feelings.

Navy crunches away on his breakfast as I prepare the omelet and waffles Charli requested. I'll make sure we're all fed, then wake up our family group chat.

I know Uncle Ivan is working today, but Caroline's schedule is all over the place, so I have no clue if she's even awake yet.

Chocolate chip waffles pile up, I also decide to warm some peanut butter as a sauce instead of a traditional syrup. Charli will lose her shit over these. Even if she doesn't, I have the old trusty ham and cheese omelet to fall back on.

My girl loves to eat.

My cheeks are flushed and warm just thinking about the fact that she's *actually* my girl.

It's not just a hopeful fantasy anymore.

I'm standing in the kitchen, grinning like a love-struck idiot. Luckily, Navy is my only witness.

When I make it to her bedroom, Charli's face lights up at the sight of her breakfast. Her excitement makes my heart do summersaults. I'll never grow tired of knowing that I'm *finally* one of the reasons for her beautiful smiles.

The fact that she's gained healthy weight since she's been here brings me massive amounts of joy. She was a withered shell a couple of months ago, and now she naturally glows. Her skin is so much more vibrant. Her hair is shinier and silkier than ever. The hollows of her cheeks have filled in. She looks so lively.

Her assessment of me was partially correct when she asked about my mother. If I hadn't been a mere infant, I likely would have done as much as possible to try and help her, too.

Do I go out of my way to help everyone I care about as much as possible? Yes.

Do I think it gives me some 'savior complex' like my uncle has called it in the past? No.

Am I hell bent on 'saving' Charli regardless? You better believe it.

Do I care if he judges me for falling for her? Eh, kind of, but I'll survive.

At the end of the day, I know my uncle wants everyone to be happy, too. He's just seen all the loss and hurt in our lives, so I know he's grown cynical. I want to show him that I'm not the same naïve teenager trying to compulsively help everyone anymore. I've grown a lot in the past few years. I've been alone and have given myself time to think about what I want out of life.

And what I want is the angel covered in peanut butter sauce across from me.

I sit and take a bite of the breakfast sandwich I made myself. My palms are clammy as I unlock my phone. Charli watches me, silently. I know she must feel how nervous I am.

**Me:** *Good morning, change of plans for this week. I*

*want to take everyone out for sushi tonight. I have some news to share.*

**Parasite:** *It's literally 8 am. Go away...*

**Me:** *Sorry, I assume you worked late last night? Are you ever going to go back and finish your degree?*

**Parasite:** *Not you too. UGH. I'm going back to sleep.*

**Me:** *Sorry, I'll catch you later.*

I'm not trying to face the wrath of a sleep-deprived Caroline, so I pull up my uncle's contact and message him directly.

**Me:** *Sorry I know it's early, and you're working but I just wanted to make sure you know to meet us at the little sushi spot around the corner from the hospital at six.*

**Uncle:** *I do hope your news is important, to be throwing off our week like this. We will see you there, Nicky. Tell Charli we look forward to seeing her again. I want to know all about her therapy session.*

**Me:** *We look forward to seeing you too. Her therapy went well. I'm sure you'll be proud of her when you hear about it.*

**Uncle:** *I'm proud of all of you. Don't think for a second that I'm not. I love you, Nicky. See you at six.*

**Me:** *I love you, too. See you then.*

Okay, that could have gone way worse.

*I can do this. She's worth it.*

"Are you okay?" Charli's hand lands softly on my leg accompanying her question.

*Shit, I forgot where I was for a second.*

"Yeah." I take a deep breath. "That was just nerve wracking, but it went well." I lean back against the headboard, settling in as we continue eating.

"So, did you tell them?"

"Oh no, I wouldn't dare tell them over a text message. That's rule number one. Never give big news of any sort over text. Things can get lost, misconstrued or even just overlooked. In person is the only way." With a final bite of my sandwich, I place my plate on the nightstand.

"I like that. You're all so open and honest with each other. Even in difficult situations." She licks a bit of peanut butter off her finger, finishing her last bite.

"Well, when you've had the shitty luck we have, you learn not to keep things pent up. You never know when your last conversation with someone may be, and the regret of not having the chance to tell someone how you feel is a heavy burden to bear." I know my words are intense, but honesty tends to be.

Charli takes my hand in hers and we sit in easy silence as she pets Navy. I can virtually hear her mind whirring with the thoughts she's mulling over. I don't push her to open up to me any more than she already has today, though.

"I really like you, Nikolai. I don't want to add stress to your family, though. Are you sure this is a good idea?"

I'm entirely aware that *this* means *us*. No way am I going to lose her as soon as I get her.

*Nope, not happening.*

"Charli." I pivot to face her, placing a palm against her

cheek. "This is the best thing that's ever happened to me. *You* are the best thing to ever happen to me. Nothing worth having comes easy. I think I've proven by now that I don't run from a challenge. Besides, it's just my overprotective uncle. At least he likes you. You should have seen the hell he gave me over Lilah."

A laugh bubbles out of her. "I just don't want to cause a rift, that's all."

"Sugar, you caused a rift the second you stumbled onto that old cabin doorstep. To be honest, you've been what we all needed. A breath of fresh air, someone to shake up the dull monotony of our lives." I softly kiss her forehead and the blissful smile she rewards me with every time appears.

She lets out a soft hum. "How do you always know what to say?"

"I don't, I just speak the truth. You're exactly where you're meant to be. So, let yourself live in the moment."

"Okay, I'll do my best." She nods gently.

"That's all any of us will ever ask of you. Now, we need to start getting everything in order for later. The day is already getting away from us." I grab our dishes and bring them to the kitchen.

Time flies when you're having fun, or something like that anyway. It's almost six, Charli and I are seated in a booth at the sushi spot I picked for our dinner. It's one of the nicest places in town for some kick-ass shrimp tempura rolls. Since we established that it's Charli's favorite, this place was a no-brainer.

A large koi pond is in the middle of the room, cherry blossom trees are painted on the walls. The air smells like rice wine and soy sauce. Soft music dances through the restaurant.

Charli is completely mesmerized by the ornate detailing etched into the border of our black and white marble table. I can't stop myself from staring. I love showing her nice places like this. The look of wonder on her face with new experiences will never get old.

"Can I get you started with any appetizers?" Our waitress breaks my trance.

"Oh, sure. We're still waiting for two more guests, but I know everyone loves pan-fried gyoza. Could we get an order, please?" I reply.

She nods and leaves us to continue our quiet admirations.

When my uncle and Caroline arrive the air around us noticeably shifts. I can feel my nerves building, and so can Charli. Her hand finds my knee under the table as I wave them over and offer the most genuine smile I can.

"Nicky! This had better be good. But if it isn't I also have news that everyone will love!" Caroline is vibrating with excitement.

"Well, don't let our news overshadow yours, it seems important. What's going on?" My brows are tightly drawn together.

"Well, you know, everyone has been all over my rear about going back to school. Charli came into our lives and really shifted my perspective. If she can overcome all the trauma she went through, so can I. Sooooo, I've decided that I'm going back to school full time in the fall!" She claps her hands together, bouncing in her seat.

"Wow, Caroline. I don't know what to say. That's so amazing!" Charli is completely awestruck beside me.

"Oh, Li. I don't know how to thank you enough. You're so strong and determined and just been so inspiring. I couldn't just sit back and let my life pass me by anymore once I saw your dedication to building a life after what you lived through." She reaches across the table, squeezing Charli's hand as they both sniffle, holding back tears.

"Caroline, you know I'll help you financially, right? You focus on schooling, and that way neither of you—" I motion between her and my uncle. "—will have to worry about anything while Caroline finishes her degree."

"Oh Nicky, that would be so awesome of you." Caroline's eyes sparkle even brighter.

"Yes, that would be a great help. I wouldn't want her to have to work those crazy hours and still go to school full time. As much as I don't like handouts, thank you, Nikolai. We'd greatly appreciate it. I'm proud of you kids for always being there for one another." My uncle's face is soft.

There's so much love and compassion going around, this is the perfect time to drop the figurative bomb.

"Speaking of overcoming trauma and building a life for myself," Charli speaks up, before I have an opportunity to get my thoughts together.

"Ah yes, your therapy. I can only assume that's why we're here tonight instead of this weekend. Do tell, Milaya. How was your session?" My uncle rests his chin on his fist awaiting her response.

"Well, the session itself wasn't great, in terms of helping the investigation anyway. But I have talked a lot with Doctor Hastings in the past couple of sessions about my life. Well, the life I am working toward now. I have been living by the motto of 'be brave' because it would have been so easy to stay shut down, denying myself the experience of new things. Sushi being a great example." She chuckles. "Anyway. Part of that has been accepting my... living situation and the feelings I have about said situation." She fidgets beside me as her courage dwindles.

*Time to step in.*

"What Charli is saying is that she's decided to take a huge step and stop resisting her natural attraction and urges. Okay, 'urges' isn't a great word." Damn it, now I'm fidgeting. "What I mean is, we talked this morning. Well...she talked, I listened and we're officially dating."

I want to bury my face in my hands to avoid their reactions, but I don't. If Charli can sit here and "be brave" so can I.

"You're dating? So not just one-time sex then?" Caroline, as always, gets straight to the point.

"Good lord, I need a vacation," my uncle grumbles, rubbing his temples.

I'm not sure if it's our relationship revelation, or Caroline's inability to read the room that has upset him.

"Uncle, just know that I didn't push for this. It was all Charli's decision."

"Nicky, my tenderhearted boy, I believe you'd never push anyone into anything." He reaches across the table and takes my hand in his before turning his attention to Charli. "Milaya, I am truly astonished by the progress you've made. I am so proud to have you as a member of the family, whether you're with Nikolai or not. Just know that I love you both, no matter what happens. I only want to see you all happy and cared for."

"You know I care for her," I cut in.

"I know you do, but you need to care for *you* too, don't lose yourself again." His voice is laced with a slight sadness.

"I wouldn't let him," Charli interjects, "I don't know the first thing about relationships, but I know that it feels right with Nikolai. Now that I've allowed myself to feel things anyway." She leans into me and I kiss her temple.

"Ahhhh! You two are the absolute cutest! I love it," Caroline squeals, half of the restaurant turns to gawk. She's entirely oblivious to the audience she's drawn.

"I'm so glad you're all making such great progress in your lives. You're going to make my old heart burst." Uncle Ivan wipes genuine tears from his eyes.

I can count on one hand how many times I've seen this man cry in my life. Most have been related to death. This is the first time I've ever seen him shed tears of joy.

Our waitress returns with the gyoza. We place our dinner orders and continue casual conversation. All my panic and trepidation had been for nothing. I know my family and had assumed this would be the outcome, but I still always prepare for the worst.

After dinner, we say our goodbyes and head home. Charli is exhausted and filled to the brim with shrimp tempura. She makes a quick retreat to her room to sleep off her overindulgence.

My studio is stale, I haven't stepped foot in here recently. Hell, the last time I did, Charli shook my entire universe on that midnight blue couch. My dick twitches at the memory.

*Down boy.*

I load my palette with a vivid spectrum of pigments, unlike my usual two to three colors. My life is brighter and more alive than ever, and I need to put all these feelings on canvas.

A dark base sets the scene for vibrant smears and splatters of electric blue, firefly yellow, a vivid magenta, and rosy pink that reminds me of Charli's flushed cheeks.

This is going in the living room, hands down.

I may be biased, but I think this is my best work yet.

# CHAPTER 27

## *Charli*

What an incredible week. Nikolai has been amazing. God I was a fool for ever resisting this. Every morning, he takes Navy out, makes me breakfast in bed—made-to-order nonetheless—then draws me a bath. We've bonded over more superhero movies and I am undoubtedly an Iron Man fan.

I have been so caught up that I never messaged Detective Hastings about any of my memories. I also haven't had a single flashback or nightmare this week, so it hasn't been on my mind at all.

I can't believe it's Saturday already. I'm cocooned in a soft blanket on the couch, reading my latest romcom. The large canvas in Nikolai's hands as he enters the living room catches my eye.

"Wow. That's so unlike your usual style. So happy yet disorderly looking all at once." I admire the vibrant splatters.

"I know right? I want to hang it in here somewhere."

He looks around at the walls, already scattered with art and movie posters. "Hmm. What if we take some of these down over the TV and put it up there?"

"We? You want my opinion?" I'm wide-eyed, stunned, completely caught off guard.

"Charli, this is your home too. You spend as much time in this room as I do now. I painted this the other night after we came back from sushi. My mind and heart were brimming with emotions, and I needed to let it out. I mean it when I say you're my muse."

"Wow, o-okay, then. Yeah, I'd like to have it over the TV, too. That way it can act as a sort of centerpiece."

"Me too, this painting is us, after all. Every stroke of my brush was fueled by my feelings about us."

My stomach lights up with flutters. God, he's the sweetest man ever.

I don't know a ton of men to be fair, but that doesn't mean I can't appreciate a good one when he's standing right in front of me.

After the painting is hung, Nikolai joins me on the couch. I actively seek out his gentle touches now so when he sits next to me, I turn and place my icy feet in his lap. Without question he immediately begins to rub them.

In seconds I feel his hardness under my heels. When he tells me that he's always turned on, it's not even close to an exaggeration. He never presses the issue though.

We haven't been sexually intimate since the night in his studio, but I feel my desire for it increasing every day.

I want him, but not in the ways I've already had him.

I want to know what his raw, unrestrained passion feels like. I'm just scared to mess it up.

What if I get in my head and freak out?

*God, I don't think I'm ready yet.*

Soon though I'll have to overcome my fears.

"So—" His voice startles me from my thoughts. "Have you thought more about what you want to do with your life? I know you were thinking about maybe volunteering at the animal shelter. Is that still something that interests you?"

At that moment, Navy comes prancing into the room from napping on my bed. I pick him up and he plops into my lap for snuggles.

"I think I would like to work at a shelter. Or anywhere that would allow me to help pups like Navy find loving families." I scratch the spot under his chin that makes his little leg kick.

"Just know, I don't expect you to go and work at some dead-end job that will suck the life out of you. You can stay home every day, and I'd support that choice too. I want you to do whatever makes your heart feel full. Life is too short to spend your time being unhappy."

"I genuinely want to help animals. This little guy in my lap brought me so much hope and joy when I needed it. We're very similar. The things I've managed to remember about my childhood are not great, they're repressed for a reason. At this point I don't care to re-member more. However, helping him helped me."

"Okay, wild question then. Please don't freak out. But

I keep thinking back on our conversation... Would you genuinely want to open your own rescue? I'd love to help run something like that. I need something fresh and rewarding to do, and if I get to do it together with you that's honestly a bonus." Nikolai smiles brightly at me.

My jaw hangs open. Is he legitimately offering this? I don't know the first thing about running a business, especially one so important.

"I'm sorry, I should have asked that a little gentler I guess." He's blushing, embarrassed that he's rendered me speechless.

*Don't leave him hanging.*

"I'm sorry. Jesus. Are you really interested in opening a dog rescue with me? I don't know anything about how to operate one." My head spins just thinking about it.

"Me either, but we don't have to do it now. I'm a planner. We have all the time in the world to research and prepare. We can hire experienced management. We can work with the state to provide summer jobs to under-privileged youth, walking dogs, cleaning kennels, that sort of thing. We could even name it after Navy and make it ultra special."

"Nikolai, you're the most wonderful person I've ever met. I'd love to." A wide smile pulls at my lips.

"Great! We can start planning soon. It'll be a while before we even break ground. We need to find a good plot of land first. Want to start looking tomorrow?"

I giggle playfully at his excitement. "How about we wait until after my session on Monday. It's going to be a rough one. But hopefully it'll be the last one I need to do the guided meditation for. I fully plan to help Detective Hastings find that cabin and arrest those fuckers."

Nikolai's mouth opens wide. "Charli, I'm rubbing off on you. You filthy mouthed heathen!"

"When in Rome." I shrug.

We watch *Cake Wars* for the rest of the night, firing off ideas to one another. By the time I lay down I'm almost too excited to sleep. I pull Navy a bit closer and eventually manage to drift off.

Sunday was another lazy day. We had breakfast in bed, watched a few more movies. Nikolai made a delicious roast in the slow cooker. I ate until I thought I'd explode. It was such a comforting day.

My breakfast this morning was light, by choice. I don't want to be sick all over Doctor Hastings' office.

*Today's the day.*

I finally reached out to Detective Hastings and he's sitting in on my session today, this way I won't have to relive everything again to tell him about any discoveries.

As warmly as ever, Doctor Hastings greets me, "Welcome, Charli. I do hope you're well. The whole hour today will be dedicated to discovering anything we can to aid the investigation."

"Okay, I'm ready when you are." I lean back in the familiar chair.

"Please, relax. Theo will observe quietly and record with your permission."

"Okay, here goes nothing." I rest my head on the pillow and let my mind regress back to the darkest parts of my memories.

"Tell me about the men. How many are there? What do they look like? Are there any defining marks or features?"

I dig in as deeply as I can. With a deep breath I will my mind to fabricate an image of all three men.

"Well, Vincent is definitely older than the others. He's probably fifty or sixty years old. His hair is dark and short with gray throughout. No marks I can remember. He's not overweight, but also not thin or muscular. He's always covered in black grease; his hands are anyway. Sometimes he would leave streaks behind when he was done. I would try and try to get it off, but it was sticky, and I only had a leaky pipe to use."

"What color are his eyes? How tall is he?" Her voice feels far away.

"Brown eyes. Dark, dark brown. He's around six feet tall. Definitely taller than me."

"Okay, very good so far Charli. Who else is there?"

"Frank and Ricky. They look almost the same, but Ricky is bigger, with a round belly and chubby face, lots of pimples. Frank is lanky and thin. I think they're related. Both have similar hair, it's either black or really dark brown, it's too dark to tell for sure. Ricky has brown eyes like Vincent. Frank's are gray, maybe light blue. I don't know how old they are, but they're not much older than I am, I don't think anyway," I spout out as much information as I can bear to give.

"How tall would you say they are?"

"Maybe five foot ten to six feet each? I'm not too sure, Vincent is a little bit taller."

"You're doing wonderfully, Charli. What can you remember about the cabin you were kept in?"

"Nothing specific, except the room I was in. There were no windows, no sound from the outside. I think it was a specially built room. I had an old TV high up on the wall that played some random basic cable channel for entertainment. They gave me a few old books to read, too. I think they were planning on having another girl eventually. Frank said something about it once, maybe twice. He'd said I was getting 'worn out' and they'd get a new toy soon." I shudder at the memories flashing through my mind.

"What was the cabin like the day you got free?"

"It was dark inside. I got free at night. I think they were all asleep."

"Nobody saw you get away?"

"No, but I still ran like I was being chased. I wasn't taking any chances." My voice trembles.

"Okay, try to really place yourself back in the moment. I know it'll be difficult but imagine the scenery around you as you breach the front door. Is there anything you can see that isn't just trees?"

*I'm trembling as I step into the crisp night air. For the first time in an unknown number of days I smell something other than the musty room I had been quarantined in. I take off directly out the door and run, nothing is going to stop me. I'll die before I go back.*

"I think there's a truck parked out front. It's dark green with four doors. I can't tell what the model is." I gasp as a detail I'd never seen before jumps out at me. "Oh my God. There's a sign on the truck. It's a ranger vehicle."

"That's amazing. Charli. If one of them is a registered forest ranger, the cabin could also be a registered residence. Is there anything else that you notice?"

My mind is unraveling. Flashbacks and tumultuous emotions have wrecked my subconscious. I can't focus on another singular detail.

"I'm sorry everything is so muddied up." My face burns from the stream of tears rolling down it. "Was it enough? I don't ever want to do this again."

"Okay, our time is almost up anyway. You did remarkably well. I'm satisfied with our outcome. Are you up to combing through some information with Theo before you leave?"

Sitting forward, I nod. "I can manage."

*Can I though?*

I want Nikolai to hold me while Navy nuzzles into me. I want to cry out the last of this nightmare, sleep for a day or two, and never have to think of that hellscape again.

"Wonderful. I'll leave you to it."

"Thank you, Claire. Now, Charli, I know you're mentally and emotionally exhausted, but I did want to just confirm some details." Theo keeps his voice soft.

"Alright, just let me know how I can help."

"I just want you to confirm the men's names were Vincent, Frank and Ricky. Correct?"

I offer him a slight nod.

"Could you verbally confirm for me? So that I have it on the recording. Please?"

"Yes. Their names were Vincent, Frank and Ricky."

"Perfect. You stated you were kept in a windowless, soundproof room in the basement of a cabin. The door was thick and bolted. Is that true?"

"Yes, Sir." Again, I nod.

"And on the evening you were able to escape, you noticed a dark green Forest Ranger truck parked in the driveway. You're absolutely certain it was a marked Ranger vehicle?"

"Yes, I remember the lettering in gold." I grip the cushion I'm clinging to.

"Charli, this information may prove monumentally useful. I'll be in contact, should we have any further questions. Do take care of yourself for the rest of the day. You did something that is undeniably difficult and handled it with such strength. Be kind to yourself."

"Thank you, Detective."

"Please, call me Theo. I promise there's no need for formalities. We're beyond that now." He smiles warmly.

"Okay, Theo. Please find them so I can sleep better at night knowing they're locked away."

"I've got the best of the best on this case, Charli. I'll walk you out."

I'm a wreck as we head for the lobby. There's only one thought on my mind.

I need to forget.

# CHAPTER 28

## *Charli*

I spend the majority of my post-session day in a zombie-like haze. My brain won't stop replaying the worst of their wickedness. Navy has had more than enough of my clinging snuggles and retreated to his bed in the corner of my room.

Nikolai has taken it upon himself to be a human security blanket for me, since I'm not mentally prepared to be alone with my thoughts. We have been curled up together in my bed for the past hour watching a movie.

His affectionate touches, the glances to check in on me silently, paired with his warmth, and pressing myself as close to his body as I can all have me reeling.

After a short deliberation, I get out of bed and step into the bathroom. After a brief pep-talk to prepare myself for what's to come, I'm ready.

*I want this.*

No, I *need* this on a molecular level.

"Nikolai," I whisper, stepping reluctantly out of the

bathroom.

He's laid back on my bed casually. When his gaze lands on my now-nude form I watch him pull in a sharp breath.

"Fuck, Charli. You're flawless." His hand moves to cover his quickly growing erection. "I know this is the dumbest shit I'll ever ask, but... Why are you naked?"

"I need you, Nicky. I don't want to keep thinking about all the shit I remembered today. Take your pants off and make me forget."

He doesn't hesitate; he never does.

He's fully hard as he lays back on the bed.

"What do you need?" His heated gaze skims over my body, unabashedly.

"I want what you promised me. You said you'd run your hands all over my body and make me forget anyone else who has ever touched me. Make passionate love to me."

"Come lay down, I've got you gorgeous."

As confidently as I can, I make my way to my bed and lay tentatively in the middle, right next to him.

I close my eyes, preparing myself as my nerves begin to overwhelm me. I trust Nikolai. I can do this without feeling like he's taking advantage of me.

I know I can.

He settles in next to me, slowly trailing the faintest touches over my entire body. Whispers of his fingertips travel up my sides, over my shoulders, down my arms to my fingers, then back up.

I realize he's desensitizing me, preparing me for the more intimate touches that are quickly approaching. Tingles, brought by his breath on my neck and soft grazes of his thumb under one of my breasts, cause shivers to run through me.

"Too much?" He whispers softly in my ear.

I shake my head, unable to speak.

Nikolai spreads his hand out as he slides it up my chest. I arch into him, seeking more pressure. His hums of approval spark heat in my core.

Tender kisses trail from my neck to my collarbone, descending to the valley between my breasts. Eventually his lips drift to a hardened nipple, I open my eyes to meet his as he traces it with the warm, firm tip of his tongue. As I moan for him his confidence peaks.

Seeming sure enough that I won't panic, he shifts over me, positioning himself between my thighs.

Now that he's on top of me I would have thought I'd feel trapped. While a minor part of me does have a flash of doubt, it fades the instant I take in his gentle gaze as he begins telling me everything I need to hear.

"Just look at you. Fuck, Charli I'm the luckiest man in the world. I damn near passed out when you came into the room." He nibbles on one nipple while pinching the other until I'm writhing beneath him.

"Such a vision. Look at these magnificent tits. So perky and beautiful. Do you like it when I play with them, Sugar?"

I nod desperately, grinding up against the ridge of his

erection, seeking out any sort of friction I can find.

"Easy now, my needy little muse. We're just getting started. You know I'm going to give you everything you want, right?"

"Y-yes Nicky."

"That's right. I want you to remember this, and only this. When your delicious little pussy aches tomorrow, you'll think about me. How good I can be, just for you."

Light kisses resume their journey down my stomach as he lowers himself. He bites my upper thigh, I squeak and squirm, only for him to chuckle and kiss his mark. Pleasure filled whimpers are the only response I can muster.

"Does my perfect muse like biting too?" He asks against my sensitive skin.

"I do, bite me harder." My voice is needy, even with such a stern demand.

I'm throbbing already and he's barely touched me.

He hums against my inner thigh before biting slightly harder this time. Testing the waters to see just how much I can handle. The stinging pain sends a thrill down my spine.

I'm on the brink of madness. "Nicky, I need to come so badly. You're doing so good for me. I'm close already. Make me come."

"Yes, ma'am." He moves his mouth to my clit and sucks while sliding two long, coarse fingers inside me. He expertly works them in and out, with skill and finesse I could only expect from a man who makes such beauty with his hands.

Mewls and incoherent screams explode from me when I feel myself start to unravel. The sensations rippling through my body are unlike anything I've ever experienced.

"That's it, gorgeous. Get ready to come like the goddess you are. Make a mess of me so I can savor you."

"Oh God, you have magical fingers." I'm panting, sweating, on the edge of being fully wrecked.

"I've barely touched you, Sugar. I'll show you real magic, just wait."

Before I have the chance to ask what he means, his fingers are inside me again, pumping steadily. He kisses up my thigh, pausing to appreciate my building wetness.

The moment he begins sucking and lapping at my clit while working against a sensitive spot inside me, my body goes into overdrive. Sensations swirl through me. Another bite to my thigh is followed by soft, soothing kisses while he pushes his fingers deeper.

"Fuck, Nicky. You're amazing." My body tenses up, preparing to detonate.

"Mmm yes, that's it. Find your release. You can do it. Just relax and let it go. Soak me, I know you want to. Fuck." He's pleading with rabid enthusiasm.

He thrusts deep and curls his fingers. When I tighten and bear down on the pressure my release hits me all at once. A flooding sensation escapes me with a tsunami like force.

Nikolai grits out deep, feral groans as he pulls his face away from me. "My muse, you're magnificent. Such a treasure to behold. You come so beautifully."

He's dripping wet when I spare a glance at him. "Oh, God. Di-did I do that to you?"

"Fuckin' right you did." He runs his fingers from my soaked pussy and trails them up his equally drenched torso, licking them clean as they reach his mouth. The rumble of satisfaction he lets out has me aching for him.

*Who am I right now?*

"Now the real pleasure can begin." He grips his cock, stroking himself as he glides it through my wetness. He bites his lip and groans as he slides the tip up to my sensitive clit. "So warm and wet, Sugar. Are you ready for me?" His eyes are locked with mine.

My legs are spread wide for him, I couldn't move them if I wanted to at this point. "Yes, Nicky. Please me."

He leans down and takes my mouth with his.

The kiss is slow, passionate, soul deep. Our tongues dance together with the same passion as they did weeks ago. He trails a hand up my side, stopping to pinch my nipples. I gasp into his mouth as he slowly pushes inside me.

I gasp against his lips from the stretch as my body works to accommodate him.

"Pure, blissful utopia. That's what you are." He pulls out and slides back in, pushing deeper. "Being inside you is paradise."

"You fuck me so well, Nicky." I graze my nails down his back.

He kisses my neck as he thrusts even deeper. "I'm not

even fucking you yet. This is just the warmup. I want you to be good and ready for the passion I'm about to unleash. If you really want it."

"I want everything. Don't hold back. Let me feel all of you. Fuck me." I bear down on him and his nostrils flare as he inhales.

"As you wish." He leans back lifting my hips, angling me so he can slide a pillow under my ass, lifting one of my legs over his shoulder. The new position gets him deeper than before. He pulls out before driving back in, grinding against me. I watch his ab muscles flex as his body rolls while he sets a steady rhythm.

"You're so thick, Nicky. God, I love the way you fill me."My walls begin to flutter around him and my hips roll on their own as he pushes harder, stroking steady circles over my clit with his thumb.

"Are you going to come on my cock, my sweet muse? If you want me to really fuck you, I'm going to need to ask that you come one more time." He pants out.

Another orgasm rips through me before I can even think about it. I grind myself into him with unexpected vigor. My body seemingly draws energy from reserves I didn't know existed.

"Just like that, Sugar. You're incredible." He throws his head back as he picks up his pace.

The sensations are almost too much to bear, yet I ache for more.

"Nicky, yes. I need you so bad." I whimper around a moan.

His eyes darken, hands grab ahold of my waist as he slams himself into me. He's shimmering with sweat and looks like a dream above me.

"Charli, fuck. You take my cock so well. I'm going to come so fucking hard for you." He practically growls, leaning back to watch himself work.

"You'd better not think about coming yet." I scrape my nails down his chest.

He leans back into me. "I wouldn't dream of it, my muse. Not until you tell me to. This exquisite little pussy of yours makes it a challenge though."

I reach up and fist his hair, slamming his mouth to mine. We become nothing more than clashing teeth and tangled tongues. He grows frantic as I bite down on his lower lip. "Fuck yes, I love the way you hurt me."

"You want me to hurt you, naughty boy?" I grit out. *Well, that's new.*

Eyes alight with yearning consume me as he rolls us over, pulling me onto his lap. "Don't just hurt me. Own me, Charli." He drags my hand to his throat, positioning my thumb and fingers exactly where he wants them.

*Oh God, he wants me to choke him.*

The throbbing between my legs only intensifies as I squeeze his throat. I rock my hips, grinding against him as he drives up into me. "Nicky, you're so bad. I love it."

As his cock twitches inside me, my grip grows stronger.

I almost stop when his eyes begin to roll back in his head, but I don't. I trust that he'll stop me when he needs me to. The power I have over him in this situation is exhilarating. A side of me I never knew existed comes alive. With everything I have, I ride him as he grips my ass.

His hips jerk unevenly as he taps my arm. "Slap me," he wheezes when I release my grip. "Please, slap me."

I'm a screaming mess on top of him as I give him what he wants. A quick, firm slap across the face and he goes wild below me. "You can do better than that. Show me how much you want it, and I'll fuck you into oblivion." He pants wildly.

I give him a solid smack; the crack reverberates through my bedroom. He growls ravenously, lifts me up like I'm nothing,  and turns me over onto my stomach.

With a quick slap on my ass, he plunges himself back inside me with unexpected intensity. I scream at the sensation of being filled so roughly.

Strong fingers thread through my hair, pulling just enough to expose my neck to him. He bites down, sucking at my pulse point as he pushes deep and hard, continuing his punishing pace. Sounds I didn't know I could make erupt from deep within me. I quiver at the feeling of him marking me while his hips piston relentlessly.

In an instant I'm sobbing from the overwhelming ecstasy and blinding pleasure. The room is filled with a chorus of our bodies slapping against each other as we take everything from one another.

Nikolai pulls me back against his chest, sitting me in

his lap. I feel myself tightening around him as he grips my breasts, plucking my nipples.

He reaches down to rub my clit, bringing his mouth to my ear. "This, my darling muse... fuck. This is exactly how you deserve to be pleased. Do you feel how hard you're throbbing on my cock? Your pussy is transcendent. So wet, so tight, so luscious. Just demanding me to fill you up. Do you want to get filled up with my cum? Tell me how badly you need it. Tell me and I'll give it to you."

"Nicky, I need it so badly. Come for me, show me how much you love to please me." I gasp as he sucks at my pulse point.

With a few shuddering breaths and jerky thrusts, he bites down on my shoulder and comes deep inside me, strumming my clit as my name passes his lips. An array of colors bloom in my vision as he brings me to a final, mind melting orgasm.

Kissing the marks he's left on my neck and shoulder, he carefully rolls us onto our sides and spoons me. He's still inside me, stroking my hair as I try to return myself to this plane of existence.

"Spectacular. You're utterly spectacular, Charli." Soft kisses to my shoulder help me come back to the moment. "Thank you for trusting me, and for not choking me to death" He chuckles breathlessly.

"Nikolai. What just happened?" I pant. "Where am I? Is this even real?" I'm barely holding on to consciousness as my body begs for sleep.

"I did as I was told, and you really let yourself get lost in the moment. It was beautiful. Now, get some good rest. You deserve it. I'm right here." His arms wrap around me and pull me close as I get lost in the warmth of his embrace.

I can't wait to do this again.

# CHAPTER 29

## *Charli*

Commotion in the kitchen startles me awake. Light filters into the room from the hallway. Nikolai must have put Navy outside and started breakfast.

Last night was exactly what I needed after the day I had. I've never felt so thankful for someone before. We may only be a week into our *official* relationship, but he's paid so much attention to me the whole time I've lived here that it feels like it's been so much longer.

My eyes are still heavy, and my body is still boneless. I roll over to try and get a bit more sleep before he wakes me up for breakfast.

*Life is good.*

The bed behind me dips as Nikolai sits down. I feel a strange sense of unease. I can't tamp down the building panic. He always makes his presence known when he comes into the room.

*Something isn't right.*

As I begin to roll over, my worst nightmare comes to

life. "Look at you, filthy fuckin' whore." A voice that has haunted my dreams steals the air from my lungs.

"V-Vincent?" I can barely choke out his name.

"You really thought you'd get away from me? You're mine, bitch."

I'm frozen in place, unable to fight him off as he stands and  zip ties my arms and legs to the bedposts.

"God you're disgusting dripping with your little boyfriend's cum. It's alright though, he's not gonna be a problem anymore."

"What? What do you mean?" My voice wobbles.

"I mean he's bleedin' out like a stuck pig all over that fancy fuckin' kitchen right now."

A sob breaks free. "You—"

'Killed him. Just like Frankie and Ricky. Those little shits weren't loyal." His words are dripping with pure venom.

"H-how did you find me?"

"Silly little girl. I got a tracker in ya. Learned my lesson after the last one tried to run. Man's gotta have a plan in case his pets try and get away."

*A tracker?*

"Y-You've been watching me all this t-time?" I stammer.

"Had to wait it out, make sure I knew what I was walkin' into. Gotta have patience, a plan. Thought you spotted me a time 'er two. Now, shut up and let me reclaim what's mine."

The clinking of his metal belt buckle is deafening. I

close my eyes, willing myself to wake up from this night-mare as he rounds the bed to position himself between my restrained legs.

There's no way this is happening; it must be a dream.

"She'll never be yours," Nikolai's strained voice destroys the dome of horror encompassing my room.

Both of our heads snap in his direction.

Everything happens so quickly.

Vincent rises from the bed, taking the first fraction of a step. Light bounces off the object in Nikolai's hand. A bright flash accompanied by a loud bang resounds through the room. A crimson spray coats my bed sheets as Vincent falls lifeless onto the carpet.

"Nicky!" I wail, thrashing against my restraints. He stumbles as he makes his way to my bed.

"Charli, I-I stopped him. You're safe—" He sputters with a cough, collapsing next to me. "—I c-called 911. You're... safe."

"Nicky, don't talk, you're hurt." I want to hold him so badly.

"It's okay. You're going to be... okay." His words are barely more than gasps. His eyes flutter as he attempts to stay alert. "Charli, I...I love you."

My heart shatters as his eyes slip shut and he goes limp. Soul splitting screams tear from my throat. I've never felt more helpless. I can't tell if he's breathing, I have no clue if Vincent is, in fact, dead. I thrash and thrash until my wrists and ankles are raw.

It feels like an eternity before the police and paramedics burst through into my bedroom. "Help! Help him please!" I scream.

Acting quickly, a paramedic assesses the scene, checking Nikolai for a pulse. She casts me a solemn look and fresh molten tears burn my eyes.

"We have a very weak pulse, he's lost a lot of blood, we need an I.V. and emergency transfusion with universal blood started immediately. I see at least two stab wounds, one to the abdomen, one to the shoulder."

The bodies in my room move in a blur as I'm freed from my restraints and Nikolai is taken away on a gurney. A coroner is called to secure Vincent's body. Nikolai's shot went directly through his heart, killing him instantly.

"Ma'am, are you injured?" A blank face asks me. His voice sounds distant, like I'm under water.

"H-Hastings." My mouth feels wrong.

"Ma'am?" The shadow asks.

"Hastings. D-Detective."

"Sir, I think she's in shock." A soft female voice breaks through the rushing waves crashing against the walls in my head. I imagine Caroline knelt before me.

"I...need Hastings. He knows."

"Ma'am, are you referring to Theo Hastings?"

My eyes spring open, I nod frantically. "Yes, he knows. I'm Charli."

"Okay, we'll call him. He'll meet us at the hospital. We're going to take you there to get checked out, okay?"

I nod a final time before collapsing. I'm faintly aware

of the movements around me as I'm transported.

The bright lights on the ceiling are blinding. I'm in bed but it's not mine. I grimace as my head pounds. My wrists ache and my body doesn't feel like my own.

I jolt as memories flood back rapidly.

I'm laying peacefully in my bed, anticipating Nikolai's tender touches as he wakes me for breakfast. The sight of Nikolai's blood-soaked shirt. My heart shattering as his beautiful green eyes faded before he collapsed next to me. The heartbreaking fact that his last words to me were the same three words I've been feeling, but have been too afraid to acknowledge.

"Charli." The voice of Theo Hastings snaps me out of my spiral. Sluggishly, I tip my head over toward him. "Charli, you're awake. Claire is here as well, you can talk to us if you'd like."

"I don't even know what to say." My throat is raw, like I've swallowed glass shards.

"Theo, Darling, could you locate a nurse to bring her some water please?" Doctor Hastings. Even now, in the presence of my chaos, she's stoic and reserved. It's reassuring, calming even.

"Yes, my love. I'll be right back." He stands from the chair next to hers and exits the room.

"Now, Charli, don't stress out about anything, okay? When Theo rejoins us, he will have some questions for you, but he's not going to expect perfection. Offer as much information as you're able to."

I nod faintly.

As soon as he returns and the water is in my hand, I gulp it down. Icy and refreshing, I've never savored something as simple as water so thoroughly before. "Okay, ask me what you need," I rasp.

"Well, what exactly happened? Can you recount the last few hours of the morning as you remember it?"

I try my best to recap everything that happened. Telling him about Vincent, the stalking, and the tracker.

"He said something about others?"

"Yes, he told me the last 'pet' tried to run so he put some sort of tracker in me as 'security' or something." I shrug. A hidden tracker isn't surprising considering how I was treated.

"So, there were others before you?"

"Apparently." I shudder.

*Those poor women.*

"And the other men, Ricky and Frank, he said he killed them?"

My heart splits into a million pieces.

"Too," I whisper.

"Too?" Theo has a bemused look on his face.

"H-he told me that he killed them too, after he told me about N-Nicky," I croak as tears stream down my face. "I thought I was paranoid; thought I was imagining things. Oh God, I got Nicky killed. My family took another loved one from Ivan and Caroline." I'm heaving, hiccupping, on the verge of hyperventilation.

"Charli, Nikolai is alive. He's—"

"Alive?!" I shriek, interrupting Theo.

"Yes. He had a rough patch, but after some much needed blood and some stitches he's expected to make quick recovery. You've been sedated for some time. You were hysterical and posed a threat to yourself when you first arrived," he confirms.

"I need to see him." I scurry to get to my feet.

Doctor Hastings speaks up. "Charli, we'll take you to see him but please, just breathe for me. Can you manage that? They won't allow you to visit him if you're acting erratically."

The cold floor on my bare feet surprises me. I nod and take a deep breath. "Can I have some socks?" I shiver as the chill from the linoleum permeates my body.

"Yes, there's a pair on your side table. We can save the rest of our questions for later. Since there's no immediate threat to safety and you're not injured beyond the minor abrasions on your wrists and ankles. I'll go get your doctor to sign your discharge papers. Sit tight for just a moment." She steps out, walking quickly.

Once she returns with my doctor and I get the all-clear, I waste no time getting to Nikolai's room.

A teary-eyed Caroline meets me at the door. "I want to be upset with you, but I know this isn't your fault. He's sleeping right now, but you can come in, just don't wake him."

Ivan is seated at the far side of his bed, meeting my gaze

as I approach. A wave of worry washes over me.

*Does he blame me?*

I don't have to speculate for long. He rises to his feet, with open arms, and closes the gap between us. "Charli, Milaya." His warm embrace soothes my nerves. I melt into his chest. "We were so worried and they wouldn't let us in to see you. I'm so sorry that this has happened."

"Y-you're sorry? I'm the problem here. None of this would have ever happened if it weren't for me." My tears soak the front of his sweater.

"Hey now, none of this is your fault. The only person to blame is no longer with us." He rubs my back as I weep.

"Nikolai killed him... Is he going to jail? Oh God, I've ruined his life." I wail loudly, choking as I cry.

"Nicky will be fine. From what I understand, the crime scene was pretty black and white. Anyone could tell what had happened. The state's castle doctrine laws mean that he was well within his right to act as he did. He's already been cleared of any wrongdoing," Ivan explains calmly.

"Is he going to make it? Do you think he'll hate me? He told me he loved me before he passed out." I continue to wail into his shoulder.

"Milaya, he would never be capable of hating you. That boy has had eyes for you since he first saw you. Everyone could see it. Don't you worry about a thing." He guides me to Nikolai's bedside.

"Caroline and I are going to head to the house and

take care of Navy. If anything changes, send us a message. We'll be back in an hour or so."

The room feels colder once they leave. The chair I'm in doesn't feel close enough to Nikolai.

Being mindful of the wires and I.V. connected to him, I slide myself up into the bed and nestle into his side. The small hospital mattress is not meant for two people, I don't care. I do my best to get comfortable curling into him.

Within a few short minutes I drift off to sleep.

I don't know how long I nap for, but feather light strokes of my hair and gentle kisses against my forehead wake me.

I tilt my head up and his gentle eyes melt into mine as he lightly kisses the tip of my nose.

"You're awake." I feel the familiar sting behind my eyes. "I-I thought."

"Shh, it's okay, Sugar. The doctors were already in to see me. You slept through it all. I told them not to disturb you. You were sleeping off the rest of your sedatives."

"Do Caroline and Ivan know you're awake again? I need to text them." I try to scramble for my phone, but he pulls me closer.

"They know. It's okay. Just breathe for me. Everything is going to be fine." His heartbeat steadily thumps against me.

"Nikolai, can I kiss you? Are you feeling up to that?" I look up at him with a pout.

He answers by pressing his lips to mine with warmth

and tenderness, humming with appreciation as I lace my fingers through his hair. "Easy now. I just got a blood transfusion, can't have it all rushing to my dick."

"Nicky! Not funny. I thought you died and the last words you were ever going to tell me were—"

"I love you." He cuts me off.

"—Y-yeah. I-I love you, too. I don't even think I realized it until I thought I'd lost you. At that moment it felt like my whole future was being stolen from me all over again. I don't have any experience with love, but I know it's what I feel for you."

"Why can't we be home right now? I want to show you exactly how fucking much I love you. This is not helping my blood flow situation."

A joyful giggle squeaks out of me as he playfully bites at my neck. "You're insatiable."

"Charli, I just survived multiple stab wounds, killed a man, and then the most incredible woman in the world professed her love to me. Today has been a wild rollercoaster ride. I really wish I could just fuck you silly and get all this adrenaline out of my system, but I'll have to settle for just being close to you." He pulls me back into his chest.

"Awe you two look so cute all snuggled up! I can't handle it." Caroline's ever excited voice cuts through our lusty fog as she bursts into the room.

"I can't wait to get out of here so I can have some peace and quiet," Nikolai groans.

"You know you love me. I brought snacks so hush!"

Candies, pretzels and meat sticks emerge from her purse.

Nikolai grabs a bag of mini peanut butter cups and tears the bag open. "You're forgiven for interrupting, but only because I'm starving. That son of a bitch got me when I was getting ready to make waffles, and I worked up an appetite last night." He smirks.

Ivan sputters, the water he was sipping sprays comically across the room. "Nikolai, please have some decency."

Caroline snorts and offers him a fist bump. I chuckle along with them.

"Oh no he's corrupted you, too?' Ivan pinches the bridge of his nose.

"How long until I can get out of here? I'm fine. Really. He didn't hit any internal organs, just sliced through some muscle."

"The doctor made it clear you need to stay for the rest of the day so they can make sure you don't have a reaction to the blood transfusion." Ivan's tone takes on a paternal firmness.

Nikolai lets out an Oscar-worthy sigh.

While we're all joking around making light of the situation, the reality that we almost lost him washes over me, dampening my joy.

"You know, my darling muse." He reaches out to take my hand "It would take a lot more than some half-assed stabbing to take me out. Scars are hot right?"

His ability to find humor in any situation is endearing but irritating at the same time.

"It's not funny though. I felt so powerless, and I was convinced you weren't going to make it. There was so much blood, Nikolai. I couldn't save you." Fresh tears burn my cheeks.

"Shhh, you didn't need to save me. I promised that you're safe with me and meant it. I'll never, *ever* let anyone hurt you again." He kisses my tears away.

He indulges on the snacks Caroline snuck in with me pressed securely into his side. My appetite is completely absent. As I lay here, listening to the steady beating of his heart and their lighthearted banter, exhaustion takes over. I lose the battle and fall asleep on his chest.

# CHAPTER 30

## *Nikolai*

The doctor isn't thrilled that Charli has fallen asleep in my bed with me—again. He'll just have to deal with it. I could have lost her. The stab wounds are nothing compared to how much it would have killed me if he'd taken her. I'll never forget the relief pulling that trigger brought.

Charli said Vincent admitted to killing the other two men who kept her locked in that room. It's a damned shame, I would have loved to end both of them, too.

I stare at her peaceful face as she sleeps. The past forty-eight hours have taken a toll on her and I'll be damned if the doctor is going to disturb her.

If I had any say in it, we'd already be home so we could rest together in my big comfortable bed. I don't think we'll ever sleep in separate beds after this. I never want to leave her side again.

Yes, I know she's safe now, but do I care? Nope.

She's mine, and I'm going to make sure she's the happiest, healthiest, safest woman on the planet—no, in the universe.

She let me love her before all of this went to shit. True, passionate, soul-melding love. She gave me all of her and let herself go completely. It was everything I could have ever hoped for.

Then, as quickly as my life had been completed, it was destroyed. The chaos happened so quickly.

One second, I was riding the waves of ecstasy, the next my world was dark and filled with dread.

I'm so thankful I keep a pistol locked up in the living room. Charli didn't even know it was there. I saw the disbelief flash across her face as the shot rang out.

I probably shouldn't have professed my undying love to her as I was quite literally in the process of dying, but she needed to know. While telling Charli I love her so early in our relationship was not part of my plans, having her wholeheartedly tell me that she loves me too was even more of a shock. I think my heart skipped at least three beats and had to jump start itself in response.

Nothing will ever get in our way again. We're going to be so good together. My life has so much more meaning with her in it. Now that I've been on the brink of death—so they say anyway—I'm determined to live it to the fullest.

Charli wanted to wait until after her therapy session to start looking at land for the dog rescue. If she thinks this will put a damper on those plans, she's mistaken. Nothing's stopping me now.

It's amazing to think about. Looking back at our first encounter, I honestly believed she'd run away in the middle of the night. Man am I thankful she proved me wrong. Part of me believes she secretly felt the same pull as I did. It's just wishful thinking, I'm sure.

Charli stirs next to me. A tiny puddle of drool has soaked into my hospital gown. She's so small and adorable, I want to squeeze her all the damned time.

Have I mentioned that I can't believe this is my life now?

*Fuck, I love her.*

"Oh, sorry, I guess I fell asleep again." She rubs her glazed eyes. I make no effort to fight the powerful urge to kiss her, drooly face and all.

"Nikolai, I'm gross," she grumbles as I pull my lips from hers.

"Nothing will ever come close to making 'gross' an acceptable description of you, Sugar."

"I know why you call me your muse, it's literal, which makes sense. But why 'Sugar'?"

"Oh, great question." I kiss her quickly again, unable to stop myself. "The second I saw you I could see how gritty you were, but also how undeniably sweet you were, too. I knew I'd be addicted to you once I had a taste."

She blushes so hard I have the urge to kiss her until we're breathless. I don't, though. She's "gross" after all and I know she doesn't want me all over her right now.

"Oh. That's um." She clears her throat. "That's way

more profound than I expected."

"Charli, I don't take nicknames lightly. Hence why Caroline is my parasite." My smirk makes her laugh softly.

"I like being your muse. However, now that I know why you call me 'Sugar' I suppose it doesn't bother me anymore."

"If it bothered you, why didn't you tell me to stop?"
*What the fuck?*

"I just figured nicknames were a thing for you. But the guys, they all had names for me. So, when the first thing you called me was 'Sugar' I immediately decided that I hated your guts... Well that and the hair thing." She reaches up and runs her hand through my messy bedhead. "I love it like this, though. Keep it this way."

"As you wish, my love."

Her eyes sparkle as she tilts her head up to kiss me softly. Apparently, she's finished being 'gross' now.

"The doctor visited again while you were asleep. If I'm still not showing signs of complications from the blood transfusion I can leave in the morning."

"Do you feel well enough to leave so soon?" Her continued concern is adorably comforting.

"I'm fine, I promise. He barely even scratched me, really."

"Nikolai, you collapsed from blood loss. I thought you died. I lost my mind with grief until Theo and Claire told me you were alive."

"Oh, you're on a first name basis with the Hastings'

now huh?" I quip.

"Not the point of the whole conversation, smart-ass." She slaps my shoulder playfully.

I poke her in the side and chuckle as she squeaks.

"I'm fine, Charli. I swear. I wouldn't do anything to put myself at risk."

"You mean, other than taking in an escaped captive that you know nothing about. Falling in love with her. Letting her slap the shit out of you and boss you around. Then getting stabbed by her ex-captor turned stalker?"

"The risks were worth the reward. The stalker and stabbing were unforeseen complications. The end result is still as I had hoped." I grin lazily at her.

"You'd hoped to almost bleed out and need a blood transfusion?" She lifts a brow with a playful, crooked smirk.

"Okay, you're not allowed to out-sarcasm me." I tickle her ribs.

She squirms for a second before hopping off the bed. "Not fair! I can't tickle you with stitches."

"Okay I'm sorry, please come back I'm cold without you." I put on my best pouty puppy-dog face.

"You're completely ridiculous. I love it." She laughs and reclaims her spot curled into my side.

"We're staying in bed all day tomorrow, just so you know. I'll order a ton of food, and we'll both rest up." I nuzzle into her. My eyelids feel like sandpaper, I'm exhausted beyond belief. "Good night, Sugar. I love the fuck out of you."

"I love the fuck out of you too, Killer."

I let out a small laugh at her nickname. I don't hate it. Hell, I'd kill for her over and over if I had to. I'll wear that title with pride.

I'm at a Taylor Swift concert.

Wait, no. That's a ringtone.

Charli's phone is ringing. Nobody ever calls her, only five people have her number. I reach over and see it's Detective Hastings calling.

*Already?*

"Hey, Charli is just waking up. Hold on, I'll hand you over to her."

She takes the phone and lazily presses it to her cheek. "Yeah? Oh..." She bites her bottom lip. "Yeah, um keep me updated as much as you can." She hangs up and stares blankly at the wall.

"Do you want to talk about it?" I ask, cautiously.

"They, uhm. They got straight to work and are confident that they know where the cabin is." Her trembling voice doesn't match the apathetic expression she's sporting.

I don't say anything. There's nothing that can be said. Instead, my arms snake around her and pull her on top of me.

"Nicky! Your stitches!" She tries to fight me, but I scoot up in the bed and cradle her against me.

"Shhh, I'm here. It's just us. Nothing else matters." Like clockwork, tears begin to pour from her beautiful gold splashed eyes. "You're safe. You're loved. You're never going to be alone again."

She wails and clenches the bed sheet in her fists. "I j-just want it all t-to be over!"

"You're in the home stretch, brave girl. The hardest parts are behind you. You've endured more than anyone should ever have to. Just know that you have a wonderful support system behind you for this final push." I gently pull my fingers through her hair, peppering soft kisses against the top of her head.

"Thank you for everything. You have no idea how much you mean to me, Nikolai."

"I don't think I'll ever be able to convey how much you mean to me either, Charli."

A throat clears from the doorway, Charli peels herself away from my embrace as my doctor approaches my bedside. "As you know, Mr. Koval, your wounds were hardly more than superficial. You suffered significant blood loss, but there doesn't appear to be any adverse effects from the transfusion, so I believe you should be in the clear to discharge at your discretion. You're welcome to stay another day and ensure you're free of complications, if you'd prefer."

"Doctor, no offense, but I want to get the hell out of here. I have an adorable pup at home that I want to love on, and this gorgeous goddess to snuggle with. Can you believe she loves me?"

His mouth forms  a straight line.

*Not an ounce of humor in this one I see.*

"I'll have your paperwork finished up, you'll be good to go in about an hour. Once that last bag of fluids is done and we can get the I.V. removed."

"Thank you. I can't wait." I give him a thumbs up as he turns and hurries away. "He must be a busy guy, yeah?"

"I think we made him uncomfortable." Charli shrugs, as if to say she doesn't give a shit.

Good. Neither do I.

# CHAPTER 31

## *Charli*

We've just arrived home. I'm relieved to see that the house is no longer considered a crime scene so we *can* come home.

I shudder passing by my door. I don't want to set foot in that room ever again. It's still taped off for cleaning anyway, but it may as well be radioactive.

"We'll come back tomorrow and check on everyone. Navy will stay with us for a couple of days so you two can recuperate. If either of you need anything, don't you dare hesitate to ask. I love you both dearly. Rest up. I mean it." Ivan pats Nikolai on the shoulder.

I take in the sight of Nikolai's room as we step inside. All this time, and I've never bothered to venture in here. Hell, I've only been in his studio that one time.

Instantly, he strips down to his boxers and plops himself onto the huge, plush bed. Dark blue blankets, gray pillows, a dark stained wooden frame. The room itself is painted a steel-gray color. It's so masculine, in a calm, comforting way.

Following his lead, I shed my leggings and t-shirt and stand in place, wearing nothing but my underwear. "Can I borrow a shirt?"

Nikolai's eyes roam over my body. He swallows hard and nods, moving to sit up.

I motion for him to stop. "Just show me where, you stay there."

He points to the second drawer in the large dresser across from the bed. His room is astonishingly clean and organized. Knowing him, it doesn't surprise me all that much.

I pull out a plain white shirt, slip it over my head and turn back toward the bed. "Holy shit, please only ever wear my shirts again. I'm going to burn all your clothes, so you have no choice."

I let out a sharp laugh. "But I like the clothes you've bought me." I pout as I crawl into the bed next to him.

"Me too, but this." He trails a finger along the hem at my neck. "This is a wet dream come to life. I want to be inside of you so badly."

"I'd like that, but you need to rest." I roll over, putting my back to him.

"What if I just slide myself inside and hold you? Would you like that?" His voice has dropped, saturated with raw desire. "I'd like that." Slowly, he shifts behind me and kisses my shoulder.

"Nicky, I don't want you to strain yourself, maybe in a couple of days."

"Okay. You're right." He huffs.

I don't want to be right, though.

I'm in his bed, in his shirt, in his arms.

Everything is *him*.

His clean, crisp scent fills my senses.

Warmth radiates from him as he wraps me in a tight embrace. "I can hear you panting and feel how fast you're breathing. You're not helping my situation, Sugar." He presses his hardness into my ass.

*Damn it.*

Unable to resist, I arch back into him.

"Charli," he grits, pushing into me again. "Please tell me I can. I'll make you feel good in return. God, I just want to feel your warmth."

"I mean, you *did* kill a man for me and almost die."

"Is that a yes? Please tell me it's a yes." He groans.

"Yes, Nicky. You can hold me... with your cock inside of me."

I hardly finish my words before he sheds his underwear and pulls mine to the side. His hand finds my clit as he pushes into me from behind. I moan at the sensation, but he doesn't move.

With just a few deliberate strokes of his fingers, and soft kisses to my neck, I come undone, rolling my hips instinctively.

"That's my girl. Damn, I love feeling you come." He presses himself as deep as he can get and wraps his arms securely around me.

"You're really just going to lay there? Don't you want

to get off, too?"

"I told you; pleasure isn't only about orgasms for me. This is just as good. I love the connection. Why? Does this bother you?" He nuzzles his nose into my hair.

"No. Honestly, I enjoy it. I wouldn't even say the orgasm was necessary. I think I understand what you mean." I wiggle into him. "Good night, Killer."

"Good night my sweet muse."

A sudden sound wakes me. I pry my eyes open and check my phone for the time. "Oh my God." I squawk. Nikolai stirs behind me. "We slept for eleven hours! How is that even possible?"

"Well, the hospital beds were shit, and I've personally never been more at peace. It makes perfect sense to me." Warm fingers glide down my side. "Thank you for keeping me warm."

The meaning behind his words doesn't escape me. I'm a little sad that he's not still inside me. I understand that it's been half a day, though. It would be insane if he was still hard.

"Are you two decent in there?" Caroline yells through the door. "We've been texting but neither of you have answered. You need to eat. We brought fried chicken. Come out of your sex den when you're ready."

Nikolai snorts and shakes his head. "Well, I guess we're officially awake now." I roll my eyes and get up from the bed. Without giving it any thought, I make my way to Nikolai's dresser and get clothes out for him.

The vibrant admiration and appreciation gleaming in his eyes could melt even the coldest of hearts. "Thank you." He swallows a lump in his throat. "Nobody ever takes care of *me*."

"I wasn't even thinking about it. It's not a big deal, really. It's what we do when we care, right?"

"It's the little shit like this that makes me love you. So, just, thank you." His lips curl into a pout.

I lean down and kiss him quickly, then realize that I have no clothes to wear. I can't bring myself to step foot in my room.

*Great.*

I grab a pair of his shorts and pull them on, since I'm already wearing his shirt anyway.

Nikolai groans at the sight. He may actually burn all of my clothes just to keep me in his. I'll have to hide some of my favorites just in case.

When I make it to the kitchen I pause and laugh. Caroline and Ivan have half a restaurant worth of chicken and sides spread out on the counter. I couldn't care less about the food though. The one thing I really want is in Caroline's arms squirming to break free once he spots me.

Once she puts him down, Navy bounces at my feet. Clearly, he's missed me as much as I've missed him. I gather him up and we smother each other with kisses.

"Save some of that for me," Nikolai jokes as he steps

into the kitchen.

"Don't worry, there's enough to go around." I hand Navy to him. The kissy face he makes while Navy melts in his arms has my ovaries ready to explode.

*I'm screwed.*

"I'm glad to see you both look well rested." Ivan's voice is full of warmth.

I was nervous he'd be upset that I'm literally in Nikolai's clothes. It can't be a good look considering the circumstances.

"Thank you, Uncle. I haven't slept that well in days," Nikolai casually replies. Evidently he's not concerned about my attire at all.

"I bet." Caroline chuckles.

"Listen, Parasite. Keep it up and I won't offer you the job I was considering."

"Job?" We both say in unison.

"Yeah, I promised Charli we'd start looking at land this week for the rescue. I think it would be amazing to hire you as our in-house veterinarian once you finish school. You have, what, a year and a half until you're done?"

Caroline sputters. "Uh, wow. I don't even know what to say."

"Say yes. I think it's a great idea. It's also motivation to finish out your degree. I'd love to have you there. Someone we know we can trust." I take her hand in mine.

Tears fill her eyes. "I'd love to."

"Great! Now that we have that settled, I have a few places set up for us to look at later this week. We obviously have a few other more pressing matters to deal with first."

"I sure hope you mean resting," I deadpan.

"Of course. They're also supposed to finish cleaning up your room today. You should be fine to sleep in your own bed tonight." Sadness fills his eyes as he casts them to the floor.

"I don't want to sleep in my own room. I am more concerned with wearing my own clothes and having my shower products. Not that smelling like you is all that bad, but I'd miss my shampoo." I chuckle to myself.

"I'm still in shock over the fact that you're opening a dog rescue!" Of course, Caroline is hung up on that. She's been envious since we originally told her about our plans. I'm glad Nikolai wants to bring her on board.

"You mean *we*. As in, all three of us. I may be funding it, Charli may be the heart behind it, but you're going to be our head veterinarian. Don't think for a second this isn't a family affair," Nikolai interjects

"Stooooop Nicky. I'm so ugly when I cry. Don't make me." Her lower lip trembles.

"I think it would be wonderful for you all to work together for such a passionate and loving cause." Ivan beams, his face glows with pure love.

My phone vibrates, interrupting the conversation. I look down to see a notification from Theo, freezing when I read it.

Noticing my change in demeanor, Nikolai places a hand on mine. "Is everything okay?"

"Remember how they thought they found the cabin?" A trio of silent nods stare with uneasy eyes.

"They found it...and the bodies. Theo wants me to meet with him so he can give me details in person. He said, 'This is so much bigger than we thought.' Whatever that could possibly mean."

"Shit. When?" Nikolai runs a hand through his hair.

"I'd like to go as soon as possible."

"Well, there's no time like the present. I'll see if you have a dress in the dryer."

# CHAPTER 32

## *Charli*

Fortunately, I did have a dress to wear. At least I didn't have to show up to the police station in Nikolai's clothes.

"Charli, Nikolai, please follow me." Theo ushers us into a back office. Several pictures are laid out on a large wooden table, names attached to them.

"Charli, do you recognize these three men?" he asks.

"Yes." I scan the faces that still haunt my dreams.

The names below each photograph chill me to my bones. Vincent Thornton 56, Franklin Thornton 29, and Richard Thornton 27.

My watery eyes snap to Theo. "Thornton? They... they were—"

"His sons Charli. They were Vincent's sons. From what I know they were virtually untraceable. He likely raised them to do his bidding. He worked as a ranger and a freelance mechanic. The cabin was provided by the state for his ranger duties. Those boys likely never knew life outside of that cabin."

"He-he told me once I was 'worthless' since my only job was to give them a son and I couldn't even do that." A sob catches in my throat. "Oh God, do-do you think h-he—"

"Charli, we found remains of several women buried on the premises in shallow graves. A couple of which have already been identified as missing campers from Kootenai National Forest. Most were reported missing over a decade or two ago. It's very likely that Richard and Franklin's mothers suffered a fate similar to yours."

"Except they 'served their purpose' and then died for it!" I screech, crumbling apart.

Nikolai pulls me into his lap and cradles me. "How many?" He asks, since I'm incapable of forming words.

"Six women so far," Theo solemnly responds, "and two infants... Charli, what happened in the cabin was horrendous, there's no other word for it. Because of your bravery, and Nikolai's, nobody will be his victim ever again."

"What was wrong with him?!" My voice cracks between syllables.

"I'm not sure, but it doesn't matter, he's gone now. He can't hurt anyone else. I'm sorry to be the one to deliver all of this, but I figured it would be best that you knew what you helped stop."

I can only nod in response, unable to speak.

"Is there anything else you need from either of us?" I've never been so thankful for Nikolai as I cling to him while he takes over the conversation.

"No, we're just going to finish investigations of the premises. But given our findings so far, there's no need to keep questioning either of you for any more information. You're free to go but do keep in touch. Claire is always available for continued sessions. If either of you ever just need a friend, please feel free to reach out."

"Thank you, Theo." Nikolai nods to him as we stand to leave.

When we get home, Nikolai lays me down in his bed and holds me. Caroline and Ivan have already left so he sends a summary text message in our group chat. They respond offering words of sympathy and support, but I'm too numb to process any of it.

"Charli." Nikolai whispers, breaking through the maddening noise in my head. "Charli, I don't know how to say this." He sighs. "I don't want to throw this at you. But I don't want you to have any reminders of *them* or that nightmare."

"I don't understand," I mumble into his chest.

"Vincent was your fathers' stepbrother. Thornton. You're a Thornton, they were Thornton's... I don't want you to be a Thornton. I want you to be a Koval. We're your family," he explains rapidly.

I pull back and pin him with an intense stare. "I can't just change my name. It doesn't work like that. As much as I wish I could just march down to city hall and say, 'I share the same name as my screwed-up family, please let me change it.' That's just not possible."

"Marry me," He spits out.

I lurch my head back as though he'd slapped me. "Wh—"

"Before you say no, just hear me out," he interrupts, "It doesn't have to be an 'official' marriage, but if it severs the last tie you have to that whole situation, please consider it."

"What would that even look like? What if you find someone else who's not a mess?"

He cups my face, staring straight into my soul. "Charli, you're it for me. I don't want anyone else. I'll never want anything more than what you have to offer. If you ever decide to find someone better for you, I'll graciously step away, but you'll never have to worry about me being unhappy."

"You don't want to marry me for real?" My chin trembles.

"I've known that I want to marry you since the day I met you. Of course I want to marry you for real, and we can definitely do that someday. I want to do it right though. Think of this as more of an act of service to help you get closure."

"Okay. Let's do it." I can't allow myself to overthink any of this. "I want to be a Koval, too."

Nikolai's eyes sparkle, brimming with excitement. "Fuck, okay. Damn it." I laugh as he argues with himself.

"I want it to be real so bad. But it's way too soon. God, what am I doing?" He sighs, exasperated.

"Then let's make it real," I state bluntly.

"You mean it? You'd want to be my wife...for real? It's not too soon?"

"Yes. I would love to be your wife, for real. I know this isn't the traditional way that any of this goes, but nothing about our whole situation has been traditional." I smile softly.

He pulls me snugly against him, peppering kisses over the top of my head, wincing slightly as his stitches pull. "The family is going to be so excited...after they're done scolding me. Still, I know they're going to love this and demand to be there when we go. We need witnesses anyway."

I beam at him. His love isn't the type you pass up, and I'd be an idiot to ever let him go.

Every woman deserves a dedicated, passionate sweetheart who will *literally* kill for them.

Bonus points if he has a filthy mouth and a naughty side that repairs your fractured soul.

As we go through the motions of our day, I feel lighter and freer than ever. Knowing I'm safe, and loved beyond my wildest dreams, puts a spring in my step.

The cleaners have finished my room, so I work up the courage and promptly start moving my things out, just down the hall to Nikolai's room—Our room.

Nikolai let Ivan and Caroline know that we needed to talk. They were supposed to bring Navy back home today, anyway.

As we're all seated around the table, Nikolai takes my hand. His loving eyes silently assure me that everything is going to be okay. He turns to his—*our*—family. "Uncle, Caroline, I'm not going to sugar coat it. Charli and I have decided to get married."

"What?!" Ivan's mouth is agape. "You two barely know each other. You've only just begun dating. Have you lost your minds?"

"Dad! Have a little faith. You and mom barely knew one another when you got married. Right?" Caroline snips.

"Times were different then. Now there's so much more to consider," Ivan retorts

"I love Charli, she loves me. That should be enough. She also loves you two and wants more than anything to be an official member of our family. I thought you'd be thrilled to have her." Nikolai stands firm.

"I am! Don't let his stubbornness reflect poorly on me." Caroline crosses her arms elbowing Ivan.

"I'm sorry, Nicky." Ivan scrubs a hand over his face. "Everything has just been so chaotic these past couple of months. I am pleased you two are happy. I just don't do well with such immense surprises."

"Will you two be our witnesses when we go sign the papers? We don't really have anyone else, and a whole wedding seems silly for just the four of us," Nikolai asks with a loving grin.

"Yeah, who else would there be to invite? Business

owners you've sold paintings to?" Caroline snorts at her own joke.

"Very funny. I know I'm a recluse. I like it that way. People have too many expectations. Easier to not let them down if I don't know them." Nikolai shrugs. "We have to apply for the license three days in advance. So, we'll do that today and make it official three days from now, if you're both available. It'll be Sunday."

"Really trying to dive right in, huh?" Caroline elbows me.

A shy smile pulls at my face.

"We will be sure to make it. Nicky, I'm proud of you. I apologize for my outburst. You and Li are wonderful together. You'll make me some beautiful grandbabies someday too." Ivan beams, his eyes crinkle.

Nikolai chokes beside me.

I pat his back as Caroline cackles uncontrollably.

"We... we haven't talked about anything like that yet. Jesus," he wheezes.

"Come on, I want to be a grandfather before I die. Caroline doesn't even look at men," Ivan grumbles

"I do too! I just have standards!" She screeches.

Nikolai leans into me and whispers, "Are you sure you want to live with this forever?"

I kiss him in response.

There is no other future I could even begin to imagine.

Emotions crash over me as we walk together through the doorway of the courthouse. My knees buckle as they work to carry me down the steps.

Nikolai catches me with a wince as his stitches undoubtedly tug. "Easy there, Mrs. Koval. I'd hate to lose my wife within minutes of signing the papers."

An amused giggle bubbles up from the deepest parts of my chest.

*I'm so lucky.*

"Joke around, see what happens. I'll divorce you right now." I try to look as irritated as possible.

He doesn't buy it.

"Grooooss. Get a room and go consummate the marriage or whatever." Caroline fake gags.

"Oh, we will, after dinner. We need to celebrate." Nikolai scoops me up, and plants me in the passenger seat of the car. "See you guys at the restaurant, for our first *official* family outing."

We enjoy a great dinner, and an even better night.

Months ago, I was lost, drowning in a sea of darkness and misery. Now I feel whole, as if the parts of me that I don't remember don't matter.

Who I'm becoming is such an improvement over who I've ever been.

# Epilogue

## Nikolai – 2 years later

The best feeling in the world is seeing the glow of my gorgeous wife as she carries our child through the doorway of the front lobby.

We're officially opening Navy's Place today.

The timeline got pushed back a bit when we discovered that Charli and I had conceived our daughter on our wedding night.

With all the chaos going on, she'd missed a few birth control doses, and we were too entranced to pay it any mind.

Ivy Theresa Koval, our little surprise gift. Those pink lines were the biggest shock, but felt so right in the moment. Our new life together, paired with bringing new life into the world, is a sort of poetic beauty.

Charli fell into motherhood with the grace I had expected. Watching her with little Ivy makes me want to put about a dozen more babies in her. To be fair, the look in her eyes when I'm in complete dad mode makes me think she wouldn't mind.

She has come out of her shell so much in the past couple of years. She's been a force when it comes to organizing everything to get this place prepared to open.

I've never seen someone with so much passion. She's so authoritative and direct, as if I didn't already know she was, but I'm still surprised by her ability to command a room. I often think back to the reserved, timid woman that curled up and hid herself away when she first stormed into my life.

I'll never take her good days for granted, and I love supporting her through her worst days. She does still have flashbacks, on occasion. Her repressed memories haven't fully come back, and she makes no effort to regain them. She has continued to visit Claire, but only once a month.

Claire and Theo have kept in touch. They're close friends of ours now, having welcomed a son of their own mere months after Ivy was born. Henderson is blonde haired and blue eyed like his parents. A chunky little bundle of giggles and babbles, he and Ivy are best buddies already.

Caroline finished her degree and, as promised, is our lead veterinarian. We also employ a veterinary assistant to help her out. Little did we know they have history. They seem to despise each other most days, but I think she'd secretly be lost without him. I catch him eyeing her, awestruck by her knowledge quite often.

Maybe it's time for me to meddle in her love life?

I kept my promise to help local disadvantaged teens

with employment. Half of the people working here are fresh out of high school, or even still in school. We've become quite the pillars in our community already and we're not even officially open yet.

Charli's case garnered a bit of media attention and she had a moment of fame within the true crime community. Occasionally, she's called for a podcast interview, but nothing extravagant.

Poppa Ivan still teaches, but he's been flirting with the idea of retirement. I constantly try to push him to do it, and he gives me hell for it. I feel like he just wants to spend time with his grandbaby. He's absolutely smitten with that curly haired, green eyed, fair skinned angel.

Yes, she's his grandbaby. While I'm not biologically his son, he's the only father I've ever known. Why wouldn't he be her grandpa? We all just call him Pop now anyway. There's no discernable difference. He cried almost as hard as I did when Ivy came into the world.

I wrestle my way out of the storage closet with bags upon bags of supplies and gifts for our adopters today. We're not a high-volume operation, but we're hoping to get there. The plot of land we settled on is right on the edge of town and there's plenty of room to expand if we ever want to. For now, we house about fifty dogs at a time.

Potential adopters line the street. Families wait impatiently up and down the block to be let in. We've been operational for a couple of weeks and have been taking in dogs. This is our grand opening for the public.

I look around at the family I'm surrounded by. So much love and compassion overflowing.

*Fuck, I'm lucky.*

I'm absolutely putting another baby in my wife tonight. If I ask nicely, she might even tie me down and do it herself.

Time to get this show on the road.

# About the Author

Rii Finley is a coffee-drinking, music-loving introvert. She finds joy in all kinds of creative outlets from painting and sculpting to writing (obviously). She loves animals and has two rambunctious boxer dogs. The Spotify team is probably concerned by how much of her listening time is consumed by Sleep Token.

Romance novels are her escape—her happy place—she's usually reading one on her phone in her down time.

If you love good banter and lighthearted humor in the midst of chaos, and prefer your books spicy and heartfelt with a splash of darkness, you've found your new favorite author!

# Acknowledgements

First off, I need to give John a HUGE shoutout. Without your love and support, I'd have never been able to dedicate so much time—and money—into this passion. I appreciate you for always believing in me, even when I didn't believe in myself.

To Enrique (Brody) and Erica (Syn) THANK YOU for listening to my rants and mindless rambles through this process! I love you both so much and wouldn't have stayed sane without you.

To Lexi, I appreciate you for always being an ear and helping me make sense of my own internal chaos.

Finally, to all the bad-ass fellow indie authors in the IAR. Thank you for all the supportive words—and aggressive love—when imposter syndrome tried to kick my butt. Being a fairly anonymous indie author with no freaking clue what you're doing is a wild ride. I'm just glad to have picked up some like-minded besties along the way!

# Keep up wtih Rii

Hi there! If you've made it this far, I must have done something right! If you want to stay up-to-date on my current and future projects. **RiiFinley.com** has all my relevant links!

Thanks for reading!